The sarcoph[...]
white robed [...]
itself so that its features and its nakedness were revealed in its full beauty. It
was no child but a woman of exquisite
beauty, so petite in every feature, her
full red lips moving as she uttered mute
words which the watcher did not hear
yet understood. A plea, looking about
her fearfully even as she spoke. *'Take
me from this place, O stranger, and the
one who loves me and is entombed back
there. Take us back to your land and
free us from the curse which has been
put upon us. I beseech you!'*

Her voice was fading away, the light
failing and the darkness coming back
again; leaving Mason lying there in the
black solitude of the cave, knowing that
it was neither dream nor hallucination.
It had all happened, there was no doubt
about that.

Also in Arrow by Guy N. Smith

ABOMINATION
ALLIGATORS
BLOODSHOW
CANNIBALS
DEATHBELL
DEMONS
DOOMFLIGHT
ENTOMBED
MANITOU DOLL
SATAN'S SNOWDROP

ACCURSED

Guy N. Smith

ARROW BOOKS

Arrow Books Limited
62-65 Chandos Place, London WC2N 4NW

An imprint of Century Hutchinson Limited

London Melbourne Sydney Auckland
Johannesburg and agencies throughout
the world

First published by New English Library 1983
Arrow edition 1988

Printed and bound in Great Britain by
Anchor Brendon Limited, Tiptree, Essex

ISBN 0 09 956390 8

For Maralene Powell
—from one who writes words
to one who sings them

He shall not be shut in along with the souls which are fettered; he shall have power to deliver himself wherever he may be; and the worms shall not devour him.

Chapter CLXIV. Book of the Dead

Prologue

'HAS IT ever occurred to you, Reverend, that you are a thief?' The small sunburned man spoke emotionlessly, his features impassive in the shadow cast by the scuffed and grubby sun-helmet which was tilted over his forehead. A dead cheroot adhered to his thin lower lip and bobbed up and down.

His companion stared at him, squinted. Arrogance except for the tone of voice. A statement of fact as Suma saw it.

'Then you, too, are a thief, Suma.' The Reverend Mason stroked his thick grey beard, his squat form hunched over the remnants of the campfire. 'Tomorrow both of us will go in through that door below. If you are not a robber then at the very least you are an accessory.'

'I'm just a guide.' Suma struck a match and attempted to relight his cheroot. 'I do what I'm paid to do and nothing more. I neither enter tombs nor remove anything from them. All I do is show my clients where they are. The natives do the digging.'

'So I have perceived.' The older man's tones were rich and gentle, a veiled remonstration such as he might have delivered during the course of a sermon. 'But I do not steal. I do not seek to acquire wealth, merely to take my finds to a place of safe keeping where they may delight an old man who attempts to understand the ways of an ancient civilisation. Take the British Museum, for example. The exhibits there could hardly be referred to as stolen property.'

'The treasures belong to the dead.' Suma stared into the fire, stretched out a sandalled foot and kicked the charred faggots so that they showered sparks and burst into flame. 'They have need of them in *Sekhet-Aaru*, the land of the dead. One day they will return for what is rightfully theirs and find that their belongings have been stolen.'

The clergyman refrained from an impulse to try and explain to Suma that in heaven one had no need of material possessions. It would have been a waste of time. Out of the corner of his eye he studied the other, a strange little man whom one might almost have taken for a sunburned European at first glance. Part Egyptian certainly, part . . .? It was anybody's guess. A wanderer of the wastelands, a desert nomad. They told you in Cairo that Suma was the best guide available . . . if you could acquire his services. Sometimes he was not heard of for months at a time, then suddenly he would be back in the city looking for work. It was all according to his mood how much he charged; some said there were times when he did not charge at all. A hunter of tombs.

'I shall not come to Egypt again.' Mason spoke sadly, philosophically. 'Not just because I am an old man but because soon there will be nothing left to take. Surely the authorities must call a halt to it soon. So far they have been too pre-occupied with the aftermath of war, but I fear that we are witnessing the end of an era. This is surely my last expedition, Suma.'

'And maybe mine, too.' The little wiry man smiled whimsically. 'Methinks I should not have brought you here, Reverend. Not to the tomb of Dalūkah and Āba-aner.'

'Dalūkah was Queen of Egypt. Apparently her tomb was overlooked by Carter and other leading Egyptologists.'

'Not queen. A descendant, but by that time the royal bloodline had gone. I shouldn't have brought you here, Reverend, but there is still time to leave. We have not broken into the tomb yet. Fortunately!'

'You've got cold feet, suddenly, Suma. Why? I'm not backing down now. Like I said, I shan't come to Egypt again. This is my last tomb and I'm going in there whether you like it or not.'

8

'That is up to you, Reverend.' Suma glanced behind him as though he expected to see something lurking in the shadows of the cave. 'As for me, my job is done. I have brought you to the tomb of Dalūkah and Āba-aner. I have watched you dig. The rest is up to you. You need me no longer. You have the natives and a truck, enough to get you and whatever you ste—— . . . take back to Cairo. I shall leave in the morning at first light.'

'D'you mind telling me *why*?' Mason found himself peering into the shadows beyond the firelight, his gaze coming back to rest on the guide, a tiny shiver running up his spine.

'It is not for me to say.'

'You're frightened, aren't you? You're as superstitious as these natives. They won't camp near the tomb. They've retreated almost half a mile into the desert. How do I know they, too, will not have fled by dawn?'

'They might.' Suma smiled wryly. 'But they are poor. The money you are paying them may well overcome their fear temporarily. On the other hand it may not. It is fortunate you have not given them any money so far otherwise I fear that they would have been gone by now.'

'You're all frightened of bogies, spooks that don't exist except in your own mind.' There was a note of reproach in the old vicar's tone. 'I am a Christian. I believe in God. He will not let anything harm me or those who accompany me. I am not a thief; the items which I take from this tomb will be used in the interests of archaeology, to benefit Mankind so that they may learn about an ancient cultured civilisation. It is God's will that I am here.'

'We are all entitled to our own beliefs, Reverend, however mistaken they may be.' Suma yawned, stretched himself, a touch of arrogance this time. 'Now I am going to turn in for I must leave early in the morning.'

'Before we break through into the tomb, eh?' Mason leaned forward. 'You're up to something, my friend. You've broken into a dozen or more tombs before this one and rumour has it that you have a collection of relics that would grace the finest museum.'

9

'There are many rumours along the Nile.' Suma stood up, his ill-fitting khaki shorts falling well below his knees, laughable in any other place except this ancient burial ground. 'I should not take too much notice of what you hear, Reverend.'

'But you expect me to take note of *your* insinuations.'

'Yes,' the guide's eyes narrowed, his voice dropped to a whisper. 'Because *I* know. But as I told you, the decision is yours. Now I'll bid you goodnight, Reverend. Sleep well.'

Mason watched the other walk away, a kind of glide on those short legs until the darkness swallowed him up.

Mason began unrolling his blankets on the soft sandy ground, found himself glancing again into the shadows. He shivered. These desert nights were cold; the wilderness burned you by day and froze you by night. But tonight seemed exceptionally cold. Maybe he should keep the fire going; a stirring of primitive man's instincts, flames to keep the wild beasts at bay. Something scuttled across the cave, hidden by the darkness, and he started. A rat probably, these excavations were crawling with them. But they were harmless, not like scorpions and snakes. He shuddered, tried to throw off an indeterminable creeping fear. There was nothing here that his own faith would not protect him from. *Yea, though I walk through the valley of the shadow of death.* . . .

His bedroll ready, he dropped to his knees, tried to shut everything else out of his mind while he prayed. It wasn't easy. That rat was running to and fro again, scavenging for scraps of food; a sudden gust of cold desert wind whipped up the sand, drove it at him as though some venomous being out there was echoing Suma's warning in its own inexplicable way. *You're a thief, Reverend, a grave robber!*

When he opened his eyes again the embers had died down to a dull glow allowing the shadows to move in on him, black shapes that were alive and seemed to touch him with icy fingers. There was a shotgun and some ammunition in the truck; he thought about going and fetching it but that would only have been pandering to his own childish fears.

Like the time when his parents had first demanded that he slept in a room of his own. The sheer terror of those first few nights, he would never forget them. Voices that whispered as he trembled beneath the bedclothes, fingers stroking the blankets and when he jumped, prodding him, taunting him. Infantile fears that eventually evaporated. Until now. He pulled the blankets right up over his head.

Listening. That rat had gone away, probably tired of its constant search for food, returning to its hole to sleep. Mason wished he could sleep. Suddenly he wasn't tired anymore. Perhaps he should go and fetch a torch and try to read. But that meant going out there into the night. . . .

Voices! Like those in his infant years, an indecipherable whispering as though demons hid in the shadows and were mocking him; closing his eyes tightly, trembling violently.

Something made him open his eyes, an awareness of light like when his mother used to check on him on her way up to bed. He saw it through the blankets, a penetrating golden radiance, its brightness making him squint. Fear, groping for a logical explanation. The dying embers had blazed up. He had to be sure. Breathlessly, almost afraid to look, he eased himself up and peered out of his bedroll.

The scene which greeted the vicar brought a grunt of amazement from his bearded lips, dying away to a moan of terror. It was impossible, it could not be! A waking nightmare in the midst of some desert fever, an hallucination brought about by his mind dwelling on Suma's superstitions, the fact that the natives would not come near this place after nightfall. He stared, again tried to reassure himself that what he saw was a figment of the imagination, the mental meanderings of an old man.

The cave had magnified many times, or perhaps it had always been this size but hidden by the shadows. But it was no longer a cave, more of a huge chamber with plain walls, a tomb such as the one which might lie behind that heavy door in the adjacent excavations. The whole scene was lit by some radiating golden light as though the rays of a setting sun penetrated this gloomy place. The Reverend Mason continued to stare, saw that in the centre of the floor stood a small plain sarcophagus. A child's coffin, a thing of sadness that misted his eyes and blurred his vision, held his gaze as though it had some kind of hypnotic power.

The temperature had dropped several degrees and the light seemed to die, bringing back the surrounding shadows. *And even as he watched the tiny coffin lid began to raise as though the infant occupant had suddenly come to life or else had not been dead in the first place.*

The Reverend Mason wanted to tear his gaze away, to scream, to rush headlong from this place of inexplicable death into the world outside. But it seemed that all bodily functions were denied him; that some unknown power commanded that he must be a spectator to the happenings in this place, the horrors of some unearthly resurrection.

The sarcophagus lid was flung aside, a white robed figure sitting up, disrobing itself so that its features and its nakedness were revealed in its full beauty. It was no child but a woman of exquisite beauty, so petite in every feature, her full red lips moving as she uttered mute words which the watcher did not hear yet understood. A plea, looking about her fearfully even as she spoke. *'Take me from this place, O stranger, and the one who loves me and is entombed back there. Take us back to your land and free us from the curse which has been put upon us. I beseech you!'*

Mason thought that he could make out another sarcophagus some distance away, a larger one from which there was no movement, but it could just have been a trick of the shadows. Like this one!

'It is no trick, stranger.' She seemed to read his confused thoughts which were still searching for a logical explanation. *'For I am Dalūkah, an enslaved high priestess of one whose name even now I dare not utter. And there lies my lover, Āba-aner the soldier, and our crime is that we love each other. Free us, I beseech you, take us away from this tomb to another land while there is still time and before we are yet again put to the sword and entombed for eternity.'*

Her voice was fading away, the light failing and the darkness coming back again; leaving Mason lying there in the black solitude of the cave, knowing that it was neither dream nor hallucination. It had all happened, there was no doubt about that.

Suma was gone when the clergyman emerged from the cave next morning, tyre-tracks leading off into the desert and when the drifting sands obliterated them it would be as though Suma had never been. Just another legend that might or might not be true.

Mason felt tired as though he had not slept the previous night, a niggling ache behind his eyes which in all probability would increase as the day progressed. Again he saw that scene in the chamber, the woman of unparalleled beauty pleading with him to take her away, to release her from some ancient curse. But how could he when she didn't exist anymore? The cave had no recesses, there were no coffins concealed in the shadows.

His troubled thoughts were disturbed by the appearance of the natives; there should have been five but doubtless the others had left, having conceded to their superstitions and cowardice. An old man and a boy, they might have been father and son but the clergyman did not consider it worth bothering to find out. Already the sun was up and the coolness of the underground would have been appealing to him had it not been for the memory of that vision.

'Others leave.' The wizened old man pointed back to the desert. 'They follow Suma. He afraid, too.'

'Well *I'm* not afraid because there's nothing to be afraid of.' The Reverend Mason prayed that his lingering fears did not show in his expression. 'Now the sooner we break into the tomb, the better. With luck we can all be away from here before dark.'

The outer entrance door was a greater obstacle than they had anticipated and it took them three hours' work with crowbars and chisels before they finally broke through into a dry, musty passageway.

Mason stood there in the interior, had the feeling that he was in a timeless void, a chamber that bridged the gap between civilizations. He held on to the wall, experienced a

13

sensation of vertigo. In the dusty gloom he saw the outline of the inner door, through which lay. . . .

'Bad place.' The old man was clutching the boy to him. 'Very bad place. *See!*' His voice rose to a pitch, an extended finger shaking.

'It's only a painting.' The clergyman was aware how his own tone shook. A kind of emblem on the narrow portal, a double-headed snake with piercing eyes that would seek you out wherever you tried to hide.

'*It is the sign of Set!*' The old native was backing away, dragging the boy with him. '*This is an evil accursed place. Let us flee now before we are murdered as Osiris was, put to the sword as were Dalūkah and Āba-aner!*'

'Leave now and you get no money!' Mason shouted, his words echoing in the enclosed space.

'Money no matter.'

'Look.' He moved with surprising agility for his age, barred their way. 'I'm not going to have everybody running out on me when the goal is in sight. I'll bargain with you. Help me smash down this door and then I'll pay you your wages and you can go. I will go into the tomb alone.'

The native sucked his toothless gums, glanced back again at that painting on the door. The boy was tugging at him, crying, and begging him to leave now.

'All right, we'll break the door for you. But then you pay us quick and we go.'

Mason nodded, gave an audible sigh of relief, and picked up his crowbar.

Now he was all alone. The vicar listened to the padding footsteps of the retreating natives and wondered if he ought to follow them. No, not now he had come this far, spent a large part of his savings in finding this tomb. It was barely noon yet; he would work for five or six hours, take out as much as he could in the time, load up the truck and be away before dark. *At all costs he had to be away from here before dark!*

He drew a deep breath and stepped over the debris,

14

aware that this was the moment when he went back in time, trespassed in the kingdom of the dead. Hollow shuffling footfalls, a torch beam that shook crazily penetrating the dust of aeons kicked up by his every movement.

The Reverend Mason recoiled, almost fled before fear deprived him of the use of his limbs. The interior, the simple undecorated chamber with the small sarcophagus in the centre, so familiar that he recognised it instantly. This was the place of which he had dreamed, the tomb of his vision!

Strangely his terror subsided as he stood there in the centre swinging the torch beam around him in an arc. The chamber was no more than twenty yards square, humble in comparison with others he had seen, simplicity as opposed to grandeur, a place where the dead could rest in peace. Or could they?

He had expected to find a second coffin. It stood there on a raised stone platform, a casket that was much larger than the first one with neither carvings nor paintings on its surface.

He swung the beam to his left, started involuntarily as it reflected two pairs of glowing eyes set closely together, an amulet depicting that double-headed serpent again, Set's malevolence glinting evilly. Beside it on the single shelf was an obsidian head the size of a cricket ball, finely carved features, nobility that eyed him proudly yet not hatefully.

'Strange.' He spoke aloud, grateful for the sound of his own voice. 'A tomb of this size and yet it is empty of treasures, with no signs of robbers having been here before. No food to sustain the *kas* on their long journey, no wealth stored here, although surely the dead were of a wealthy line.'

He found himself approaching the smaller of the two coffins as though some force drew him, as if his actions were not his own. His fingers smoothed along the lid but found no fastenings of any kind, merely a hinge which moved as easily as if it had been oiled yesterday. It lifted noiselessly, swung back. And in that moment his terror returned! *For here lay Dalūkah who had pleaded with him only last night!*

He didn't want to look, wanted to slam it back, leave this place and flee just as Suma and the natives had done because now he sensed the oppressive evil, the cold cloying unseen force, those double eyes boring malignantly into him like laser beams. The dust was thicker, his torch beam fainter as he shone it down on the still form inside the sarcophagus, saw her features staring up at him from amidst a mass of loose swathings as though somehow she had torn them from her because she was not really dead and needed to breathe.

Such beauty, unmarred by the passing of thousands of years, eyes that had not dulled, long dark hair that had not lost its sheen. Then the horror as he saw the wound, an ugly incision below her left breast where a cruel sword blade had pierced and disfigured, been wrenched free as she had fallen bleeding to the ground.

Eyes that still saw and understood. He held on to the sides of the coffin, fought off a wave of dizziness, saw those lips move and heard her gentle tones like the rippling of the tide on a deserted beach.

'You have not failed me, stranger. Now take myself and Āba-aner, the soldier, away from this place to your own land where we shall be freed from the curse placed upon us. Do not delay for every second that we remain here we are in danger!'

There was no thought of refusal in the old clergyman's mind, just how he was going to manage the task of taking these two up above on his own. But he knew he would make it somehow. They were not happy here and possibly elsewhere they would be at peace. The girl had pleaded and he would not fail her.

The mummy of Dalūkah presented no problem for she was no heavier than a child and he lifted her easily, stumbled through the outer chamber and up the long flight of steps with her cradled to his breast. Without pausing for breath he returned for the coffin.

Now it was the turn of Āba-aner. The Reverend Mason felt the coldness of the tomb as he re-entered it like an icy barrier trying to repel him. *Yea, though I walk through the valley of the shadow of death I shall fear no evil, for Thou art with me. . . .* Yet all he experienced was a sense of loneliness.

The man was tall, a handsome specimen of his time, his features fierce yet the eyes reflected an underlying kindness. Something more, a deep sorrow. Muscular, a fine figure spoiled only by that same sword wound that Dalūkah bore, an ugly gash that went right into the heart.

A hiss; it could have been the desert wind soughing down the open tunnel where it had been denied access from time immemorial. Mason told himself that that was what it was because the serpent on the amulet was an inanimate object. Those eyes just glinted in the torchlight because they were jewels and for no other reason.

This time he had to drag the body because it was impossible to lift it, wincing as the legs caught on the rough stairs, feeling every bump on his own body. Yet somehow he made it, then went back for the coffin.

The sun was low in the western sky when the Reverend Mason made his last trip down below. He didn't have to go, he didn't know why he did; some kind of compulsion or was it avarice because of the four jewels that scintillated in the double head of the serpent of Set? Or because the obsidian head would grace his own collection?

Fearful now, breathless from the physical strain which he had undergone, his tired muscles twitching. The torch was almost gone. In his haste he had forgotten to search the truck for new batteries.

Yet down in the tomb his artificial light was superfluous. An irridescence lit up the chamber with that same glow that had illuminated his vision. The eyes of Set alive now with the fire of triumph, the amulet cold to the touch yet burning his fingers as though with frostbite. Clutching it to him, grabbing up the sculptured head and running for the exit.

He fell, banged his head, felt the warm trickle of blood but ignored it. Fearing that the outer door might somehow have closed and entombed him in this devilish place. It hadn't. Barely had he the strength to mount those steps for the last time, thanking God that he had been spared to gaze upon the saffron evening sky and breathe in the dry hot air of an Egyptian desert.

17

Tired as he was he was determined to drive through the night and make it to Cairo without a stop, almost as though he feared pursuit.

And as he started up the truck, listened to the battered worn-out engine noisily ticking over, he was reminded once more of his words to Suma. *I shall not return to Egypt.*

Now they were a vow. He had no wish to come back here to this land of unexplained mysteries. For in many cases it was better not to know the truth.

'Those *things* of yours in there are gettin' a bit niffy, Reverend.'

Mason sighed. Mrs Barker was renowned for speaking the truth and equally renowned for a lack of tact.

'It ain't right, to my way o' thinkin',' she continued, dusting among the objects on the ornate study desk with unerring accuracy, giving the obsidian head a quick wipe with obvious contempt. 'Gives me the creeps, them Egyptian things do, Vicar. Them mummy-things are just like bodies dug up out of their graves.'

Which of course they are. Mason raised his eyes heavenwards and wondered how he would possibly cope without his daily help. A bachelor's life wasn't as easy as some people were inclined to think; there were so many mundane chores to be done.

'I will admit,' he cleared his throat, 'that they aren't exactly *fresh*. On the other hand they are valuable souvenirs of a civilisation which was more cultured a few thousand years ago than ours is today.'

'Which is as good a reason as any for gettin' rid of 'em.' Mrs Barker had moved on to the wide windowsill, her back to the clergyman so that her expression was hidden from him. 'My 'usband tells me there's a job goin' up at the 'All . . .' She paused, rubbed energetically at a small stain. ''E works there, as you know.'

'Maybe you're right.' The Reverend Mason fitted a new nib into a pen-holder, dipped it in the inkwell and made a pretence of scribbling on the foolscap sheet in front

18

of him. 'I'll do something about those mummies, Mrs Barker. Don't you worry, I'll see to them. There's no need for you to consider getting a job up at the Hall. As a matter of fact I was also considering giving you a small rise. How would an extra two shillings a week suit you?'

Mrs Barker smiled to herself. She had always prided herself in being able to handle the Vicar. All that was required was a bit of *tact*!

A three-quarter moon cast its ethereal silvery light across the spacious vicarage garden, creating weird shadows amid the shrubbery and orchard, glinting on the black sluggish water of the river which wound its way through the thick reed beds below the furthermost boundary. A silent landscape even though the town was less than a quarter of a mile away, the squat tower of St Edith's Church outlined against the clear sky.

The Reverend Mason donned his Norfolk jacket, a somewhat worn garment which had recently been relegated to the status of garden apparel and pushed his feet into his patched wellington boots for the ground was inclined to be muddy down by the river. He went out to the shed, found a spade and crept stealthily down through the orchard.

The thought of the physical work involved never daunted him for on several occasions when Jakes, the regular gravedigger at the cemetery, was suffering with his back Mason had done the job himself. You took your time, didn't rush it and in the end you finished the job; maybe not with Jakes' expertise but nobody had ever complained.

A fitting site, the vicar decided; level ground adjacent to the dense trees, the soil soft enough to dig without having to use a pickaxe. And in a way it could be likened to Egypt for was not that country once known as *Kamt* or *Qemt*, meaning dark in colour, because of the black mud of the Nile? Of all the places he could have chosen to inter this long-suffering pair who had died by the sword, there was nowhere more suitable than here beside a wide reedy river. In a way he was restoring them to their rightful place, giving them an honourable and Christian burial.

He worked steadily, taking off his jacket after the first half-hour and hanging it on a nearby branch; just the squelch of the spade as the soil became wetter deeper down, thuds as he threw the sods up on to the growing pile.

A sadness misted his eyes as he finally completed the second grave. It had taken thousands of years for Dalūkah and Āba-aner to be laid to rest in a proper manner and obviously God had chosen him to do it. It was an honour; the thought gave him the necessary strength to go and fetch the two mummies.

He stood there breathing heavily; his back was hurting and he felt slightly dizzy. The sweat chilled on his body and he shuddered, found himself glancing around just as he had done that night in the cave after Suma had left; a feeling of being . . . *watched*!

A sudden gust of wind. The suspended jacket swung, something jingled and for one moment Mason saw a glow in the half-light as though he had inadvertently put a lighted pipe into his pocket and the material was smouldering. That amulet, of course, the one with the emblem of Set engraved upon it! Those serpents' eyes glinted, night or day, as though they . . . *lived*! He found himself stepping back, stumbled and almost fell into one of the open graves. A gasp of fear escaped his lips.

This whole business was madness. Two mummies, long-dead people who had begun to decompose once they were away from the dry atmosphere of Egypt. That was logical. So they had to be disposed of. Nevertheless there was something unhealthy about a secret nocturnal burial. Like that time during the war when two wounded soldiers up at the hospital in town had died from some kind of plague; the details were never released but they had been buried after dark. Mason had objected but the authorities said it was best because otherwise rumours would have spread and they could have created mass hysteria. Half the population lived in fear of unknown diseases. Now it was the same all over again.

He took the man first, wrapping him in an old bedsheet, rolling him into the grave because there was no way he could lower him, wincing at the thud — so undignified. One last glance down through misted eyes, an indistinguishable whiteness; it was impossible to see how the mummy lay. Now feverish haste again, shovelling in the mud and soil.

The woman; he didn't know whether he could go through with it. There were no outward signs of decomposition, the features starkly white and beautiful in the gentle moonlight. Maybe he should take her back to the house, hide her in the attic where Mrs Barker wouldn't find her. No, that would have been sacrilege.

'*Bury me, stranger. Lay me to rest and free me from the curse as you have done Āba-aner!*'

The vicar heard the words clearly, bent lower to see if those lips had moved but they were still rigid. He had imagined it; the whole business was playing on his nerves. Nevertheless, he would not fail Dalūkah; he would keep his word and carry out her last request.

He felt the impact in his own body as the mummy hit the bottom of the grave, lay still. He dropped to his knees, was aware of a wetness on his cheek as he mumbled a short prayer, crossed himself. May God have mercy on her *ka*!

That glow came again, seeming to spread out and touch him, a cold fire that burned, had him crying out with shock and pain; pinpoints of blazing eyes like glow-worms, commanding his attention. *The wrath of Set was very much alive!*

'*Bury me with Dalūkah, my servant!*'

Mason scrambled across to where his jacket hung, fumbled in the pocket until he found the amulet, a circular piece of icy metal no larger than the palm of his hand. Like that strange light it burned him with its coldness, the double-headed serpent's eyes flickering with the fires of evil, an ancient hatred rekindled.

This time he did not kneel and look upon the corpse in its grave with remorse; he flung the amulet from him, clasped his hands to his ears as if anticipating the scream from below. A piercing shriek of sheer terror and hopelessness; a sound that hurt his brain, had him moaning his own fear. *What have I done? Dear God, what have I done!*

He knew he must fill in the grave without delay, panicking as he shovelled and pushed the soil back; heard the rectangular hole filling up. Movements, as though a desperate struggle was taking place down there, those cries still ringing in his ears, muffled as though they came from afar.

'You have betrayed me, stranger. Tortured me with the promise of freedom only to imprison me once again with my oppressor!' Words that hung in the still night air like distant echoes unwilling to disperse.

At last the grave was filled, Mason leaning on his spade for support, weak and trembling, glancing around him as though the shadows hid lurking evil beyond his comprehension. Remorse at what he had done, a secret which would haunt him for the rest of his days, a Judas who knew that his work could not be undone. And as if to hide his shame a bank of dark cloud passed across the face of the moon.

It was some time later when the Reverend Mason made it back to the vicarage. He had recollections of stumbling, falling, crawling the remainder of the way across the wide lawn. Muddy, his waistcoat stained and torn, fingernails black and cracked. And that pain in his left arm which had nagged him throughout the return trip from Egypt had travelled up into his shoulder and downwards. There was not much time left.

Somehow he reached his study, pulled back the curtains and saw that dawn was breaking. There was enough light to see by. He found his diary, just two pages left; scratching with a bent nib, ink that ran and blobbed because his gnarled fingers shook so that he could barely form the letters. Illegible perhaps, but would it ever be read? Did it matter?

An apology to Dalūkah and her lover Āba-aner, that he had condemned them to the eternal purgatory from which he had temporarily freed them. The pen moved slower and slower, ran out of ink and he had not the strength to reach across for the inkwell again. And then came the explosion inside his chest, an eruption in a sealed volcano trying to burst its way out, blinding him with agony.

Breathlessly he slumped forward, knew that he would write no more but it was enough. Dalūkah and Āba-aner would know that he had tried, that he had done his best, but in his foolishness he had failed them.

Tortured screams, bodies writhing and flaying in a damp grave because they were dead and yet lived. Crying out, accusing him; cursing him. Then silence, except for the hiss of a venomous serpent that had two heads and four eyes from which there was no hiding place.

And somewhere close by the river lapped its reedy banks, its slow deep current an eternal passage to the oceans of the world, linking far-off lands; another Nile, another Egypt.

BOOK ONE

THE LIVING

Chapter One

The Buried Mummies

'I HOPE you haven't come inside in your wellingtons.' Emily Brownlow's shout from the landing was habitual as though her vocal chords were operated somehow by the opening of the kitchen door; a dominant bleat which she had practised to perfection with an everyday recital. And always the same answer from below.

'No.' George Brownlow had long since dropped the "dear". 'They're in the corner of the coalhouse and I haven't put them on the carpet, either.'

Rumours that the Brownlows had a carpet in their coalhouse were not without foundation; certainly not an Axminster but the six by six square of material would certainly have graced more humble abodes than their detached house on River View. Remarkably that piece of chequered material was kept reasonably clean, not due entirely to the fact that it was vacuumed once a week, but rather that the coal was hosed down before being stacked inside. By an uncomplaining George; at least, his wife never *heard* him complain.

George Brownlow remembered to wash his hands thoroughly in the sink before wiping them on the roller-towel. He was due to be reminded of that requirement shortly when his wife came downstairs.

He studied his reflection in the mirror while he dried his hands, wrinkled his pointed nose in time with his constant nervous twitch that created the impression that he was winking. He had to admit that he did not like what he saw; a complexion that was dark red, the veins standing out like contours on an Ordnance Survey map, a mop of unruly greying hair that dictated its own style. Heavy rimmed glasses that gave his eyes an owlish appearance, reflected a fanatical gleam, an anger that boiled within him because where Emily was concerned he dared not show it. The nagging bitch, she was driving him into his grave, an early one at fifty-two. *'Don't come inside in your wellingtons, George. Don't dirty my carpet in the coal-house.'* Bloody carpet in the coal-house! Somebody had given the old cow a piece of second-hand carpet, *'so we'll have it in the coal-house, George, and if you wash the coal down before you carry it in we can keep it nice and clean in there, not like those dirty old outhouses that some people have.'* All part of keeping up with River View and trying to go one better.

He was getting round-shouldered, too. And there was a thickness creeping into his waistline. He grimaced, and twitched again.

'Put the kettle on, George.' That meant that she would be downstairs in a minute. Then *'make me a cup of tea; one sugar and just a splash of milk.'* The way it had always been for the past thirty years except she had only started instructing him on it these last few months. It was all this façade of an upper-River View image which was sending her round the bend, he decided. They were living a lie for the sake of being snobbish. She'd gone to the extreme to keep the fact a secret that she'd won the *Place the Ball* competition in the *Mercury*. Eighty grand and a car the week after he'd been made redundant; she'd gone and pleaded with the paper not to publish her name. No commoner's wealth for Emily Brownlow; *she* wasn't going to be labelled one of the *nouveau riche* who had come up out of the semis estate on the other side of town. She'd got it all worked out, had spread the lies and both George and their two teenage children, Barry and Sheila, had been conned into going along with it. George had *not* been made redundant, she'd told everybody. He'd started up in business on his own, *'design work'* (that could mean anything) and he was working from home; doing so well that they'd been able to move up to River View.

The kettle started to boil and George Brownlow switched it off. His wife would, likely as not, chide him because there was a film of condensation on the kitchen window. *'I've told you before, George, switch the kettle off before it comes to the boil else you steam up the windows and I only cleaned them this morning.'* And every other bloody morning for the past week!

'There's a draught coming from somewhere, George. We'll have to do something about double-glazing. The Evans's have got it, you know.' Emily Brownlow came into the room, instinctively checked that her husband hadn't actually sneaked indoors with his wellington boots on. She remembered the occasion he'd done it last winter; she would not forget that for a very long time. She had made him wash the kitchen floor again.

He filled the teapot, glanced up at her. Not exactly unattractive, she'd got some of that weight off she'd been threatening to lose for the past month; some American high-protein fruit and veg. diet. Her shoulder-length hair was black, too black, so you knew it wasn't its natural colour. Her features had hardened . . . no, sharpened, blended in with all this bickering. That made her look her age. Forty-eight. Maybe she was going into the change and all this nonsense was biological. In which case it wasn't her fault except that she could get hormone treatment, only she'd never admit to the change, not even to Doctor Horne. So it was all her bloody own fault and he couldn't muster a grain of sympathy.

'There's something I want to talk to you about, George.'

'What's that?' Wincing and twitching. There was always something Emily wanted to talk to him about.

'It's about Sheila. I don't like that boy, Adrian.'

'He seems all right to me.'

'"All right" about sums him up. You know where he comes from, don't you?'

'The Firs Estate.' George found himself swallowing, instinctive guilt when his wife started up like this because in the end it always turned out to be *his* fault.

28

'There's nothing wrong in . . .'

'Oh yes, there is. It's a *council* estate. Council houses, and you know what sort of people live in them. No background. George, it's letting *us* down. Neighbours notice things like that. You've only got to look at the boy; long hair that straggles all over the place, jeans that are not only dirty but frayed. My God, you can almost see his knees through them! And his *accent* – there's no prizes for guessing where *he* comes from.'

George Brownlow's left eye was twitching a shade faster than usual. His mouth had gone dry and he found himself staring down at his feet. Wait for it, any second and *I* get the backlash.

'I'm surprised *you* haven't done anything about it, George. Do you always have to wait until I point the obvious out to you?'

'Sheila's seventeen.' His lower lip trembled as he spoke and he hated himself for it. 'A lot of girls nowadays leave home at that age, get married or . . . or go and live with some feller.'

'That's exactly what I'm driving at.' Emily Brownlow's mouth curled into a contemptuous sneer. 'The next thing'll be Sheila will be walking out and shacking up somewhere with . . . with this *yob*! Him apart, it's immoral!'

George had an awful feeling that he was blushing; fortunately with his complexion it was difficult for an observer to be sure. Except Emily. She never missed a thing. 'She's only been going out with him a few weeks.'

'Which is all the more reason why it should be stopped now, before they get too involved. Doubtless people are already talking. I can't for the life of me guess what a daughter of mine sees in somebody like *that*!'

'Times have changed.' He began to pour the tea, it was sure to be either too strong or too weak. 'You can't tell teenagers what to do these days or like you say they'll just up and walk out. If we put pressure on them Sheila's likely to do just that. She's headstrong.' He refrained from adding '*and it's no secret who she takes after!*'

29

'Well, you'll have to do it tactfully then.' Emily sipped her tea, grimaced. 'I want you to speak to her tonight, George.'

'Why don't *you* have a word with her?' It was the nearest he had come to open defiance for a very long time. His cheeks were a bright flush, a combination of anger and high blood-pressure. His whole body tensed, his fingers curling and digging into the palms of his hands. 'Talk to her, Emily, woman to woman, if that's what you want.'

She started, an expression of amazement on her features, then her eyes narrowed and a white spot appeared on either cheek. 'That is your job, George. And don't try to shirk it.'

'Because I'm supposed to be the head of the family?' His neck was craned forward, stretched out of his shirt collar so that the blue corded veins were visible. 'You only want me to take charge when something difficult crops up.' His eye was twitching rapidly now, the pupil seeming to bulge behind the thick lens.

'George!' Stepping back a pace, a physical and psychological retreat.

'George this, George that.' He raised a fist and it seemed for a moment that he might strike her, but he lowered it again. 'I'm getting bloody sick of this game you're playing. Just because you won a small fortune and you're scared that everybody might get to know that you did it in the least intellectual way possible, you think our roles have been reversed. "George is working for himself these days, a design something or other. Works from home!" What a load of crap. I'm redundant like three and a half million other poor buggers in this country. Out of work, on the dole, call it what you will. And I'm not ashamed of it. And I don't care either. Do you want to know why I don't care, Emily? Come on, tell me, do you want to bloody know?'

Her head moved, he didn't know whether it was a nod or a shake. He didn't care, because this time she was bloody well going to hear him out.

'Well, I'll bloody well tell you. Because before many more months are out nobody in this world is going to give a monkey's because none of us will have a job. We'll either be dead or dying from radiation fallout. D'you understand me, Emily, there's going to be a nuclear war one way or the other. We've had crises over Afghanistan, Poland, El Salvador, the Middle East and a dozen other spots. Now it's Libya and any fool could see that was coming this last few months. Sooner or later that madman was going to get hold of a nuclear weapon, it was only a matter of time. And there's no prizes for guessing who supplied him with it! America's warned him to expect the worst if he uses it and there are nasty threats coming from behind the Iron Curtain about what will happen if they intervene. Can't you see what will happen? Libya will blast Israel off the map and the Yanks will wipe out Libya. Then in come the Russians and, hey presto, it's all started and that's the end of all of us.'

'You're mad!' Her voice was a whisper, an expression almost of fear on her pallid face. 'It's just a threat. We've had threats hanging over us for the last twenty-five years. Libya's just another threat and that's all it will ever be. A threat.'

'You poor fool!' he laughed harshly. 'D'you think anybody's going to worry about your pedigree when the flashpoint comes? Of course they bloody well aren't. We're all going to be the bloody same, a dying, classless society wiped out by one madman.'

'Stop it!' she shrieked.

'No, I won't stop it.' He moved forward another pace. 'You've had the power in this household because you've got the money, but money won't be any good to anybody when the world goes up in smoke. So I'm going to get myself something that will be, and you'll come crawling and pleading to me, Emily. Believe me, you will.'

'Whatever . . . whatever are you talking about?' She was leaning against the sink unit now, holding on for support. 'Are you feeling ill, George?'

'Oh, don't run away with the idea that this is something I've just thought of because you've got me wild. I've had this in mind for the last few months and tomorrow I'm going to make a start on it. I might not have a job but I'm going to bloody well work eight hours a day, seven days a week. Hard physical labour.'

'What . . . what *are* you going to do, George?' Subdued now, frightened, glancing behind her as though judging her distance from the door and wondering whether or not to make a run for it. But she didn't.

'I am going . . .' he paused for effect, '*to make a nuclear fallout shelter in that bloody big useless lawn which you keep nagging me to mow twice a week!* I'm going to dig it up, have the whole place looking like an open-cast coalmining site and I'll enjoy every second of it!'

She almost said "you're mad" again but thought better of it. Instead she muttered, 'nuclear shelters cost a lot of money and even then there's no guarantee that they will be effective. Anyway, if the worst does happen, and I don't for one moment think it will, but if it does, then what is the *point* in trying to survive and face the aftermath?'

George Brownlow felt a sudden surge of elation. She wasn't dismissing his idea out of hand, no backlash of contempt; she was stating a reason, an argument, albeit a negative one but he had known her long enough to sense those odd occasions when he actually had the upper hand. And this was one of them.

'Well, *I* am going to build a shelter.' He drew himself up to his full height. 'Whether you or anybody else likes it or not. In Switzerland they are compulsory in order to obtain building permission for houses. We shall have one and I will make every bit of it with my own hands.'

'You're not the practical sort.' She appeared to have recovered some of her composure. 'Besides, shelters cost a lot of money . . . which *you* don't have and *I* am not financing this ridiculous obsession.'

'I'm not asking you to,' he smiled. 'I have the necessary tools to dig it out and I shall construct it from the best materials I can lay my hands on. There's some local firm advertising every night in the paper trying to get rid of a surplus of asbestos sheeting. That demolition site in town is only too glad to sell off second-hand bricks and timber to clear the site. Don't you worry, I've made my mind up on this. Give me six months; I'll have it habitable by winter, you mark my words. I only hope I'm in time.'

'Whatever will the neighbours think?'

'Frankly, I don't give a damn what they think. For once I'm going to do what *I* want to do. You can tell 'em what you like — tell 'em it's a project in connection with my "design work" which you've put about.'

'You're impossible. I . . .' She broke off, heard the back door slam. 'That'll be Barry. He's home early.'

'I expect old Matheson has sent him home early so that he can get on with his studies. More likely he'll spend the evening tinkering with that damned motorbike.'

'At least he has a good class girlfriend,' Emily Brownlow retorted. 'I only wish Sheila would take a leaf out of his book. Rita's a real nice girl, it's just a pity that she has to work at that awful research laboratory. I've never stopped worrying about her since that smallpox germ killed that girl in Birmingham a few years ago.'

More likely you're worried about yourself in case she brings some disease here, George Brownlow thought. 'That was a freak accident. It will probably never ever happen again.'

'Hi Dad, Mum,' Barry Brownlow came into the kitchen, a smile on his freckled face, his dark ruffled hair spilling down over the collar of his dark suit. 'Any tea left in the pot?'

'Your hair needs brushing,' Emily was already scrutinising him. 'And your suit could do with a good pressing. Really, Barry, it isn't fitting for somebody working in a solicitor's office to travel on a motorbike. Whatever does Mr Matheson think about it?'

'He says he wished when he was my age he could have afforded a machine like mine.' Barry grinned, poured himself a cup of tea.

'And I'll bet you didn't tell him it was on HP,' she retorted icily. 'The best thing you can do is to forget all about motor-cycles, get on with your studying and qualify as quickly as you can so you'll be able to afford a *respectable* car.'

'You two been rowing again?' He sipped his tea. 'God, you could've cut the atmosphere in here with a knife when I walked in.'

'You may as well know,' Emily sniffed loudly, a habit of hers when she was defeated on any issue, 'your father has had a brainwave, or rather a *brainstorm*. He's going to dig up the lawn, make an unsightly mess of the garden and build *himself* a nuclear fallout shelter.'

'Good for him.' The youth sensed an opportunity to side with his father, a chance not to be missed when his mother was in one of her moods. 'I reckon we might need it before long.'

'Don't let's go into all that again.' Mrs Brownlow brushed some imaginary obstacle from in front of her, an angry impatient gesture that signalled a personal defeat on some family issue. 'I just hope Rita will be able to make more of you than I've made of your father. Such a nice girl. At least she doesn't waste her time and let us all down by working in a supermarket like Sheila.'

'Pack it in, Mum.' Barry drained his cup, rattled it down on the sink unit. 'If you're not going on about her job at the supermarket you're running Adrian down. And he's a nice guy, take it from me. As a matter of fact he's coming round tonight to give me a hand with the bike.'

'You're all mad.' She raised a hand to her head, drew her fingers slowly and meaningfully across her forehead. 'I think I've got a migraine coming on. And it's no wonder the way you lot carry on. There's a salad in the fridge, you can help yourselves. I'm going upstairs to lie down.'

'What's got into her?' Barry glanced at his father as they listened to Emily Brownlow's rapid footfalls going up the stairs.

'The usual, I guess.' George Brownlow sank down into a chair, suddenly felt weak, a sensation as though he ought to burst into tears and get the frustration of the last quarter of an hour out of his system. 'She's going into the change for sure. Either that or she's really going mental.'

'These obsessions of hers are getting on top of her.' Barry began unfastening his tie, pulled it off in one quick movement. 'I reckon a carpet in the coal-house and washing the coal are about the limit. She'll be hanging oil paintings in there next. The worst thing that ever happened to us was her winning that fortune. Now everything's geared to keeping up with everybody else on River View and trying to go one better. Which doesn't make for a very happy home. Are you *really* going to make a shelter, Dad?'

'Yes.' A sudden tightening of George Brownlow's lips, those hands clenching again. 'If everybody else is prepared to sit around and get blown up then I'm not. I've nothing else to do, anyway. You don't expect me to hang around the house all day and listen to *that*, do you?'

'No, but this family is getting obsessional. It's like living in a madhouse most of the time. Why d'you think I spend most of my time out with the bike? Why d'you think Sheila's always down at Adrian's and he doesn't like coming up here?'

'Then you'll understand why I'm going to dig a shelter.' God Almighty, I might even go and live in it, shut myself away. And if there is a nuclear attack you lot will all come spilling down into my refuge: *'What a brilliant idea of yours, Dad.' 'Now keep the place tidy, George.' 'We ought to have a carpet on the floor.'* Jesus Christ Almighty!

'There's supposed to be some Egyptian mummies buried somewhere hereabouts,' Barry paused in the doorway shrugging himself out of his jacket. 'At least, if what that article in the *Tribune* the other week said is true. There used to be an old vicarage on this estate with a huge garden running down to the river. The old vicar was obsessed with tombs and the like and he brought some of his finds back here. The story goes that a couple of mummies started to go off a bit so he laid 'em to rest in a proper reverent manner. Mind you don't dig 'em up, Dad!'

'Huh!' Brownlow grunted. 'When there's no local news worth reporting they dig up some old story and if they can't find one then they invent one. Makes you sick!'

Barry Brownlow closed the door and mounted the stairs, found himself tip-toeing past his parents' bedroom. The door was shut and he could imagine his mother lying there on the bed ready to put on her migraine act if anybody came in. Dad was just as bad except that he was kept in check by mother most of the time.

He entered his room, closed the door and began to search for his denim overalls. Damn it, that cow had been tidying up in here again, put everything where *she* thought they ought to go. Eventually he located his overalls; they had been washed again, the second time this week. The latest issue of his biking magazine protruded from the waste-paper basket and with a muttered oath he retrieved it. Aggro, that was what it amounted to. His lips tightened. The best thing he could do was to look for a place of his own; at least a bedsit somewhere, however tatty, would give him peace of mind.

A noise outside, like metal striking stone, attracted his attention and he crossed to the window. Below him the spacious garden with its immaculate lawns and shrubberies ran down to the edge of the river, enclosed on all sides by a high wattle fence. And in the centre of the main lawn was one pathetic shirt-sleeved figure wielding a pickaxe, hacking at the lush turf as though he bore some personal grudge against it, was determined to take his revenge on it and destroy it.

Barry Brownlow gave a hollow laugh, felt a little shiver run up his spine and goosepimple his neck. It reminded him of that afternoon a few weeks ago when he and Rita had gone for a stroll in the churchyard. In a far corner they had come upon an old gravedigger just starting his excavations, picking away at the grass just as George Brownlow was doing now.

'One more, one less.' The fellow had given them a single-toothed grin, spittle stringing from his lower lip. 'The only certain thing in life, boy, is that this is how we'll all end up.'

And for some reason Barry Brownlow couldn't get the story of those mummies out of his mind. It was true what the old grave-digger had said, there was only one place you were going to finish up.

Chapter Two

The Amulet of Set

GEORGE BROWNLOW cursed, paused to rest. He could feel his heart pounding away inside him like a distant voodoo drum. He was sweating heavily, the perspiration cooling and chilling him, and fleetingly he wished that he had not embarked upon this foolishness. In a way it had been a kind of fantasy, something to switch his mind on to when Emily started nagging, like some people dreamed of a Robinson Crusoe existence on a tropical island but carefully overlooked all the hardships and inconveniences. Life was all about trying to con yourself.

Everybody was too concerned with living. No, that wasn't quite right — staying alive. Survival. But they did damn all about it, governed by The System which dictated whether you lived or died in a variety of ways. A political issue and you were suddenly at war, a clash of major powers with no thought for human life. So you had to do something about it yourself. In the end you only had yourself to rely on.

He hadn't intended to make a start right away though. Certainly not tonight. That had been Emily's fault, pushing him into something again. *'Go and mow the lawn, George, there's rain forecast for tomorrow. And the garden shed needs tidying.'*

He had never liked physical work, not because he was lazy but because it was all so boring. You mowed the lawn and in a week it wanted doing again, sooner if Emily noticed it. You got aches and pains, tired yourself out needlessly. Nothing to show for it. And now the enormity of his task was all too apparent. Too hasty. He should have sat down and drawn up some plans, taken a few measurements. Perhaps he should go inside now and make a start, get something down on paper. He almost dropped his tools and reached for his jacket. Only one thing stopped him: Emily again.

Her migraine would undergo a miraculous cure the moment he went back indoors. *'Soon gave that idea up, didn't you, George? You're not cut out for real hard work. Have you got over your little bit of bad temper? Worked it off, eh; you'll be laid up for a week. That'll teach you a lesson. Now you can darned well go and put the lawn back as you found it and when you've done that you can mow it. Nuclear shelter, indeed!'*

He swung the pick again, gasped aloud as it struck a stone somewhere below the surface and jarred his arm and shoulder. He tugged it free, struck again. And again. This was one job he wasn't chickening out of. He'd no idea how to construct a fallout shelter but he'd make something even if it was only on the lines of the World War II dug-out air-raid shelters. Anything. But he wasn't giving in. And if it wasn't radiation proof he'd use it as a 'den', a refuge to get away from Emily. He'd rig up a light and a heater of some kind, find himself a comfortable old armchair from somewhere and make it into a cosy little house all of his own.

He would have to be more methodical, though. It was useless just hacking out lumps of grass and soil; cut the turf out in squares, stack them in a pile. Then scoop out the soil and stones, heap them up like he was digging a . . . *grave!* He shuddered. It could become just that if he didn't get it right. He'd have to get a book on nuclear preparation from somewhere. He remembered vaguely having seen advertisements in the newspapers for HMSO booklets on the subject. Yes, he'd have to go into the matter more thoroughly. But in the meantime there was no harm in beginning the initial excavations for Emily's sake!

He paced out fifteen yards, used the heel of his boot to mark the spot; eight yards across, that should be wide enough.

Do the job properly, get your lines straight. He went up to the shed and found a garden line.

Now he was working more systematically, slicing out squares of lawn, religiously following that length of taut string. It was going to be a long job but he had until winter to get it finished and he wasn't going anywhere in the meantime. The exercise and fresh air would do him good. He had meant what he had said: seven days a week, morning till night. If it wasn't so bloody hot. . . .

George glanced up at the sky. The sun had sunk below the western horizon but there was still an hour or so of daylight left. The weather looked settled, no sign of rain although nothing short of drifting snow would force him to abandon his project now. Come to think of it, it hadn't rained much since the end of March, and May was two-thirds gone. That was why the ground was so hard, making digging difficult. That long dry summer of 1976 had started this way. Christ it was going to be bloody hot, hard work if there was another drought like that! It wasn't likely though; you only got a real scorcher every ten years or so, a '1976' every couple of centuries, if that. All the same, the authorities had imposed restrictions on the use of water, no car-washing or watering the garden. George laughed softly to himself. That bloke three doors away had been caught using a hose on the car. Silly bugger, it was some sort of Sunday morning obsession; wash the mud off in winter and the dust in summer, and if the bloody car was clean then wash it just the same. Bloody masochism! He probably thought a £10 fine was money well spent. It was the likes of Threadgold who were making the country bankrupt but very soon it wouldn't matter anyway. When Libya pressed the button all the water in the world wouldn't douse the fires.

Take each spadeful as it comes, don't think about the next. Pace yourself. You're not tired but your muscles need to get used to the sudden shock of navvying. Fifty-two's a dangerous age for men, the time when you're likely to drop dead from a sudden heart attack. Don't think about it, you're fitter than most. That spot of blood-pressure last year was nothing that a few tablets couldn't clear up. Dr

Horne said you were fine now, needed a bit more exercise. Well, this is just what the doctor ordered.

Dusk was deepening, another ten minutes and it would be too dark to see. He'd have to pack it in then. I'm having an early night, Emily, because I've got to be up and at it early in the morning. You stop in bed and get that migraine better. Or do what the bloody hell you like!

A metallic clink; his spade struck something below the surface, something that wasn't just a stone. Mild curiosity, cutting out another square of turf, turning it up.

Then he stopped and stared. Something in the soil flashed as though the sunlight was reflected upon it — but there was no sunlight. A harsh light that dazzled him briefly, would have made him look away except that for some reason he could not remove his gaze from it. Like fire that burned, died down to a dull glow then flared up again. You had to watch it whether you liked it or not.

George Brownlow stooped down, scraped with his spade. Soil and stones were moved away and he was able to see the object clearly. A disc of some kind, roughly the size of a coffee-jar lid except that its shape was uneven as though it had been roughly cut out of a sheet of metal with a hammer and chisel. Yet why was the initial workmanship so poor whilst the engraving upon it was undoubtedly the fastidious work of a master craftsman? Snakes, God they were repulsive! No, just one. That was silly because no reptile had *two* heads. He reached down for the object, shuddered and almost snatched his fingers away. He didn't want to touch it, it was vile; you could almost see those snakes wriggling, rearing up to strike at him with their fangs! Those eyes, both pairs, small and beady, flashing hatefully. *Seeing him!*

A little cry escaped his lips as his fingers closed over the thing, lifting it clear of the soil. The coldness which emanated from it had his skin prickling, his mouth going dry. Heaving, tasting bile at the back of his throat, he could *feel* those carved serpents wriggling in his grasp. He wanted to fling them from him, run for the house and slam the door behind him. But he couldn't, he was compelled to stand

and stare at the object nestling in the palm of his hand. Feel an inanimate life, four glinting orbs holding his gaze . . . *holding him prisoner!*

And suddenly it was all over; a trick of the imagination, a tired brain succumbing to infantile terrors in the darkness. The thing was cold, certainly, but it couldn't be anything else if it had been buried in the ground for God knew how long. Slippery with moist earth, creating the hallucination that the double-headed snake moved and wriggled. Those eyes . . . he wiped the mud clear of them, gasped his astonishment aloud. Surely they were jewels, they could not be anything else.

Bemused he stood there in the darkness broken only by the glow of the streetlamps on the road more than fifty yards away. It was unbelievable, he'd dug up some item of treasure, a jewelled trinket that had somehow lain buried for perhaps centuries. It might be worth a fortune. His euphoria cooled as he remembered some law about buried treasure belonging to the State. He'd keep it then, clean it up and hide it away. His digging, his tools were forgotten as he glanced back towards the house. Emily was still in bed, she wouldn't be coming downstairs again tonight. Barry and Adrian were in the garage tinkering about with that damned motorcycle. Possibly Sheila and Rita were in the house watching telly. There was no bloody privacy anywhere.

He put on his jacket, dropped the strange object into his pocket like a child that had discovered an exciting toy on a walk in the park, guilty because it belonged to somebody else, afraid that it will be taken off him and he will be punished. Hiding it, seeking an opportunity to go someplace and play with it.

George Brownlow went back indoors furtively. Sheila was in the kitchen, a shapely fair-haired teenager dressed in tight-fitting jeans and a sweater, setting some mugs out on the table. She smiled at him and he saw again Emily when they had first met, features that had not yet hardened with bitterness, unscarred by the constant battle for acceptance in higher social circles which was to leave its mark in later life. That hadn't happened to Sheila yet.

'Does the navvy want a cup of tea?' she laughed good-naturedly.

'Thanks.' He resisted the temptation to fling himself into the nearest chair. His back ached, lumbago pains which had left him untroubled for months suddenly protesting at this unexpected manual labour.

'Rita's in the lounge watching telly.' She began filling the kettle. 'Needless to say the two fellers are mechanicing again. Lord knows how long they'll be at it tonight.'

'How's Mother?' He winced at his own reference to Emily, a sexless term that had grown up with the children.

'She's got a migraine, so she *says*.' Sheila switched the kettle on. 'You two have been rowing again, so Barry tells me. Not that I blame you, Dad. She's getting impossible lately. In fact . . . I'm considering looking for a flat.'

'Oh!' A sickening punch below the belt, an awful thought that Adrian might be moving in with her. He still clung to the hope that his daughter was a virgin. Unlikely in this age of sexual freedom but Sheila wasn't like that — she couldn't be, she was his daughter. Still his little girl.

'I haven't fully decided yet.' She was watching him carefully now, looking for a reaction. 'It all depends on Mum.'

'We ought to try and persuade her to see a doctor. I think maybe she's . . .' suddenly not able to put it into words.

'Going into the change?'

He half-nodded, glanced away. How could any man admit that he didn't know without confessing that he and his wife had no sexual relationship. A gradual process; single beds, next it would be separate rooms. And when that happened marriage was all over, clinging on to a façade of companionship, and even that might die.

'I can't stand much more.' Almost a sob of pent-up frustration. 'She goes on and on about Adrian, every pernickety little fault she can find and tops it all up by saying "what else can you expect from a working-class background." I try to tell her that that's what we were before she won that damned money. Christ, I hope I never get like that. But I'm not giving up Adrian to pander to her little game of make-believe.'

42

'Don't go, Sheila.' It was a desperate plea, a fleeting instant of panic in case she walked out and left him all alone. '*I* like Adrian. He's a nice boy.'

'As I said, I haven't made up my mind yet.' She filled the tea-pot, draped a cosy over it. 'But I will if I have to.'

And I'll go too, he thought. If I only move out to live in that shelter. If I ever finish it!

'Hi.' Rita glanced up from the television as George carried the tray through. 'You've been gardening late tonight, George.'

'Got to make the most of the daylight,' he mumbled, didn't want to enter into explanations. It sounded silly, digging a nuclear shelter without any plans. An obsession that seemed frail in the company of ordinary people.

'Gaddafi's told his people that Israel's for the chop,' Rita pursed her lips, her freckles seeming to dance in the moving glow of the television screen. 'He hasn't even given the Israelis an ultimatum. It's as though he's made his mind up to blast them anyway and TASS are backing him. It's sheer lunacy, he'll never *really* go through with it. Surely he realises the implications . . . unless he doesn't care. The US President has been on American television telling the world that if Libya does carry out her threat then there will be no holding back, not just angry murmurings and trade sanctions like there were over Afghanistan and other places. Our own government's giving the Americans full backing, and don't forget we've got American missile bases in this country. But in all probability it's all hot air and will blow over like everything else in a week or so. Hopefully. Surely one madman can't start a holocaust just on the strength of hatred and a whim?' Her features had gone much paler and it wasn't due to the light reflected from the screen.

'There's more behind it than that.' George Brownlow searched for his glasses, touched something hard and cold in his pocket and snatched his hand away. 'They've niggled one another for years now. Any time now one of 'em's going to overstep the mark. Then that'll be the end for all of us!'

Rita Hendon regarded him with a quizzical expression. Short jet-black hair, she had an air of capability about her, a firmness around her mouth in a different way from Emily Brownlow. Determined, yet not stubborn for the sake of being stubborn. Sex appeal because she was the kind who had to do everything well or not at all. On a number of occasions she had turned George on but that, he decided, had as much to do with Emily's shortcomings as Rita's qualities. She was six years older than Barry but it was a match that would work because he needed somebody firm, somebody to mother him because that was what he had lacked in his upbringing. There was more to bringing up children than discipline; affection played a part in it too.

George was aware that he was sipping tea and watching a television screen. Neither really registered; abstract, wondering how long it would be before the lads gave up their bike repairs for the night and everybody either pushed off home or went to bed. *'Now don't you leave any of them downstairs on their own, George.'* A stock instruction of Emily's if she went up to bed before everybody else. *'It's not right putting temptation in their way.'*

If they want to to do it, they'll do it, he had always longed to reply but had never got round to it. Because he was still trying to convince himself that his own children wouldn't do things like *that*! But tonight he wasn't going to leave them to it because he needed the kitchen to himself. Damn these youngsters. Adrian would hang on until the last possible moment and then spend half an hour saying goodnight to Sheila in the porch. Barry would see Rita home and take about an hour over it. Damn the lot of them.

George Brownlow was determined to sit them all out. The evening dragged on. Eleven o'clock. The boys came back in. Emily would have gone beserk at them coming into the lounge with oil smeared on their hands and faces. The roller towel on the kitchen door was probably black with it too. Go on, get off home or go to bed! But nobody was in a hurry, because Emily wasn't around.

Finally the gathering broke up. Rita showed no qualms about going home on the pillion of Barry's bike, a fact which always astounded Emily. *'When I was her age I wouldn't have gone on your bike, George.'* No, because I never

44

bloody well had a bike. Perhaps I missed out on something. *'And this snogging in the porch is getting disgusting. It could lead to other things!'* Something else we missed out on but it's too bloody late now for sure.

Waiting. The temptation was to get that thing out, whatever it was, begin polishing it slightly on a handkerchief, drop it back in his pocket if anybody came. Pulses racing; too risky. He thought he felt a movement, like something ... *wriggling*. Ugh! All the same, he couldn't wait to have a good look at it. What the hell *was* it?

It was cold in here, which wasn't surprising because Emily had turned the central-heating off last month. *We shan't need that again until the autumn, George.* Another sacrifice to assist her in keeping up a River View image. Kippers and curtains, an old saying; you ate kippers and kept the curtains closed so you could boast to your neighbours that you'd eaten Dover sole.

A door slammed, footsteps going upstairs. That would be Barry. A few minutes later George heard the muffled sound of a record. It wasn't fair with Emily ill. *If* she was ill.

It was half an hour before Sheila came in, kicking off her shoes in the hall and going straight through to the kitchen. A few minutes later he heard the kettle boiling. A bloody nightly ritual as though going to bed was something to be delayed until the last possible moment. Neither of the children would come in here, though; they never did. A kind of guilt complex. They might be asked what they had been doing this last half hour. But they wouldn't do anything like *that*, George was certain. He decided to try and put it out of his mind.

At last the house was quiet. He glanced at the clock. A quarter past twelve. The Brownlows never went to bed on the same day that they got up. Except Emily, of course.

His breathing was shallow and he was glancing about him nervously, listening intently because somewhere a floorboard creaked. It would be just like Emily to sneak downstairs, fling open the door suddenly, her expression ready in case she caught him at the cocktail cabinet helping himself to the bottle of Dimple which they kept specially

45

for River View callers. *'Whatever are you doing sat there in your gardening clothes, George? Anybody would think you objected to sleeping in the same room as me.'*

But she didn't come.

Feverish haste, scrabbling that thing out of his pocket so that it slipped through his fingers, bounced on the carpet and rolled, clinked as it hit the table leg and came to rest. Staring at him, four venomous eyes glinting in the subdued lighting. It really hated him!

He caught his breath, was aware how his heart was pounding. I'm sorry, I didn't mean to drop you like that. I hope you haven't hurt yourself. The snake eyes lost some of their fire, those fangs could almost have been smiling. *Pick me up, then. Don't be afraid.*

He advanced, stretched out a hand nervously, touched the strange metal with trembling fingers, almost dropped it again. He crossed the room, laid it on the flat top of the cocktail cabinet. Emily would go beserk if she came in now. Sod Emily!

He examined it more closely, used his handkerchief to wipe away some of the clinging mud, those eyes following his every move — there was no getting away from them. No matter where you hid they would search you out.

It was an *amulet*! He wondered why he had not realised that before, probably because he had only seen it in the half-light. Old, very old. And very dirty. It needed cleaning, that was the first job and it had to be done right away.

He crept into the kitchen, holding the amulet as though it was a piece of antique crockery, laying it carefully on the table while he searched Emily's cupboards for some kind of cleaning substance. Ah, Duraglit, that would do fine. He remembered using it in the army to clean his brasses.

It wasn't easy, there was mud caked in all those peculiar little grooves and he had to use a pin to scrape them clean. *Hieroglyphics*! That was feasible if indeed this was an amulet. Now how the deuce did this thing come to be buried in a River View garden, a modern housing area where . . .?

Something flashed across his memory, Barry's words coming back to him like distant echoes in the mountains.

46

'There's supposed to be some Egyptian mummies buried somewhere hereabouts . . .'

George Brownlow's scalp prickled and he looked towards the window. For once the curtains were not drawn, a sure sign that Emily wasn't around. Outside there was the blackness of a summer's night; the darkness could have hidden anything. He swallowed, wondered whether or not to break off from what he was doing and go and close the curtains. He had that awful feeling that he was being watched!

Temporary relief mingled with his fear. He was being watched all right — by that double-headed serpent engraved on the amulet, its eyes redly afire again, blood red jewels which blazed an uncontrollable hatred for him. It held his gaze, he could feel its power numbing him like some potent drug, shutting him off from the rest of the world. Just himself and . . . *that*!

Mumbled incoherent apologies for disturbing its last resting place, for *daring* to clean it with some modern substance, for treating it like some object of curiosity. He promised to re-bury it, not to dig any more in case he came upon those mummies, injured them with a pick or a spade; knew he'd said the wrong thing and caused offence by the way those eyes filled with the liquid fire of some terrible wrath.

'You must dig. And dig. Make this place which I have already commanded you to make!'

George Brownlow nodded dumbly. He didn't understand how the serpent knew about his plans but at least it approved of them. He could not think why. It was as though it could read his mind and that was a terrifying thought.

He finished cleaning the amulet, wondered where he should keep it. There was nowhere private in this house; his wife was likely to go poking in the most unexpected places. There was only one sure place — on his person.

The eyes dulled, he felt their force being withdrawn from him, an almost physical sensation like something was being sucked from him, allowing him to think more freely. One last brief flicker from those eyes. 'Do not underestimate me. I never sleep, for I am Set.'

Trembling violently George Brownlow picked up the amulet, felt once more its icy coldness, the ancient life which emanated from it like some power-charged massager. And he knew without any doubt that he was its slave, committed to absolute obedience. He must dig for he had been ordered to do so, complete his shelter for some purpose besides his own instinct to survive the holocaust which he knew must come before long. It was an unnerving thought!

George Brownlow paused at the foot of the stairs, rested his hand on the rail, felt the sudden surge of exhaustion which until now had been checked as though by some psychological dam. He needed to sleep. His eyelids began to close, flickered open again; looking about him as though he expected to see some nameless horror creeping upon him, some giant double-headed serpent with burning red eyes which hissed and commanded him to go out there in the stillness of night and excavate that shelter because his master had need of it. Cringing, dragging himself up the stairs, mutely pleading to be allowed a few hours' rest so that on the morrow he might work all the faster.

Stealthily easing himself through the bedroom door, leaving the landing light on because he feared the blackness and the evil which it held. He saw the outline of Emily's body on the far twin bed by the window, a still shape that might or might not be breathing. And he did not care whether she lived or died because she did not figure in the plans of the one who called himself Set.

George Brownlow knew that he would not be allowed to rest, that the snake god had ordered him to go out into the garden and dig, had endowed him with a strength beyond that of the average man of fifty-two, would spare him the perils of pushing his body beyond its limits.

He swung the pick, winced as his muscles became shock absorbers, shovelled at the loose soil and stones, threw them up on to the growing pile. A kind of rhythm and once you eased into it your tiredness disappeared. This way one could go on digging forever.

The big hole was getting deeper. More moist, too, which was only to be expected so close to a river. George wondered what time it was, how soon it would be dawn. But time did not matter, he had to keep on digging because the serpent god would be very angry if he shirked his task. Silence, except for the thuds of soil, the trickle of small stones like a miniature avalanche.

Now the hole was so deep that he had to reach right up to toss each shovelful clear, the night sky above dark with no hint of the coming of a new day. No stars, like the entire universe was dead and George Brownlow was the only remaining living being, the sole survivor after some terrible catastrophe which had destroyed mankind. He wanted to cry but the tears would not come, just a burning sensation as though he, too, was dying from radiation poisoning, but he was forced to keep on working until that happened. And even when it did there was no guarantee that he would be granted the peace he craved.

Still digging, sensing the hopelessness of it all but working fervently because he dared not slacken, a robot who had no control over his own actions.

Stones were showering back faster than ever now. He had dug so deep that it was impossible from where he stood to throw the earth far enough back from the hole. He would have to climb out, shovel some of that mountainous heap away.

And in that one awful instant George Brownlow became aware that there was no way in which he could clamber out of the pit which he had dug for himself!

Sheer terror at first, whimpering and resigning himself to his fate, trying to shout but no sound came. Cringing in a corner, his back damp from sweat and moist earth. Then came the panic, a desperation that had him jumping at the sides, trying to claw a handhold, slipping and falling back. Sobbing.

His foot kicked against something hard and a sudden ray of hope infiltrated his crazed brain — the spade and the pick; he still had them. He could dig his way out!

It wasn't easy trying to swing the pickaxe in the confined space of that grave-like hole. There was no room

49

to manipulate it so he began using it as a lever, gouging. Despair again; solid rock and he had not the force to smash it.

The pick dropped from his hands, crashed on to his foot but the pain went unnoticed. He seized the spade, stretched up with it and began loosening the surface soil. Perhaps he could move enough of it to give him a shelf which he could reach and haul himself up on to. Soil and stones began to shower back on him, forcing him to turn his head aside.

He heard the avalanche before he saw it; a noise like a tipper truck of rubble being emptied. Then the full force of the excavated soil hit him, threw him back, flung him to the floor. In those few seconds his terror reached a peak. His vocal chords functioned again but his scream was cut off by a mouthful of foul earth. He fought against the tide, knew he was buried beneath it and could still hear the rumble of falling soil, feel the weight on his body becoming greater until surely he must be squashed and suffocated.

An instinctive gasping for air, astonished that he was still able to breathe. He tried to move his limbs but they were securely pinned down. And all around there was unpenetrable blackness.

Buried alive. Catalepsy! How long would it take him to die?

Now that he was immobile his brain was functioning logically, torturing him. Nobody knew where he was, *normal* people were asleep in bed. Emily would certainly never dream of coming into the garden to look for him. *'If you're fool enough to dig in the middle of the night, George, then you can damned well stop out there. And don't expect me to come bringing you cups of tea. You should see the doctor!'* Doctor? It was an undertaker George Brownlow would need. But if he was still alive in this grave then what was the point of burying him again? Oh God, somebody cremate me. *Let me die!*

Time passed. Minutes or hours, he had no conception. Just lying there, his mind a turmoil again. Maybe they would never think to look for him in here, would not realise. They'd list him as a missing person and wait for him to turn up. And if for some reason he *didn't* die. . . .

He thought he heard something. It was impossible, he was buried too deep. His imagination was playing tricks on him again. He held his breath . . . if in fact he breathed. Or was he already dead and this was the Stygian blackness of an eternal hell.

Definitely he heard something, a kind of slithering sound like a snake might make — a double-headed one! Trying to shy away only he could not move, not knowing whether his eyes were open or shut. Waiting, trying to whimper his fear again.

Something touched him! Oh Jesus God, it was vile, cold and slimy, easing its way up his leg as though whatever it was was feeling him out, exploring him. This time he was sure he screamed for he heard his own yell of terror. Now he knew without a doubt what the thing on his body was — *a human hand, as cold as death itself!*

Pressing, probing. *Another one coming to join it!* His last attempt at a logical explanation before his mind snapped. They'd found him, dug down to rescue him. But he knew he only lied to himself because those icy fingers were exploring him with obscene lusting pleasure, broken fingernails gouging his flesh in their eagerness.

'*Are you my beloved, Āba-aner? Answer me, my beloved, for it has been so long since I last set eyes upon you that I fail to recognise you. Have you changed with the passing of time?*'

Somehow George Brownlow found that he could see in the darkness. A strange radiance penetrated the gloom, showed him the heaped earth interspersed with tunnels just wide enough to crawl through as though some giant mole had burrowed down here. That was why he could still breathe, because there was a current of air coming down from above. If only he could free himself from the heap of earth that pinned him down. . . .

And suddenly he saw it, had a full view of the creature which knelt over him, pawing at him with hands from which the rotting flesh hung in strips. Revulsion mingled with terror, his brain unable to accept that such a thing could possibly live. Human in form; at least it had a head, and arms and legs, the whole body swathed in dirty frayed bandages which unravelled as it moved, revealing flesh beneath that was green with decomposition and giving off a stench of putrefaction. A female, because breasts sagged from it like empty pouches.

'You are *not* Āba-aner!' Disappointment and grief mingling in that harsh croak.

Don't look at the face. For God's sake don't look upon those features!

His crazed brain made one last attempt to save his sanity but he ignored it. He could not hold back a cry which incorporated pity and fear as he gazed upon features from which the swathings had unravelled. Beautiful once but now they were horrific for the parasites of the soil had already begun to ravage. Things that wriggled and crawled as they feasted upon human carrion. An eye dangled from its socket, still living, *still seeing*, trying to twist its way round so that it had a view of the human who had trespassed in this place of the dead. Nostrils that bubbled some kind of yellow mucus, wheezing as the frail lungs fought to hold on to life. A creature that was dying, only its willpower giving it the strength to crawl, some strange obsession keeping the spark of life kindled within that awful body. A mouth that had no lips, just even white teeth wobbling in the shrunken gums as it spoke.

'*Who are you, stranger, and what have you done with my beloved Āba-aner? You have harmed him, stolen his body as it was stolen once before by a holy man who did not keep his word!*'

George Brownlow tried to shake his head in denial, attempted to speak but the sound he made was unintelligible. She was becoming angry. He must convince her that he had not seen this Āba-aner, whoever he was. She gave a hiss of rage and he smelled the foulness of her breath, an icy blast that had him retching.

Now she was upon him, puny skeletal fists beating at him, pummelling his body in a frenzy of blows.

'*Tell me where Āba-aner is? Set himself has sent you to steal him, to take his body from me just as he was taken in life!*'

A denial was impossible against the windmilling arms, bony fists inflicting pain, her fury escalating as she attacked him. He tasted blood, tried to cry out that he would help her search for Āba-aner, but nothing could penetrate that hurricane of inhuman rage. The blackness came at him again as though that strange light had been suddenly extinguished, leaving him a helpless victim of this strange woman in the terrible unending darkness.

'George, for God's sake wake up!'

George Brownlow writhed, managed to get a grip on one of those wrists, held it. Strangely it didn't feel cold anymore. He twisted it, was rewarded by a shriek of pain.

'I tell you I have not stolen Āba-aner,' he screeched. 'And I don't know who the hell he is. Now let me go!'

Suddenly the light was back again. Not the soft indeterminable glow this time but the harsh dazzling brightness of an electric bulb. He still smelled that rotting human carrion fanned by her stinking breath but the flesh no longer peeled from her body. Harsh features, certainly, but they belonged to *Emily*!

He relaxed his grip on her wrist and she snatched her hand away, rubbed at the red weal. He stared around. His own bedroom, lying on his own single bed, the blankets a rumpled heap, damp with sweat. Emily watched him carefully with narrowed eyes, stepped back a pace and glanced in the direction of the door.

'You've been having a nightmare, George,' her tone was reproachful yet there was no disguising the relief. 'What a din you kicked up. I wouldn't be surprised if you've woken Barry and Sheila. Not to mention me, just when my migraine was beginning to ease up.'

'I'm sorry.' He was trembling with relief. He could still taste that horrible cloying grave soil. He licked his lip where it was bleeding.

'Never mind about being sorry, just look what a disturbance you've created. You're overdoing it, George. I've never had to say that to you in your life before but now you've gone barmy. Digging a nuclear shelter, indeed! As if *you* could make one. The most you've ever been able to do is dig the garden and even that gives you lumbago. This nonsense will have to stop otherwise I'm going to have a word with Dr Horne about you. I reckon you're going senile.'

But George Brownlow wasn't listening. Words echoed in his brain, but they weren't Emily's *'What have you done with my beloved Āba-aner?'*

And he knew that tomorrow he must continue with his excavations, a compelling inexplicable obsession for which the construction of a nuclear fallout shelter was but a façade. He shuddered to think what he might discover deep down in that riverside soil.

Chapter Three

The Plague of Frogs

'YOUR OLD man's going round the bend.' Adrian Capper kicked a stone idly, watched it skim along the narrow path and then plop into the river. 'I reckon it's the heat, but if it isn't it soon will be, digging all day in this temperature.'

'It's Mum that's driven him to it.' Sheila squeezed his hand, found herself wishing that she didn't ever have to go back to her family, that she and her boyfriend could remain in this peaceful river setting forever. Idyllic, but one had to face reality. 'You've no idea what it's like at home, nagging and bickering all day long. I said to myself the day Dad got made redundant that something was going to snap between him and Mum. She never lets up.'

'Why can't we find a place of our own?' He slipped an arm around her, pulled her close. 'Hell, we don't *have* to get married. And to hell with your mother.'

'I'd like to.' She was watching a group of water boatmen in a clearing in the thick reed-bed which bordered the bank. 'It's just that . . . well, I don't like walking out on Dad.'

'Jesus Christ he's old enough to look after himself!' He almost added '*too bloody old, if you ask me.*'

'He's got Barry and Rita,' Adrian added, pulling her close to him.

'I know. Maybe I've been too indoctrinated at home, Adrian, but I feel like I'm walking out on them. I can't explain it but . . . but there's something wrong. I'm worried about Dad. D'you know what he said at breakfast, Adrian?'

55

'No, but I'll make an intelligent guess,' he grinned. '"Pass me the marmalade."'

'You're just being silly.'

'I'm sorry, but I didn't mean it. Go on, what *did* he say?'

'It was ever so queer. Mum was going on about a nightmare he'd apparently had last night and telling him, as usual, that he wasn't cut out for hard physical work, when suddenly he stared at us and said "I am the one who has been chosen to lead you out of the wilderness. We shall suffer plagues, famine and drought but I shall lead you to safety." I know it sounds stupid but I felt little shivers running up my back. It wasn't just what he said, it was his expression. His eyes were all glazed as if he was in a trance or something.'

'Let's sit down and have a rest.' Adrian steered Sheila away from the path to where a patch of springy grass still showed green, protected from three weeks of burning sun by the overhanging foliage of a spreading willow tree. "It's too hot to walk far. I guess most folks have stayed at home. Usually this track is crowded on a summer evening.'

They stretched themselves out on the grass. So still, so windless, the sun already sinking in the west. It was hard to believe that only a few hundred yards away stood the housing estate. No noise except for the chirping rasping sound of grasshoppers and the croaking of frogs in the rushes. A swallow swooped down after flies, circled, tried again. Then it, too, went away and didn't come back. The heat was affecting everything and everybody, Adrian decided. That was why old Brownlow was digging his ludicrous nuclear shelter. When the weather broke he'd pack it in. But according to the forecasters the drought was going on into its fourth week. The experts had said that 1976 was a freak, that it could never happen again. The unpredictable British climate was doing its damnedest to prove them wrong.

'I told Dad I was thinking of moving out.' Sheila turned her face towards his and he saw that her eyes were misty. 'Oh Adrian, I want us to be together. I was hoping that maybe you'd come back from the Jobcentre with some good news today.'

He wanted to say *'we could manage on your money from the supermarket'* but only his pride, his self-respect held him back. 'Perhaps I could find some casual work.'

'Half the population's moonlighting as it is. No, I guess we'll just have to carry on as we are for a bit. I could afford a bedsit though, just to get away from home. There's a limit to loyalty.'

He kissed her, was suddenly glad that he'd brought her down here. Courting one of the Brownlows wasn't easy.

Sheila almost said *'stop it'*, pandered to her upbringing as she felt his fingers unflip a button on her blouse, move on to the next. She felt her body go tense, rigid, tried to stop that repetitive bleat of her mother's intruding. *'Don't you go making yourself cheap. Take it from me, no man respects a girl who lets him do those sort of things to her.'* Oh God, shut up, mother. We've already done it before. Twice.

Defying Emily Brownlow in her own mind, easing herself up so that Adrian could pull her blouse right off, assisting him with the clip-fastener on her bra because he wasn't used to those sort of things. You keep out of this, mother.

Closing her eyes because she felt embarrassed for him, wanted him to view her nakedness without inhibition. So cool without her clothes. She heard him undressing, squinted through half-closed eyes. Curiosity. She couldn't imagine Mum and Dad ever having done anything like this. They must have, though, because of herself and Barry. The thought was repulsive. She pushed it from her mind.

Adrian was kissing her again. She could tell he was apprehensive, possibly her own nervousness rubbing off on him. The first time, the first time *ever*, she reminded herself, it had been like this. She had tried to kid him that it had been great. Certainly it hadn't hurt as it was supposed to, if one believed everything one heard, but it had been sort of . . . well, *negative*. It was a bit trying having it on the floor of the living room in Adrian's house with his parents in bed directly above them. Listening all the time, not really paying attention to what they were doing. She had faked an orgasm, wondered if she had really fooled him but no way was she able to come like she did when she masturbated.

Now her nerves were troubling her again. Suppose somebody came, a casual stroller along the riverside exercising their dog. Oh God, the shock, the embarrassment, fumbling to get dressed. Surely either herself or Adrian would hear anybody coming. Listening again. The grasshoppers had gone silent; just the frogs, a chorus from the bullrushes.

Damn it, she could hear her mother's whining voice. *'Girls who do things like that are likely to get themselves pregnant and just think what a disgrace that would be for us. We should have to move out of the area.'*

God, mother, you're ruining this for me! Now I'm feeling guilty. Next thing I'll be going to church again.

Adrian was on top of her now. She felt his lips brushing hers, opened her mouth to receive his tongue, a movement that was an invitation to him to go ahead. Damn it, she was all tense again and that wasn't making it any easier for him.

'I love you,' he whispered.

'And I love you, Adrian.' Oh God, I'd love to get pregnant right now, have your baby, and to hell with mother and her prudishness and snobbishness.

A rhythm that slowed. They both found themselves listening again. The frogs seemed louder, nearer. A distraction. It was almost dark now and somehow the night air seemed alive as though an electric storm was brewing. But that couldn't be because there hadn't been a single cloud in the sky for days on end.

Sheila tried to pick up the rhythm again but it had slipped away. That tension had returned and now their love-making was purely a physical function that was no longer sensuous. She wished Adrian would hurry up and finish and maybe next time she would respond more eagerly. Emily Brownlow's voice echoed in her brain again. *'I always say sex is the most over-rated thing in the world. Women only do it to please their husbands and I sometimes wonder if men get anything out of it. I reckon they only do it to try and prove something!'*

Damn, it was all gone now and Adrian seemed to be experiencing difficulties. She wanted to say *'why don't we*

58

pack it up and try again another time' but she was afraid in case she offended him. Blast you, Emily Brownlow, this is all your fault!

The night was noisy. She wouldn't have believed that frogs could make so much din. She shivered and her naked body goosepimpled. Repulsive little things, so cold and slimy. She would never forget that time when she was seven when Barry had come home from a fishing expedition. *'I've got a surprise for you, She,'* he had grinned. *'Close your eyes and open your mouth wide.'* She had done so, anticipating a sweet or something pleasant. Oh, even now the memory of it made her retch. Something had popped into her mouth, a tiny cold slippery thing that had jumped and almost gone down her throat. She'd been violently sick, then fainted when she'd seen that awful little creature attempting to extricate itself from her vomit — a baby frog about the size of her thumbnail! Goodness, they were making the devil of a row tonight.

'Are you OK, She?'

'Yes.' She opened her eyes again, saw his outline as he knelt over her. 'I'm OK. Just tired, I suppose.'

'I'm not much good tonight.'

'It doesn't matter, I wasn't much feeling like it anyway. Maybe we should go somewhere more secluded next time. But I love you, Adrian.'

'I love you, too.' He reached out, groped for the scattered garments in the darkness. 'Let's get dressed and go back to our place for a coffee.' Not *your* place although we're in spitting distance of it.

He tossed her blouse across to her and even as she caught it, something fell out of it, landed squat on her bare stomach; hopped. And Sheila Brownlow screamed because she recognised the feel of a frog!

A loud shriek of sheer terror and revulsion and even before the echoes had died away the whole area seemed to come to life. Frogs, dozens of them, jumping, squatting, jumping again.

'Shut up. It's only a frog. . . .'

She was becoming hysterical, leaping up, treading on something soft and cold that burst beneath her foot, oozing

59

a slimy substance from the squashed flattened body. Another one. She slipped and fell, yelled as she fell among them.

She was up again, screaming and running blindly, Adrian Capper in pursuit. Two naked people who had completely forgotten their clothes scattered in the long grass. Headlong flight, feeling the small reptiles being crushed beneath their feet, out on to the path that ran parallel to the river, trying to shut out that maddening chorus. It was as though the frogs mocked them as they ran the gauntlet. The track narrowed, a steep bank on one side that went down to the river below; dangerous if you missed your footing.

Desperately Adrian tried to catch Sheila up. His greatest fear was that she might fall into the deep sluggish current. She had an inherent fear of water and the most he could swim was a length at the baths, and he had only managed that because he had been afraid of the school swimming instructor.

'Wait for me, Sheila!'

But Sheila wasn't waiting for anybody, her mind crazed by a nightmarish fear that had suddenly become reality. Ahead of her she saw the lights of the River View estate and only there would she be safe.

Adrian trod on a frog, slithered and almost fell into the river. Sheila gained another ten yards, gasped her relief as she saw the outline of her parents' garden fence, prayed that her father hadn't put the padlock on. In the glow of the orange street-lighting she saw the reptiles for the first time, experienced a wave of nausea that had her slowing to a halt, feeling faint. *They were everywhere, hundreds of them, a living slippery carpet that barred her way to safety!*

'There's no way through!' She screamed and would have turned back had not Adrian caught her, pulled her to him.

'Pull yourself together,' he shook her roughly. 'They're only *frogs*. They're harmless.'

'They're horrible!'

She was straining, trying to break free. There was no knowing what she would do if he didn't restrain her;

somehow they had to get back to the Brownlow household. All around them eyes glinted in the distant glow of the River View streetlamps, thousands of orange orbs, a myriad of revolting shimmering yellowish-green evil! The creatures hopped, checked, hopped again. As though they *knew*, sensed human fear and were bunching to surround the fugitives, cutting off their escape route.

'We're going through them.' Adrian stooped, exerted every ounce of strength he could muster, and lifted Sheila, cradling her to him.

'No!' she screamed.

'They can't hurt us.'

She was struggling, kicking and flaying her arms. 'Adrian, no, *no*! For God's sake let's run!'

'There's nowhere to run to, Sheila, except back to your house. Now close your eyes and hold on tight to me. I'm going through that lot!'

Adrian had never before been frightened of frogs or similar reptiles. Suddenly they were repulsive to him, those eyes watching him almost as though they anticipated what he was going to do. Jesus Christ, if only he'd stopped to put his shoes on it wouldn't have been so bad. Try not to think about them, don't look down, keep your eyes fixed on that garden gate. Once you're through there you're OK. You'll be safe.

He dared not run in case he slipped; a fast walk, long strides. Something soft and spongy beneath his foot, bursting. Ugh! Then another . . . and another. Just keep going. A carpet of them in front of him where the path narrowed. He held Sheila tight, prayed that he wasn't going to throw up all over her.

It was like walking on pieces of waterlogged foam rubber, the water squelching, squirting up over his bare feet. Frog's blood, if there was such a thing. And that noise, a symphony that filled the still night air, more aggressive now. *'Stop them . . . stop them . . . stop them. . . .'*

Adrian Capper wasn't stopping. His feet skidded on the remains of flattened reptiles, once he almost fell, but somehow he kept going. The gate was less than twenty yards away.

Sheila experienced a wave of nausea, felt again that tiny frog which her mischievous brother had popped into her open mouth, its cold slimy texture and the way it had almost hopped down her throat. She almost vomited, heaved and tasted bile. If Adrian fell or dropped her . . . it didn't bear thinking about.

He came to a halt. She heard the metallic click of a latch and opened her eyes. They had made it, they were inside the garden. *But the frogs were here as well!*

The big lawn appeared to move in jerky waves and the reflection from the streetlamps showed a shiny mass of tiny bodies, eyes turned towards the newcomers. Seeing and understanding.

'Oh, my God!' Her fingernails gouged Adrian.

'Don't worry, it's not far to the house.' His eyes were searching for a path through them, a route where they were more sparse but there was none. 'Hold on, we're on the last lap now.'

It was like wading through blancmange fresh from the refrigerator, a sea of reptiles converging on the fleeing couple; kamakaze frogs, one died and another ten took its place.

Up on to the patio, kicking them aside to reach the back door, feeling them hurling themselves against his bare legs, a futile attack because in the end strength would win the day. Sweep them back from the step, get the door open and slam it behind you. Then you'll be safe.

Only the door was locked!

Adrian felt the frogs milling around his feet, crawling over them. He kicked them away, felt another batch come at him.

'FOR CHRIST'S SAKE OPEN UP!' he screamed.

For the first time he felt helpless, abandoned. Sheila was starting to panic again. He drew back his foot, drove it hard against the lower panel of the door, gasped with pain. Where the hell was everybody? Frogs were hopping up the steps as though massing for a final assault, a wave of cold slime which would overrun the cowering humans. Adrian remembered a film he'd seen once on TV about giant

62

man-eating frogs in a swamp. But these were ordinary frogs, they couldn't hurt you.

'Mother always locks the back door after dark.' Sheila buried her face against his chest. 'They're probably watching telly and can't hear us.'

The croaking was growing in volume, a vibrant noise that came up from the river and beyond, deafening. And then the fugitives heard a key turning in the back door.

Adrian was pushing inside, Sheila clasped to him, bundling a startled George Brownlow out of the way. The door slammed shut again.

'Oi, what's going on?' Brownlow's astonishment turned to anger as he surveyed his naked visitors.

'Never mind that now,' Adrian lowered Sheila to the floor. 'Doubtless I can borrow a shirt and some jeans of Barry's. *But d'you know what's happening out there?*'

George Brownlow's gaze was riveted on the lower half of Adrian's body, disgust mingling with anger. Have you been doing something with *my* daughter?

'I'll get you some of Barry's clothes, Adrian.' Sheila made for the door, gasped her alarm and embarrassment as she met her mother and Rita coming in from the hall.

'George, whatever's happening, what's going on?' Emily Brownlow shrieked. 'Don't open the door else those frogs'll get in. Oh my God, that boy's *naked*!'

'Just shut up for once, Mother,' Sheila pushed passed her, ran for the stairs. 'There's a perfectly ordinary explanation.' Sheila didn't know one right now but she'd think up one. She was trembling as she raced upstairs, her legs suddenly weak and threatening to buckle under her. But the frogs couldn't get them in here.

'I won't stand for this in my house!' Emily shrieked. 'George, get that boy out. I won't have it, d'you hear me?'

But George Brownlow was peering out of the window, shielding his eyes against the reflection of the lighted room. He pursed his lips, whistled tunelessly.

'Where on earth have they all come from?' Barry appeared behind Rita, grinned at the sight of Adrian busily wrapping the roller-towel around his waist.

'From the river.' George Brownlow's voice was suddenly low, his eyes glazed as though an instant cataract had formed. 'Where else d'you think they've come from? Out of the bulrushes that hid Moses, swarming in their millions. *The Plague of Frogs is upon us for we are the accursed! Have I not already warned you?*'

'You're mad!' Emily ventured into the room now that Adrian had the towel around him, her angry eyes picking out a couple of slimy bare footmarks just inside the back door. 'You're all mad. The garden is full of frogs and my daughter comes home naked! It's disgusting and I won't stand for it. I want an explanation as to what you two have been up to, why you haven't got any clothes on. D'you hear me?'

'The Plague is upon us.' George Brownlow's features were ashen. 'The frogs first but there will be others, you mark my words. The gods are angry with us!'

Silence. Nobody in the room spoke for everybody was listening to the growing cacophony of the frogs outside. For once not even Emily Brownlow could dispute her husband's words. The Plague was certainly upon them.

Chapter Four

The Rod of Moses

GEORGE BROWNLOW was up long before the rest of the household the following morning, fearfully peering out of the bedroom window. He gave a grunt of relief as his eyes searched the garden below. There was not a frog in sight, they had returned whence they had come. A sign from the gods — a warning! Tonight they might come again.

He dressed quickly and quietly, and with a swift glance at the sleeping form of Emily he went downstairs. A slight headache, due doubtless to the restless night he'd had, flitting nightmarish dreams that were gone before he could remember them, leaving in their wake a growing depression.

He went into the kitchen, poured himself a glass of fresh orange juice from the fridge. It was going to be hot again today, and tomorrow, and the day after. All the same he shivered for this was only the beginning. Of what? He was but destiny's pawn and all he could do was dig. And dig.

George Brownlow went outside, looked around apprehensively. The frogs had left little evidence of their coming, just one or two squashed patches of unrecognisable morass that the early morning sun was already drying up. On a sudden impulse he decided to check the river first. They had gone back there undoubtedly to seek the cool of the rushes by day. And tonight. . . .

Footsteps accompanied by a clanking and rattling of glass bottles, a quick step and a tuneless whistling had him whirling round. The milkman. Damn the fellow, he'd taken to bringing the milk round the back lately, presumably to leave it in the patch of shade temporarily offered by the rear of the house.

'Mornin'. Lovely morning.'

'Yes.' George regarded the other impatiently. 'The whole country is being scorched up. Looks like another '76.'

'Mrs Braithwaite has been tellin' me about the frogs.' Lowering the crate, extracting three bottles, suddenly dawdling. Gossip was a perk of an otherwise mundane job. 'She reckons 'er garden was alive with the things last night. She even 'ad to sweep 'em out of the 'ouse. What d'you make o' that?'

'Nothing to get worked up about.' George Brownlow spoke tersely; he was in no mood to gossip with tradesmen. 'It's just the heat that caused it, nothing else. Freak weather conditions do strange things to animals. No different from when we had that tremendous thunderstorm last summer. The gardens were swarming with frogs then and nobody gave it a second thought. The creatures went back down to the river afterwards just as they've done now. They don't do any harm.'

'No, I suppose not.' The milkman straightened up, made as if to say something else but George Brownlow had already turned away. He was like most of the other residents on River View. Bloody snobbish. Beneath him to talk to the milkman. Bugger 'im. Bugger 'em all!

George Brownlow listened to the other's receding footsteps, the way the gate slammed shut after him. Good riddance! Then his thoughts returned to Sheila and Adrian. Their story *could* just be true and to satisfy his own conscience he preferred to believe it. They'd gone for a stroll along the river bank and the evening had been so sultry that they had been tempted to bathe. Ugh! There was sewage in this river, the water was always black and muddy, sluggish. Uninviting. And neither of them could swim properly. Points against them. Points *for* them: down by the ox-bow the water was shallow, safe if you didn't venture too far out. Which meant it wasn't deep enough to swim there anyway so there was no need to strip naked. But they might have done that because the evening was so hot. Yes, that was it! Not that George Brownlow approved because the sight of a naked body of the opposite sex *could* lead to other things. But he believed them; just a bathe, nothing else. Because Sheila wouldn't do anything like *that*.

Cautiously he let himself out of the garden gate, scrutinised the winding path that followed the course of the river. A couple of crows flapped up, cawed angrily. They had been feeding on dead frogs, a delicacy to which they would return in due course. Black wings outstretched they glided across the river, perched in the branches of a dead elm, watched him balefully. Vultures. He licked his dry lips. Vultures always came in the wake of a plague.

In the distance he heard the whine of the milkman's electric vehicle. So mundane, out of place. He stopped, listened intently. Grasshoppers chirping but not a sound of frogs. They would rest by day and come again at nightfall. Harmless, unless you got too many of them and then there was no knowing what they would do, what the side-effects would be on the balance of Nature.

The touch of cold metal in his pocket brought with it a feeling of guilt. He should be digging, not wasting his time down here. Also, he would have to find a safe hiding place for the amulet.

He turned, began to retrace his steps. And that was when something lying on the side of the path attracted his attention. A dead stick, nothing more. He was on the point of ignoring it but his gaze came back to it. Ornate for such a trivial thing; Nature was truly a perfectionist. Greenish-brown as though some vestige of life still remained in this length of broken branch, with a dark zig-zag pattern running the whole way down its two-foot length. Curiosity, a desire to examine it closer, had him stooping down to pick it up.

And in that instant it came to life! A rigid stick that his fingers closed over suddenly became a writhing spitting venomous thing, securing a grip on his wrist by wrapping its body around it, a head that turned on him with tiny flashing eyes and fangs that opened, hissed.

67

Terror, not just because he was being attacked by a repulsive angry snake but because it had materialised out of a harmless branch. He screamed, fell back and cried out again with pain, almost blacked out. Trying to knock it off his arm, knowing that already it was too late because he had been bitten, a sensation like a clumsy injection that had snapped the needle and left it in his flesh.

And then the snake had gone, releasing itself and diving for freedom, wriggling away into the scorched undergrowth with unbelievable speed, leaving its human victim to nurse his wound.

George Brownlow stared horrified at the swelling red mark on his hand, the oozing trickle of blood. Oh, Merciful God it *had* bitten him, injected its venom into his blood-stream! A wave of dizziness engulfed him at the thought. He might die!

He staggered to his feet, swayed and almost fell. Maybe it was too late already. Something registered in his brain, an article he'd read in a magazine somewhere, possibly one of those journals that you look at in the dentist's waiting-room but don't really take the contents in because your mind is on what you might have to have done to you. The fear of pain again! Snakebite, a warning, some advice on first aid. Suck the poison out of the wound!

His stomach churned. God, he'd throw up. Spew or die, that was his choice. He closed his eyes, pressed his lips to the wound, somehow forced himself to suck. A bitter taste like iron. He spat it out, stared down at the blob of pink spittle in the dust, almost fainted. Then he was retching, vomiting that orange juice with incredible force.

He had to get help quickly. If he collapsed here he would be dead by the time they found him. Don't run, it makes your heart work faster, pumps the poison round your system. Lurching from side to side, staring intently at the bleeding snakebite, wondering if he had the courage to suck it again. He hadn't.

George Brownlow slipped, had to use his wounded arm to save himself from falling, left a skidmark of squashed frogs across the pathway. The crows were still watching him, cawed again as if mocking him, flapped their wings. Vultures impatient to return to their carrion.

A red mist hovered before his eyes, an illusion that it drifted in from the river. He saw the gate, gave way to a sudden fear that it might be a mirage, almost shouted his relief aloud when he touched it and found that it was solid. One fearful glance back in case that snake was following him, but all he saw was a frog corpse and a pair of corvines gliding back down to finish their breakfast.

Across the lawn, barely glancing at his diggings, he shouted as he reached the patio steps.

'Emily . . . Emily. . . . I've been bitten by a snake. Where the hell are you?'

No answer. A silent kitchen greeted him, that empty tumbler on the table still with orange dregs in it and he almost vomited again. Mouthing curses; they didn't care if he died, his slothful family would lie in their beds while he writhed his last on the floor.

As he burst through into the hall he heard footsteps coming downstairs. Sheila, her blonde hair in disarray, her flimsy nylon negligée a reminder of how he had seen her last night. 'Whatever . . .'

'Quick,' almost a scream. 'I've been bitten by a snake!'

'Oh, what rubbish, Dad!' Disbelief and annoyance on her pert features, then her eyes widening as he held up his arm. 'Oh, God!'

She came closer, paled. 'I'll phone for the doctor. Now sit down here on this chair.'

His vision spun and he had to hold on to the sides of the chair, vaguely heard her dialling and a distant phone ringing out somewhere. *Brr-brr-brr*. Like grasshoppers chirping. Any moment he'd hear the frogs starting up. Sheila was sucking in her breath, it reminded him of the way that snake had hissed. He closed his eyes. *The Rod of Moses — he, George Brownlow, had performed that same miracle, only the serpent had been angry and turned upon him!* He saw it again, that snaking blur too fast for the eye to follow, *an evil spitting head that might have been two*! He couldn't be sure.

He shifted his position and the amulet in his pocket clinked faintly. He almost felt it to be sure that it was safe but he didn't, sheer revulsion at the mental picture of that repulsive carving. At the first opportunity he would get rid of it, throw it in the river. No, he wasn't going near the river again. No way. There were other places surely. A feeling of guilt. He had no right to dispose of it.

Sheila was talking, listening, talking again. Her words didn't register, he couldn't concentrate. She dropped the receiver back on to its cradle. 'Doctor Horne's coming round right away. You're to lie and rest on the couch until he gets here. Now, take that dirty old jacket off or Mother will go mad if you soil her best settee.'

The amulet clinked again in protest as George Brownlow shrugged his frayed garment off and he knew then, without any doubt, that he was not going to dispose of the Amulet of Set. It would not let him.

'You'll be all right.' The grey-haired taciturn Dr Horne permitted himself a faint smile and returned his syringe to his bag, gave the dressing on George Brownlow's arm a final cursory check. 'Adder bites are rarely fatal in this country provided they're treated in time. Your arm will be stiff for a day or two and you'll have to rest. Please see that he does, Mrs Brownlow.'

'He'll rest,' Emily vowed with smug satisfaction. 'I'll see to that, Doctor. If he'd stopped in bed until a civilised hour he wouldn't have been bitten in the first place, would he? Beats me what he was doing down by the river at that hour!'

'I was checking on the frogs.' Weak defiance that sounded trite. Brownlow closed his eyes, felt suddenly very tired and his arm was throbbing worse than it had done before Dr Horne had treated it.

'A lot of frogs came up out of the river last night.' Emily Brownlow felt that some explanation was necessary for her husband's seemingly irrational statement. 'The garden was alive with them and we had to keep the doors shut. But they've all gone now, thank goodness.'

Horne nodded. He wasn't interested in frogs. Or snakes for that matter. It was ten years since he had last been called out to treat a viper bite. 'It's the freak weather that's to blame. Adders are fond of basking in a warm place and their natural camouflage makes them look like a piece of dead stick. They're usually harmless unless somebody treads on them by accident. People don't *usually* pick them up, though. Anyway, if the swelling and the ache hasn't gone in a couple of days pop down to the surgery and I'll have another look at it.' *Don't call me out because doctors only give home visits in an emergency,* he added to himself before leaving.

'I almost told him about this other business.' Emily moved to the window, waited until the doctor started his car up as though she was afraid he might overhear her. 'The plagues of Egypt, indeed! You'd better rest up, George, and maybe you'll feel better. We can't afford any *scandals*!'

'The plagues have arrived.' He was lying back on the couch, eyes closed, his voice a whisper that was barely audible. *'I have handled the Rod of Moses and it has spurned me. Yet I still have work to do, for Set has commanded me!'*

'You stop where you are.' Emily glanced around, wished that Barry and Sheila did not have to go to work and leave her alone with George all day. 'You've got to rest like Doctor Horne says you have to.'

There was no answer. George Brownlow might even have been asleep. And for the first time ever Emily Brownlow experienced a fear of her husband, a chilling sensation that had her skin prickling.

Chapter Five

Locusts!

'LOOK, YOU'VE got to get a flat and get out of that mad household!' It was the first time Sheila had ever seen Adrian really angry. His voice was raised and surely his parents in the bedroom directly above would come down to see what was going on. 'It isn't safe and I can tell it's playing on your nerves. Your old man's going right round the bend. He must have been up to *something* else he wouldn't have got a snakebite at five o'clock in the morning.'

'I can't just walk out like that!' She felt the tears welling up behind her eyes. Normally sensitive, she would be crying soon. 'You can't desert your family when they need you.'

'Need you!' he shouted. 'They've never needed you before. Your mother's a right bitch and if she has driven your dad crazy then it's up to *her* to do something about it. If he wants to go and dig craters in the garden then that's his business but once he starts involving you then I reckon it's mine. And you know damned well your folks don't believe that yarn we spun them about bathing in the nude because it was hot, and having to make a run for it when the frogs came up out of the river. We look bloody stupid! Christ, we should've thought of something more feasible than that. Well it's too late now and to hell with them. See this,' he picked up a folded copy of the *Evening Mail*, indicated a place in the classifieds which he had pencil-marked, 'this bed-sit is cut out for you. No palace, but it's warm and clean. Take it and give ourselves a breathing space to look round

72

for something better. Jesus Christ, you've already hinted to your dad that you might be leaving home!'

'No.' She was having to fight to hold back the sobs now. 'I won't because it isn't right. And I'm beginning to think that you only want me for *one* thing.'

'That's a lie!' His cheeks flushed, a blow below the belt which had really hurt. 'I've never once pushed myself at you.'

'I was a virgin before I met you.' She glanced away, picked up her handbag. 'Oh, happy days! Anyway, I'm very tired and I'm going home to bed. I'll give you a ring in a day or two.'

'What about tomorrow night?' A sinking sensation in his stomach; they had never missed a night together ever since they had first started courting.

'I'm stopping in tomorrow night. I'll ring you Thursday.'

'Whatever, you're not going home on your own. I'm coming with you.'

'I'll be all right.' She tried to shake him off but he was holding her too tightly. 'I can look after myself, Adrian.' Tight-lipped, turning her head away.

'Sure, and what if the place is crawling with frogs again like it was last night?'

She sighed, knew she could not go through all that again. 'I suppose so. But I'm not changing my mind. I'm not leaving home, Adrian.'

They walked in silence across the recreation park, a couple whose relationship had suddenly fused. Adrian glanced sideways at her, saw her strained expression, the way she kept peering into the shadows. It wasn't just frogs, it was a culmination of everything that was happening up at River View. Adrian had a strange sort of feeling about George Brownlow — the guy wasn't just going mad, something was *happening* to him, something that had taken place without anyone knowing and had changed his whole life. That was how Hitler had started, an obsession that had plunged the whole world into war and cost millions of lives. Whatever Sheila might say or do, Adrian Capper wasn't going to be relegated to the role of a bystander.

'Listen!' He stopped, still grasping her hand firmly. They were on the River View estate now, parallel to the river, a quiet secluded cul-de-sac of executive houses in which everybody appeared to have retired for the night. There wasn't even a light showing from the Brownlows'.

Sheila strained her ears, picked up a distant sound like a throaty buzz, low and yet the still night air vibrated with it. 'It's . . . it's the frogs again.'

'They sound a long way off and maybe they haven't come up as far as they did last night. Anyway, I'll see you to the front door.'

'All right . . . but no further. Promise?'

He nodded, sighed and led the way in through the drive, the gravel crunching softly beneath their feet. Something darted into the shadows; probably a mouse. He felt Sheila tense, begin fumbling for her doorkey.

'Tomorrow?' Almost a plea, still holding on to her in case she suddenly rushed inside and slammed the door in his face.

'I told you I'll *ring* you Thursday. Now be satisfied and don't pester.' A peck on the cheek and she was gone, the oak-panelled front door clicking shut almost silently and leaving Adrian Capper outside in a lonely desolate world.

The moment the door closed behind her Sheila Brownlow gave way to her tears, the sobs shaking her body as she stood there in the darkened hall. Oh God, what *was* happening to her? She wanted Adrian, wanted to be with him all the time, yet *something* was compelling her to divorce herself from him. Her mother's indoctrination? *'You can't let us all down by marrying a boy off a council estate, Sheila! It's making your dad and me ill.'* Emotional blackmail. No, it wasn't that, something much deeper, much more sinister — *something that was determined to chain her to the Brownlow household!*

She took off her shoes, crept upstairs, stood listening on the landing. The sound of heavy rhythmical breathing from her parents' bedroom; they were both fast asleep. Silence from Barry's but she knew he was in. For the first time in months he hadn't switched on his record player.

A sense of foreboding had Sheila tip-toeing away to her own room. It was as though something was happening to the Brownlows, trapping them here on River View, uniting them for an unknown purpose, ostracising them from the rest of society.

And Sheila Brownlow didn't want to leave anymore, not even for Adrian. He was an outsider.

Barry Brownlow lay for a long time staring up at the ceiling in the darkness of his bedroom. So many things to worry about but right now his main concern was for Rita. She hadn't been well all week. At first she had denied it, trying to shrug it off. 'Maybe I've got a cold coming, you know how nasty these summer bugs can be. I *do* have a bit of a sore throat but it's nothing really.'

Then tonight when he had called to pick her up she had smiled weakly and expressed a desire to stay in. 'I don't feel too good really, Barry. Nothing serious, that sore throat hasn't gone yet and I've got a headache. It could just be because my period's due.'

Which was rubbish. He knew it and she knew it. So they had stayed at the Hendon's, relaxing in deck-chairs on the lawn. Twice Rita had fallen asleep, her cheeks flushed as though she was running a temperature.

'You'd better see the doctor tomorrow.' He'd noticed how hot her mouth was when he kissed her goodnight.

'Maybe.' She squeezed his arm, was virtually holding on to him for support. 'It might just be the heat.'

It might have been but it wasn't, of that he was sure. He'd set his alarm half an hour earlier than usual for tomorrow. He would give her a call before he went to work.

And Dad was certainly acting strangely. Like the frogs and the adder which had bitten him, George Brownlow was the victim of some strange obsession and Barry was sure it wasn't just because mother was always on at him. He was half resigned to staying away from work tomorrow and keeping an eye on them.

Then he heard Sheila come in, heard her sobbing downstairs and almost went to see what the trouble was.

Probably some tiff with Adrian and it was none of his business. All the same, it was something else to worry about.

Eventually he drifted into an uneasy sleep.

Rita Hendon tossed restlessly in her bed, threw off the single damp sheet. Her naked body was wet with sweat, her eyes felt as though they were burning their way out of their sockets as she stared about her in the darkness of her bedroom. She could not make out whether she was asleep or awake. She concluded after a time that she was awake. And very ill.

She tried to sit up but her strength failed her. Perhaps she should shout for her parents even though it wasn't fair to disturb them. She'd be all right if only she could get back to sleep. And suddenly she got the feeling that she wasn't alone in the room.

A creeping fear, all the greater because she was so helpless. She could neither cry out nor move, couldn't see properly either. A shadow that was darker than the others seemed to detach itself and glide across to the foot of her bed. She tried to swallow but her throat was too dry and her eyes were hurting so much that her vision was distorted.

Now the shadow seemed to split, to divide into two: a man and a woman dressed in strange flowing robes, embracing. A sound like somebody was sobbing, and the murmur of comforting words that were to no avail for the crying continued. Then they turned, still holding on to each other, and stared down at the bed.

'Oh, Āba-aner, is there no hope for our child?' The woman's voice, trembling and barely audible.

'We must pray to Set, ask his forgiveness because only he can save her, for are you not his high priestess, Dalūkah?'

'I am, yet he has failed me, Āba-aner. I am forbidden to see you because you are only a common soldier and now that I have conceived by you the penalty for us all is death, myself, you, and already the curse of Set is upon our child also. We have nothing to lose now — *let us beseech Horus to save us and our offspring!*'

'No, we dare not. That is treachery.'

'Set's treachery. Did he not try to murder Horus? Horus is our only hope if we are to save the child, Dalūkah, whom I have named with my own name so that she may carry on my work.'

Rita pressed herself back against the headboard. It was as though her whole body was burning, being consumed by an inner fire that was rapidly eating her away. Her terror was at a peak. Who were these people who were trying to make out that she was their child, calling her Dalūkah? It was madness. She tried to shout, wanted to call her parents but no sound escaped her parched throat.

'I will not let you call Horus!' The man known as Āba-aner was struggling with the woman, and in that instant the room seemed to fill with dark shapes. Cries of anger, a scream. Something glinted and even at the height of her fever Rita recognised it as a sword blade, saw it plunged deep into Dalūkah's breast, the distraught girl slumping to the floor, her attacker struggling to tug his weapon free whilst his companions held Āba-aner. And in those few seconds it was all over for Āba-aner, too, blood pumping from his ruptured heart, his dying curses filling the room.

Rita wanted to close her eyes and shut out this awful scene. It could not be happening; it was but a nightmare brought on by her raging fever. But she was forced to watch, saw the murderers retreating, fading into the shadows as though they feared retribution for their terrible crime.

It was darker now. She could not even make out the corpses on the floor, told herself once again that it was all a figment of her imagination and that it had never really happened. Yey somehow she sensed that she wasn't alone, that something still lurked in the darkness.

Suddenly she saw it, a writhing angry shape materialising out of the blackness, a thing that reared up at the foot of the bed, a giant snake whose head seemed to split apart and grow into two, four tiny eyes that glowed redly, fangs wide in an expression of sheer malevolence. She screamed. At least she thought she did.

She felt the power of those venomous orbs scorching into her crazed brain, knew that there was no escape; that she would die as surely as Dalūkah and Āba-aner had, because she was their child.

'*The vengeance of Set is terrible and none can hide from it.*' Words that hissed like water being poured on to glowing embers. '*Dalūkah and Āba-aner have paid for their foolishness and so must you, my child, for you have been conceived by one who sought to betray me. The curse of Set is upon you and your body will burn until you plead for the coolness of death. But even after death you will suffer the agonies of a ka consumed by eternal fire from which there is no relief. The Plague of Kamt is as the sting of the asp!*'

Alone now, writhing in that damp sheet, trying to extricate herself from it, weakening by the second. Vague tortured memories. The predictions of George Brownlow and how the snake had bitten him too. Uppermost was the desire for water, to slake her thirst, to splash it on her burning flesh. Determination overcame her physical weakness momentarily and she flung off the sheet, swung her feet to the floor. Somehow she made it to an upright position, staggered towards the door. She stumbled, fell against the wall, caught her foot against something heavy which sent her sprawling. Of course, the bodies of Dalūkah and Āba-aner, her parents. She clutched at them, moaned her grief and terror, peering into the blackness of the room and wondering if that awful serpent lay coiled in the shadows mocking her. But there were no glowing eyes, nothing. She groped around, could not even locate the corpses now.

Crawling, dragging her naked body along the floor and out on to the landing, sensing the nearness of water as does one who is lost in a desert wilderness, a driving force that overcomes human frailty. Tongue swollen and protruding, scrabbling frantically into the bathroom, grabbing at the side of the bath and having to make several attempts to haul herself up, falling into it. Struggling with the tap, cursing. A sudden gush of water, her gasps of relief being drowned by its force as she twisted herself round, got her mouth open beneath the jet.

It should have quenched her thirst, cooled her fevered flesh but it didn't. Water and more water, vomiting it back because her stomach could not take any more. Desperately splashing it over herself but it only seemed to kindle the fire within her.

The water was no longer cool, turning tepid, then warm. Hot so that it scalded her, steam rising like a thick grey fog, creating weird shapes before her eyes. She saw Dalūkah and Āba-aner again, writhing in their death throes, feebly coming towards her. And that serpent spitting its venom, a liquid that burned and blistered as it hit her.

And Rita Hendon managed one final scream before she finally blacked out, floating in an abyss where hot desert winds whipped her body and the wails of the damned rang in her ears. And her flesh blistered and steamed.

George Brownlow crept stealthily from his bed, took his clothes out on to the landing to dress. His hand still ached but the swelling had gone down. He'd be OK; once he got the muscles working again he'd be fine. He had to get back to the digging; yesterday was a day lost and he had to make up the time.

He felt slightly unsteady on his feet and had to hold on to the stair-rail. He felt weak, but a day in bed always made you feel that way. A drink of water at the kitchen sink, he couldn't face orange juice again. One brief moment of indecision. Perhaps another day in bed would help him to regain his strength and tomorrow he would be back to full fitness. No, there was no time to waste. The amulet, still in his pocket, clinked faintly as though to urge him on, commanding him. Hurry!

He went outside. It would be hot again in an hour or two and it was best that he got started before the real heat of the day set in. His movements were slow, an unwillingness because his body protested, demanded rest.

He stood looking at his excavations, experienced a feeling of futility and hopelessness. The area resembled an oblong of sunken garden with the squares of turf piled up around its perimeter, no more than a foot deep at the most.

He would have to go down at least another ten feet and no longer would he be able to cut the soil out in chunks. Rock would have to be broken up with the pickaxe, carried out in buckets and piled far enough back so that there was no chance of an avalanche. Oh God! Beads of sweat began to trickle down his forehead. Suppose there *were* mummies buried down there! After all he had found the amulet and undoubtedly that was part of the legendary vicar's Egyptian treasures. No, the old boy wouldn't have buried the mummies, that was all a rumour started by the locals. He wouldn't be allowed to because this was not consecrated ground. All the same it was a disturbing thought. Revolting, like that adder. Definitely the thing he had stooped down to pick up had been a length of stick, a rod. Instant transformation into a living entity, a miracle that had to be seen to be believed. It was all very well Dr Horne going on about how adders were able to camouflage themselves so that they looked like a piece of dead branch but it *had* been an inanimate object before George Brownlow had touched it. The Rod of Moses, the Curse of Set. First the frogs had come. . . .

Something attracted his attention on the lawn beyond the shelter diggings. He shaded his eyes, thought at first it was a frog, a dead one that the crows had overlooked. No, it was the wrong shape and colour; a narrow dark body that had glassy wings interlaced with bright yellow fibres. Red eyes that reminded him of the serpent on the amulet. Watching him, sending a tiny shiver up and down his spine.

He moved forward, approached it warily. Whatever it was he wasn't going to *touch* it. But he had to know.

Its eyes followed his every movement as though it not only saw but *understood*. Like an overgrown grasshopper.

George Brownlow stopped a yard or so from it, pursed his lips in bewilderment. In a way it was familiar, an insect he'd seen *somewhere*. Maybe in one of those geographical magazines that Barry received by post from America, or on television.

Suddenly the computers in his brain clicked into action, processed the data, threw out the answer. One that had him recoiling in horror and disbelief. That creature squatting on the grass was a *locust*!

George backed away slowly, the insect's gaze following him. Don't make any sudden movement or else it might fly away. He had to be sure and he had to have *proof* otherwise he was merely inviting the scorn of everybody else. It was a locust all right and he needed to capture it.

He went inside the shed, began to grope around with hands that trembled with haste. God, what a bloody mess it was. If Emily ever came in here for anything he'd never hear the last of it. '*Clean it out, George, and maybe we can find a piece of carpet from somewhere to put on the floor. You'll never be able to find anything in here and just look at the filth!*'

Objects slid and fell, a tin of nails spilling all over the floor but he ignored them. A pile of pea-canes were propped untidily in a corner encased in cobwebs. He began to sort through them. Ah! Muttered excitement and satisfaction, unable to believe his luck. An old fishing or butterfly net, whichever you chose to use it for, its mesh black with dirt but still intact. He remembered buying it for Barry a few years ago and Emily had refused to have it in the house. It had remained in here ever since.

Searching again. An empty jam-jar; he blew the dust off it. The hunter was primed for action.

Back outside. The locust was still there, eyes fixed on him unblinkingly. George Brownlow grasped his net purposefully. Any second the insect might take to the wing. Of course there would be more but he had to catch this one, his proof to his family that yet another plague was beginning. He took a step forward, then another. Don't rush it, take your time.

When he was within striking distance of it his breathing speeded up, the fingers holding the cane began to tremble. You'll only get once chance, make sure of it.

Its tiny red eyes were fixed unwaveringly on him, no hint of fear. And he knew then that it wasn't going to make any attempt to fly off.

A quick swoop and the insect was pinned to the ground, his grunt of satisfaction merging into one of revulsion. So

81

far so good, but now he would have to handle it in order to transfer it to the jam jar. The thought almost had him retching and he recalled again the feel of that snake as it had wrapped itself around his wrist, the way it had wriggled . . . and bitten! And the sliminess of those dead frogs on the river path, cold jellied blood.

Tense, his mouth dry, his pulses racing, easing his fingers beneath the net. Horrible little bastard . . . got you! No struggling movements, no frantic flapping of those wings, only the eyes regarding him balefully with an expression of almost contempt.

A sigh of relief as it went into the jar and the lid was snapped on. Suffocate, you little bugger — you're a locust, alive or dead. He held it up, studied it through the thick glass, noted the way it perched unconcernedly upside down.

There was a triumphant gait to his otherwise shuffling walk as he retraced his steps to the house. He glanced at the clock on the kitchen wall. 5.35 a.m. It would be another three or four hours at least before he could begin checking on his specimen. A phone call to the Ministry of Agriculture, they would know for sure. One locust, it could be the fore-runner of swarms moving in to decimate a scorched-up Britain of its sparse struggling crops. And following in the wake of the locusts would come — *famine*!

George Brownlow went back outside, returned to the scene of his digging. There was no time to waste for surely the weeks were closing in on civilisation now. And the amulet clinked again in his pocket as if in agreement.

Chapter Six

The Curse of Set

RITA WAS dimly aware of movements around her, a sensation as though her body floated in the air then alighted; vehicular vibrations, voices but she couldn't make out what they were saying. And still the eternal torment as though wriggling fiery serpents devoured her body from within.

She remembered Dalūkah and Āba-aner more clearly now, almost knew what their faces were like although they had remained in shadow when they had visited her. The man reminded her of a Greek god, handsome and strong yet unable to fight against the power of the double-headed serpent. The woman was beautiful and gentle, prepared to die for her child. And in the end her sacrifice had availed her nothing. Because nobody could win against Set.

Jumbled flitting recollections, difficult to grasp because of the agony, the way her body burned inside and out. Hands touched her in the darkness but she did not have the strength to push them away. On fire as though she had bathed in sulphuric acid.

A wailing noise that would not let up, a magnification almost of that hissing snake, and in the blackness which enveloped her she saw the glint of its four eyes watching her. 'The curse of Set is upon you, and your body will burn until you plead for the coolness of death. But even after death you will suffer the agonies of a ka consumed by eternal fire from which there is no relief!'

Airborne again, a sensation that would have been pleasant under different circumstances. Blinding white light beyond her closed eyelids so that she could no longer see the glare of those four red orbs. And this was how it would be for eternity, for surely she was dead and this was the living hell with which they tried to frighten you as a child. It was real, and Rita Hendon was very much afraid.

An ashen-faced Julian Hendon did his best to comfort his distraught wife. The loneliness of a hospital waiting-room, white-coated figures coming and going, a bustle of activity that might have nothing to do with you. Or, on the other hand, it might. But they wouldn't tell you. You were just a number, not supposed to have emotions.

Rose Hendon stared at the wall, red-eyed, biting her fingernails, something which she hadn't done since she was twelve, an instinctive preparation for the worst. Why does it have to be my baby who's in there, why can't it be *me*? At fifty-five she was looking forward to Julian's retirement from his firm of accountants but suddenly her whole world was caving in. Oh God, the shock of waking up in the middle of the night, hearing those screams coming from the bathroom. She would never forget the awful sight which had greeted her and Julian as they had rushed in — Rita, naked, scalding herself in a boiling hot bath, screaming; not recognising them, even trying to fight them off.

They'd got her out, phoned for an ambulance, but there was something else wrong with their daughter which bore no relation to her blistered flesh. Delirious, almost impervious to the scalding because *something else* was causing her tremendous pain. Ranting about two people named Dalūkah and Āba-aner, screaming her terror and babbling about some double-headed serpent.

'You don't think she was trying to . . . er . . . you know?' Julian Hendon muttered as they had waited impatiently for the ambulance to arrive.

'Of course not, I don't know how you could say such a thing.' Rose was trying to rub Nivea cream over her daughter's growing rash of blisters, but no way would there be enough cream in the tin to complete the job. 'Rita wouldn't commit suicide, no matter what. Oh, my poor darling, whatever happened to you?'

By the time the ambulance arrived Rita was in a deep coma. The Hendons went in the back with her, prayed in silence to a God they had almost forgotten.

'Mr and Mrs Hendon?' A well-built man wearing a long white coat, a surgical mask draped around his neck, opened the waiting-room door. His expression was impassive, a diplomat who delivered news, good or bad, with habitual equilibrium. He was just a number, too.

The Hendons came to their feet, had to hold on to each other. Julian wanted to scream *For God's sake tell us the worst, don't just stand there* but he didn't. Waiting. Trying to concentrate because they had to hear it right, good or bad.

'I'm afraid we've transferred your daughter to the intensive care unit. She's badly scalded but she is also suffering from some kind of infection that is causing a high temperature and considerable internal pain. We hope to discover what it is and treat it as soon as possible. In the meantime, rest assured we are doing everything possible. If you would like to remain at the hospital please do so.'

'She's . . . she's going to die, isn't she?' Rose Hendon whimpered. 'For God's sake, tell us.'

'She's very seriously ill.' The surgeon moved back towards the door. This was the worst part of the whole job when you didn't know yourself whether a patient was going to make it. Another thing, he'd have to get a second opinion on the girl. Not all of those lumps on her body were blisters — they were like open cancerous growths and had nothing whatsoever to do with the flesh being immersed in very hot water. This was one time he really had to stall.

Then he was gone, a dignified cowardly flight, leaving the duty-nurse to fix up with the Hendons whether or not they wanted to stay. Afraid to go back into that unit, into the incubator with the girl. He'd seen her record card. Occupation — Laboratory Assistant, Centre for Research into Tropical Diseases. And that was what worried him most.

'George, whatever do you think you're doing out of bed, and

85

what's this repulsive thing in that jam-jar on the sink unit?'

George Brownlow straightened up, dropped his pickaxe and glanced at his watch. Ten past eight. Damn, it only seemed a few minutes since he'd started digging and now Emily was up and about, the whole household stirring. He drew his hand across his forehead, he was lathered in sweat but he didn't feel shaky any more, neither was his arm throbbing.

'I've a good mind to ring Doctor Horne right away and tell him what you're doing, George. How long have you been up?'

'Just shut your bloody mouth!'

The expression in his eyes had her backing away. Suddenly, it seemed, she wasn't the boss of this household any longer. She turned away, heard him following her into the house.

'What is . . . *that*?'

He followed the direction of her pointing finger, saw that the huge insect in the jar wasn't perched upside down now. It might even have been dead but that didn't matter.

'It is . . .' he paused for effect, 'a locust!'

'You're mad!'

'You'll see.' Smug now, enjoying this encounter. 'As a matter of fact I'm just going to ring the Ministry of Agriculture about it.'

'Doctor Horne said you were to rest.'

'Doctor Horne is merely a GP.' George had the telephone directory in his hand, began thumbing through it. 'And I am *not* taking orders from *him*!'

She stared at him, felt herself starting to tremble. He had never turned on her like this before. She almost said *'don't forget I'm the breadwinner here and without me your dole money wouldn't go far'* but she thought better of it. He wasn't well, that was the trouble. His back was towards her now so that she couldn't see his expression. He dialled a lengthy number and she heard a phone starting to ring out at the other end, was answered almost immediately.

'I'd like to speak to somebody in connection with pests.' Emily had never heard George speak so authoritatively before; she found it quite disconcerting.

A pause, then a man's voice, the line crackling so that she could not hear what he said.

'I have discovered a *locust* in my garden. There may be more of them.'

The other spoke for some time, but the line was bad. Emily ventured a step closer.

'Thank you, I'll give them a ring right away.'

'What did they say?' Her voice quavered.

'Nothing much. Just gave me the number of the Centre for Overseas Pest Research in London.'

'Weren't they *worried*?'

'No.' George Brownlow was carefully dialling the digits which he had scribbled down on the jotter pad. 'They're only concerned with pests like rats, and moles, and rabbits.' He stuck a finger in his free ear, an action designed to shut his wife out. Christ, wasn't anybody going to answer? Maybe Britain didn't have any overseas pests so nobody bothered.

'Centre for Overseas Pest Research. Good morning.' A man's voice, a slight cockney accent.

'Good morning.' Momentarily feeling rather foolish, 'I . . . I've found a locust in my garden.'

'Oh yes, sir. Which area?'

'The Midlands. North of Birmingham.'

'I see. Well, in fact we have had quite a few reports of locust sightings already this summer.'

'And what are you doing about them?'

'They have all been investigated, sir. In *normal* British summers a sighting as far north as yours would have been quite remarkable, but this drought is now becoming quite serious and we *do* expect a few freak sightings. There's nothing to worry about at the moment because in this country they're quite harmless. One or two turn up in the south of England every summer. The longest recorded flight by desert locusts was in 1954, from the Canaries to the British Isles, a distance of over fifteen hundred miles, but only a very small proportion of those that started the flight finished it. In no way do they represent a threat, sir, but perhaps you would like to keep an eye on those you saw If they increase to any great extent then give us another ring and we'll get somebody out to you.'

'Thank you, I'll keep a watch on them.' George Brownlow dropped the receiver back on its cradle. He sighed; the Pest Research Centre were trying to make light of it but he had detected a slight apprehension in the other's tone. You watch them for us, sir, but for God's sake don't start a panic. Because we don't *really* know.

'So it's not the catastrophe you *hoped* for!' Emily folded her arms, glanced back towards the kitchen where Barry and Sheila were washing the breakfast dishes. 'God knows when we'll finally get some sanity in this household.'

'*We are the chosen ones.*' She retreated a couple of paces as she saw that vacant glaze over her husband's eyes again; he was addressing her but staring past her at the blank wall. 'Whether the locusts are harmful or not is immaterial. They are a sign from the gods, just as the frogs were. The land will be scorched to a bare wilderness, whether by nuclear fire or by the power of *Ra*, and multitudes will die. Famine is nigh!'

A soft thud on the hall floor had him whirling around, the letter box clinking. The morning paper had arrived, skidding on Emily's polished wooden tiles, the headlines facing him as though they carried a personal message addressed to George Brownlow, Esq.

'LIBYA WARNS ISRAEL TIME IS RUNNING OUT. T.A.S.S. SAYS WE'LL BACK YOU. THE WORLD WATCHES AND WAITS.'

'The writing is truly upon the wall,' Brownlow whispered. 'There is no time to be lost. Today I must dig throughout the daylight hours and pray that I am in time.'

Emily Brownlow sighed, knew that there was no way she was going to prevent her husband from going out there in the burning sun and working in his increasingly unsightly crater. The thought of leaving crossed her mind but she dismissed it. This was *her* home, made possible by *her* money. Hers was the impression created among the residents of River View. And she was determined that it was not all going to be destroyed in a moment of rashness.

'See you later, Mum.' Barry had his crash helmet in his hand, Sheila a polythene carrier bag containing the overalls she had washed yesterday evening. Both items were a snub to Emily Brownlow's River View image.

'I . . .' The phone rang shrilly, interrupting her. Rang again, a harshness, an impatience that seemed to convey urgency. And for some reason Emily experienced a sense of foreboding, did not rush to answer it as she usually did, hanging back, looking at the others.

A few seconds of indecision among the Brownlow family as if they all sensed . . . something. And were afraid.

'Who can that be at this hour?' Emily muttered, felt the muscles in her stomach beginning to tighten and remembered that there was a huge repulsive insect which might be still alive in a jar by the kitchen sink. Life was becoming nauseating all round — frogs, snakes, and now of all things a *locust*!

'Well there's only one way we're likely to find out.' Barry pushed forward, suddenly pale and tight-lipped, grabbing the receiver. It seemed to come alive like that adder which George had picked up, twisting its way out of his trembling hands, would have crashed to the floor had not the flex checked its fall. He grabbed it, caught it, and when he spoke his voice quavered.

'62309. Barry Brownlow speaking.'

A pause. Someone was saying something at the other end but none of the watchers could hear because the line was crackling and buzzing. Probably the heat, George thought to himself. It affects everything, the television and. . . .

Barry lurched, would have fallen had the wall not been there to prop him up, his complexion a ghastly pallor, mouthing words that would not come. Everybody was staring at him as though they too had been struck dumb, turned into human statues of inexplicable terror.

The phone swung like a crazy pendulum, bouncing and catapulting on its flex, chattering insanely to a background of electronic interference, screaming its own words over and over again so that in the end they became audible. 'Barry . . . Barry . . . *are you there . . . can you hear me*?'

George Brownlow's hand was stretching out to grab the swinging plastic mouthpiece, but he had not the courage. He remembered that stick which had transformed itself into a snake. The Rod of Moses might have many shapes.

Emily beat him to it, caught the swinging instrument just as it went dead. One moment of awful silence in which three pairs of eyes were fixed questioningly on the swaying Barry, mutely asking what they dared not put into words.

Finally Barry spoke, an anti-climax because he did not scream or whisper, flat expressionless tones that conveyed the full horror of his expression.

'She's dead . . . Rita's dead!'

Then he slumped forward, hit the floor with a sickening thud. And Sheila Brownlow began to scream hysterically.

Ten days of blistering heat that went unnoticed by the Brownlows and the Hendons, a kind of countdown to grim finality that was to have its climax in the stark drabness of the crematorium. Days that seemed years; the autopsy and its findings. A rare tropical disease, the first of its kind in Britain. Maybe the research centre would be reprimanded, maybe not. Just a tightening of security, but everybody who worked there knew the risks. You experimented with bacteria and you accepted the dangers. It was a one in a million chance of it ever happening, but that chance was always there. So Rita had died. There would be compensation but one thing the scientists could not do was to create life out of death. And Rita was dead.

A pathetic group that sweated and wept, a chaplain who appeared unmoved by it all and over-acted his mourning tones. Because for him it was the third funeral service today and he was succumbing to boredom in the oppressive heat. He didn't even know what the girl had died of, that wasn't his business.

Emily Brownlow made a pot of tea in the kitchen. The lounge was too formal, too sombre. Sheila, red-eyed, stared out of the window at the scorched lawn and its mountain of rubble. A blackbird was idly pecking in search of insects but the soil had baked too hard and in the end it gave up and flew off to the shade of the shrubbery.

George had loosened his tie, his ruddy features shiny with perspiration, a vacant expression which might have been interpreted as shock and grief. So far nobody had spoken. They had expected Barry to go straight up to his room; he would not be coming downstairs again today.

'They had no right to do that.' George Brownlow's lips barely moved, the words so faint that they were no more audible than the constant buzzing of a bluebottle on the window.

'Right to do what?' Emily began to pour the tea. It was weak, needed to mash another minute or two, but she had to do something. Anything. Nobody would notice anyway.

'To cremate her.'

Shocked silence, the two women staring at him in disbelief, Emily's lips slowly moving into an expression of contempt. 'What a horrible nasty thing to say, George! It's a good job Barry's not here to hear you.'

'They had no right.' A deeper flush to Brownlow's cheeks, the beginning of anger. 'But the harm is done now. It cannot be undone, or if it can I know of no way.'

'What d'you mean, Dad.' Sheila swivelled round to face her father. 'We all know that it was best for . . . for the body to be cremated after . . . *that*!'

'It matters not. The body is of no consequence. It is the *ka* which matters. Now it has been left to wander aimlessly for eternity, unable to depart this earth for *Sekhet-Aaru*!'

'You're mad!' Sheila snapped. 'And I'm not going to have you talking about the dead like that.'

'Except that Rita is *not* dead.' George Brownlow's knuckles showed white where they gripped the edge of the table. 'Because they have bungled it. *Do you know what she died of?*'

Sheila passed a hand across her forehead, felt the way her temples pounded as her headache raged. She ought to go to bed. 'Do we have to go into all this? You know as well as we all do . . . she had a rare type of galloping cancer.'

'Which is one way of putting it.' Brownlow rose to his feet, had to hold on to the table for support. 'The authorities have conspired to hide the facts. It is no coincidence that Rita worked in the laboratory of the Research Centre for Tropical Diseases and that a cancerous cell, maybe a bacilli, somehow got into her system. Not contagious in itself but deadly to the direct recipient.'

'This is all stupid supposition.'

'*No, it is the Curse of Set which is upon all of us. One by one we shall be struck down unless we obey his commands.*'

'For God's sake shut up, Dad!' Sheila leaped to her feet, slopped some tea on the table. 'I can't stand anymore of this. I'm going upstairs to bed!'

She ran out of the room, slamming the door behind her, and they heard the vibrations of her feet pounding up the stairs.

'It's most unfair of you, George.' Emily said. 'At a time like this, too. Have you no feelings?'

'I'll go and get changed. I've got work to do.'

'Surely you're not going to dig today. Show some respect for the dead, George.'

But George Brownlow did not reply. Time was running out for all of them. It was the living who mattered.

Chapter Seven

Rita's Return

GEORGE BROWNLOW worked steadily until darkness fell, not hurrying but pacing himself in the heat, a human robot controlled by his own obsessions. Rita's fate worried him. The fools, the bloody fools, they did not realise! Set had destroyed her for some purpose and they had played into his hands by cremating her. Now her *khaibit* was his, destined to do the double-headed serpent's bidding just as George Brownlow was compelled to do in life.

George's mind went back to that afternoon he had spent among the archives of the town's Castle Library. A week ago, the day of Rita's autopsy. God, why hadn't he thought to go there before?

The rumours about the Reverend Mason's mummies; the old curator swore they were true.

'See here, Mr Brownlow, almost all of these Egyptian relics were brought back by the Reverend Mason in the early 1920s. That obsidian head, a fine exhibit, and these trinkets of lapis lazuli, and that green schist amulet; all willed to the Castle by one who gave his life's work for the town and its people. Now, my mother used to clean for the Reverend and I can remember her telling me how he had a couple of mummies that he brought back from his last expedition. They started to go off a bit and Mother complained, threatened to leave the old boy. The next day they were gone but we couldn't say what he'd done with them. Only Jenkins, the gardener, reckoned there were two fresh graves in the garden, and putting two and two together, Mother reckoned the old chap had given those mummies a proper Christian burial, and that about sums up the Reverend Mason.'

'But do you know anything about the mummies?' George Brownlow insisted. 'Who they were, for instance.'

'Well, I've done some research myself.' Barker stroked his pure white moustache, smiled proudly. 'Always have been interested in Egyptology. Now, this obsidian head came from the tomb of two people called Dalūkah and Āba-aner according to the Reverend Mason's notes. This Dalūkah wasn't *the* Dalūkah, queen of Egypt, but only a distant relative about whom little is known except that she forsook the worship of Horus for that of Set . . .'

George started, felt his skin prickle.

'Anyway,' Barker went on, 'it's all a mixture of legend and supposition, but the story goes that this Dalūkah became a high priestess of Set and got involved in human sacrifice and all that sort of thing. Then she went and got herself pregnant by this fellow, Āba-aner, one of the queen's soldiers and a commoner. The cult discovered this after the birth of the baby, also named Dalūkah just to confuse everybody.' The curator grinned. 'High priestess and soldier were put to the sword and their baby developed some kind of plague and was shut up alive in the tomb with the corpses of her parents. The proper rites weren't administered so the souls of the unfortunate would remain close to the bodies, becoming *khaibits*, sort of shadows of the *sahus*, condemned to a prolonged haunting.'

George Brownlow stretched out a hand, steadied himself against a cabinet of exhibits as the room started to spin, that whirling obsidian head seeming to smile, mocking him. It *knew*, if nobody else did.

'Are you all right, Mr Brownlow?'

'Yes. . . .yes. . .' Everything slowing down, the Big Wheel shuddering to a halt. 'Just a little dizzy. Doubtless it's the heat. . .'

There *had* to be a connection somewhere, George decided as he threw another shovelful of soil up on to the

94

pile. Just suppose those *were* the mummies which Mason had buried, then they would still have their *khaibits* with them. Like Rita. . . .

Hours passed. Late evening eased into dusk, dusk to darkness. Only then did George Brownlow haul himself up out of his growing crater, shuddering as he recalled that cataleptic nightmare. The hole was so deep now that it could just happen. Scrambling clear with a hint of panic as some small stones avalanched.

He squatted there, sweating and trembling. The digging was almost done, another week's labour at the most. And then he would have to find out something about the construction of fallout shelters.

George didn't want to go indoors yet. Emily would be depressed and start bitching. Maybe she would have an early night, with Barry and Sheila already in bed. He made his way across to the shed, flicked on the light and flooded the tiny wooden building with the yellow glare from a dusty sixty-watt bulb. A pair of eyes glinted, seemed to focus on him but that was impossible because the locust in the jam-jar was almost certainly dead by now. And he hadn't seen any others. They would surely come, though, in spite of what the man from the Centre for Overseas Pest Research said. Oh God, they'd all come, locusts, frogs, snakes, famine, disease. All leading up to the end of civilisation. That was why he had to get a move on and finish the shelter. One of the reasons, anyway.

The amulet! He pulled open a drawer, had to force it because the wood was warped. He scrabbled among the contents, eagerly pulled out a hard, flat object wrapped in tissue. He could sense vibrations like the panting of a hunted beast about to spring on the hunters now that it had lured them into its lair. The sweat was chilling on his body, trembling. . . more afraid than he had ever been of it before.

The light bulb swung slightly, flickered and dimmed. Four tiny eyes shone redly through the thin paper, cold hell-fire that burned, had him muttering his subservience, tearing off the tissue because it was angry at being wrapped.

The serpent writhed, hissed, and he felt its freezing vapour, smelled its evil, dry mustiness of an ancient tomb.

Something else . . . *the stench of death!* A numbing of his brain, an understanding that could not be put into words. *Dalūkah and Āba-aner had fled their prison tomb, their stolen corpses rotted in the damp soil of a foreign land, but their* khaibits *had not been freed from their mortal bodies. It was still possible to entomb them, their child also, who had died of a terrible plague. They must be reincarnated, slain again. As before.*

George Brownlow understood nothing except that on the morrow he must dig again with renewed energy for Set was becoming impatient. And very angry!

George Brownlow found himself back in the house. He could not remember leaving the shed and walking across the lawn but he was here so he must have done. Exhausted, his eyelids threatening to close. He must sleep the sleep of the dead tonight for tomorrow he must work harder and longer if Set was to be appeased. For only then would he and his family be saved.

He began to mount the stairs, came to a halt as voices reached him from above, found himself straining his ears to listen. A low, virtually inaudible buzz of conversation like bees swarming in a chimney pot, certainly not Emily's whine.

Tip-toeing on to the landing, that incessant spate of words slightly louder now, but he was still unable to make them out . . . coming from Barry's room! George pressed himself up against the door. His son was speaking continually, a flow of words that speeded up, slowed, conveying an alternate mood of urgency and sadness, desperation and pleading. Still he was unable to pick out a single word, and when realisation came he straightened up with disbelief. Barry Brownlow was conversing in some foreign language that was totally unrecognisable! *Which was crazy because the boy had not passed 'O' level French, had not even studied German, Greek or Latin!*

'What is it? What's going on?'

George whirled, blushing with the instinctive guilt of an eavesdropper. Emily stood in the doorway of their bedroom, a housecoat clutched about her as though she feared her husband might catch a glimpse of some intimate part of her body through her nightdress, her features pale and strained. Edgy.

'Shh!' He raised a finger to his lips. 'It's Barry.'

She advanced a couple of steps, tilted her head to listen, spoke in a hushed voice. 'He's having a nightmare, and no wonder after what he's been through these past ten days.'

'It's no nightmare.' George's expression was one of incredulity. 'Listen he's laughing now.'

'He's talking gibberish!'

'No, it's a . . . foreign language.'

'Rubbish, he doesn't even know French. He can't be.'

But he was. A spate of words in a deep nasal accent, a pause as though he was listening to a reply. A short laugh, speaking again.

'We'll have to wake him. It isn't good for him to get all worked up like this.' Emily's fingers closed over the door-knob, hesitated as though she instinctively sought her husband's approval, was afraid to go into that room alone.

'No!' He grasped her wrist. 'Leave him in peace.'

'In peace! Hark at him now, he's getting all worked up, it could do him untold harm.' Her nostrils suddenly flared. 'What's that smell?'

George Brownlow smelled the odour for the first time, tried to identify it, knew that it was only too familiar like the strains of a catchy tune that you knew you'd heard somewhere before but couldn't quite place it. Musty, like dry rot, so pungent that you found yourself coughing as though you had suddenly stirred up a cloud of dust. And then he recognised it, knew without any doubt that it was the odour he had smelled in that cataleptic nightmare, the stench that had come from that awful entity — the same cloying one that had assailed his nostrils the time he had found the amulet. *The smell of ancient death!*

'Whatever is it? George, are you sure you're all right?' Fear in Emily Brownlow's wide eyes, suddenly afraid that her husband might be about to suffer that sudden heart attack which Dr Horne had hinted at that time he had treated him for high blood-pressure.

'Maybe we'd better check him.' Reluctance, hoping that Emily would go into that room first. 'We don't need to wake him, just make sure he's OK. Go on, then, take a look.'

She was hesitating again. Barry's voice was louder, almost shouting.

'What are you waiting for, Emily?'

She closed her eyes momentarily, knew that she had no choice, grasped the knob and tried to turn it. It resisted her. *The door was locked from the inside!*

'It's locked, George!'

He wanted to shout *'It can't be, you haven't turned the knob properly'* but he knew she spoke the truth.

'George, whatever are we going to do?'

He couldn't think of an answer, didn't want to. Barry was old enough to lock himself in his room if he wanted to. It was no business of theirs; thousands of youths Barry's age had left home, married with families of their own. It was an invasion of his privacy to burst in on him in the middle of the night. Excuses, because he was frightened of finding out what lay on the other side of the door, what was causing that stench.

'Maybe we'd better leave him alone,' he said weakly.

'We can't. He's in distress . . . there's no knowing what he . . . he might *do*!'

'We can't . . . break the door down!'

'No, but we can bang on it, wake him up.' Again she hesitated as though willing him to strike the first blow.

George Brownlow clenched his fist, felt suddenly inadequate like the time when Barry was a small boy and he had locked himself in the toilet because he was in a tantrum. It had taken them half an hour to coax him out. George checked the impetus of his intended blow, rapped meekly on the woodwork with his knuckles, his voice no louder than a whisper. 'Barry . . . Barry, are you all right? Unlock the door . . . .' Paternal habits died hard; fifteen years had elapsed since the last time. Oh God, if it had only been possible to go back in time.

A moment's silence then Barry was talking again, slow sad tones interspersed with sobs. And the dry smell of putrefaction grew weaker, or perhaps they were becoming used to it and hardly noticed it now.

'Barry, *wake up*! It's us, your mum and dad.' Emily screeched, began thumping with both fists as though she needed to get her frustration out of her system. 'It's all right, it's only *us*. Open the door. *Please*, Barry, open the door!'

The talking inside the room went on, staccato words now as though Barry was asking questions and being answered. Which was ridiculous because he was alone in there.

A shadow fell across them, had them jumping round.

'What is it?' Sheila stood there, still clothed in the dark dress which she had worn at the funeral, crumpled and creased because she had not bothered to undress before flinging herself on the bed. Dried salty grief stains marked her cheeks, her eyes were black rimmed.

George and Emily stared at her, trembling with relief, both tried to say something and failed.

'What's that awful smell?' She glanced about her.

'I don't know.' George Brownlow looked back towards the door, experienced a sense of futility. 'Barry's locked himself in his room. He's having a . . . dream.'

'He's talking to somebody!' Sheila breathed, suddenly clutched at her father's arm. 'Oh, Dad, *there's somebody in there with him!*'

George Brownlow's flesh went cold, every muscle starting to weaken and tremble. He made as if to deny her statement but knew that he would only lie. There was somebody in there with Barry! But *who*?

Three frightened people staring at one another, trying not to look at that locked door, their brains refusing to accept that Barry could not be alone in his room, the nature of that low rambling conversation defying logic.

Then silence, so sudden and so terrifying. They wanted to turn and flee, rush out into the mundane sanity of a lighted cul-de-sac, gulp the balmy night air into their lungs in an attempt to rid themselves of that cloying smell of evil.

A slight vibration such as modern floorboards make when walked upon, an awareness that somewhere somebody moved. The three of them bunched together, instinctively seeking protection in numbers, bracing themselves for . . . *the metallic click of a knob-release, the doorknob beginning to turn . . . the door easing open on well-oiled hinges. . . .*

'Barry!' Sheila's gasp that was a combination of relief and terror. Relief because it was her brother who stood there in the doorway, terror because of the expression which was stamped on his pallid features.

Grief had left its mark, a frail body where the flesh had wasted away rapidly in less than a fortnight, hands that shook uncontrollably. Eyes wide and staring out of black sockets, lips that were fixed in a smile, moving, uttering soundless words.

'Barry.' Emily backed away, pulling the others with her. 'Oh my God, look at him, there's something terribly wrong!'

He stood there but did not appear to be aware of their presence, a vacant gaze that met their frightened stares without seeing. Starting to talk again, that strange dialect, so chilling in its inexplicableness.

'*Barry!*' Sheila's piercing scream, a javelin of sound that seemed to strike her brother visibly, throw him back, his eyes rolling, clearing. Seeing.

'Rita. Where are you, Rita?' He searched about him, his gaze flicking over his mother and father, hesitating for a moment on his sister before moving on, grief and desperation. 'Rita . . . don't leave me. *Please* don't leave me!'

Emily rushed forward, caught him, but he did not seem to notice her encircling arms. Wildly roving eyes darting all around.

'It's all right, my love.' It was the first time Emily Brownlow had demonstrated compassion since Rita's death, unashamedly beginning to sob. 'She's not here, Barry. You know that. She's gone!'

'No, she hasn't,' he spoke calmly, that smile crinkling the corners of his lips once again. 'I thought she'd gone but

I was wrong. She came back to me tonight, as lovely as ever, asked me to go somewhere with her but now she's disappeared. How can I join her if I don't know where she's gone? You *must* have seen her.'

'Let's get you back into bed.' Emily signalled to her husband to help her. 'You just lie down and take another of those tablets which the doctor left for you. Then you'll go to sleep, and when you wake up you'll feel better.'

'*No!*' Sudden anger, a physical resistance. 'I won't let you drug me because Rita needs me. *My God, you don't realise what they've done to her!*' His voice rose to an hysterical pitch. '*They've taken her to be one of their priestesses because they've lost somebody named Dalūkah. They want her, they want me . . . all of us. We've got to go to her!*'

George Brownlow stiffened, felt a blackness closing in, obscuring his vision — dark choking dust clouds that stank of ancient cloying evil so that he gasped for breath, felt consciousness slipping from him. His legs finally weakened and buckled, throwing him to the floor in a faint.

And for the third time that night Sheila Brownlow screamed.

Chapter Eight

Pestilence!

'I'M AFRAID he'll have to stay in hospital for a while.' Dr Horne meticulously wiped his glasses, looked through the lenses, wiped them again. 'A nervous breakdown, but nothing that a good rest and the right treatment won't put right, Mrs Brownlow.'

'Does he have to stay in that place, Doctor.' Emily Brownlow licked her dry lips, felt that she might be sick. 'I mean, we could look after him here, in his own surroundings.'

'Mental hospitals aren't like the old lunatic asylums.' Horne smiled wanly, hopefully reassuringly. 'A lot of people go inside for a rest nowadays, you know. Quite *ordinary* people. There isn't the stigma attached to them that there was twenty-five years ago. You leave it to us, Mrs Brownlow. A week or two and he'll be as right as rain.' Or a month or two. 'In a few days you'll be able to go and visit him.'

Emily stood in the bow window, watched the doctor's departure, an expression on her lined features which blamed him for Barry's stay in that awful place. What on earth were they going to tell people to explain his absence from home? A lie was easy enough but somehow these matters had a habit of coming to light. She had a vague recollection of somebody down at the other end of River View having a relative in Shelderton. This was something that would have to be thought out very carefully.

Crossing to the opposite end of the long lounge she was afforded a view of the rear garden, her expression hardening

102

at the sight of that huge mound of soil and rubble. George had stated at breakfast that with a bit of luck he would finish the excavations today. What then, what other foolishness was he about to embark upon in order to construct a nuclear shelter? She seriously contemplated speaking to Dr Horne about her husband; George actually believed what Barry had said about Rita! But she could not risk the shame of having her husband in Shelderton as well. His mind was made up on these ludicrous matters and nothing she could say would deter him. In which case, she winced at the thought, perhaps it would be better to humour him. At least she'd give it a try; everything else had failed.

She went outside, stood on the patio. Earth and stones showered up as though some giant mole was digging frantically beneath the lawn. A scraping sound, more debris. The neighbours must be aware of it by now, must be gossiping.

Emily advanced slowly, picked her way through loose earth and stones, testing each foothold before she put her weight on it. She peered over the brink, gasped with amazement. So deep, surely it was ten feet down to the bottom, a pair of step-ladders propped up against one side to enable George to clamber in and out.

She regarded him with contempt. He was wearing just a singlet and shorts, a pair of old scuffed sandals on his feet, scraping the bottom with his spade, using a spirit-level as he strove to level the surface. That meant he wasn't digging any deeper. He had nearly finished.

'How's it going, George?' She squirmed inwardly at her own patronising tone, gave him that same smile which she reserved for the unexpected River View caller.

'Emily!' He almost dropped his spade in amazement. 'You startled me.'

'I am not forbidden to gaze upon your handiwork, am I? I thought I'd come and take a look. My goodness, you've put some work into this.'

'You can say that again.' *What's the cunning bitch up to now?* 'I'll have the excavations finished today. Then I can begin the construction.'

'You . . . you've got it all planned out, then?'

103

'Of course I have. In fact most of it is going to be built from junk you'll be glad to see the back of. That old door that's propped up behind the shed will come in useful and I'll need all of that polythene sheeting which came off the new lounge suite. There's enough timber on that pile at the bottom of the garden which the builders left behind and most of it is good enough to use. In fact, I don't think I'll have to buy much in the way of materials at all.'

'That's nice.' Particularly as you don't have anything apart from your dole money to buy them with and *I'm* not contributing to this foolishness. 'I'm going to make a cup of tea in a minute.'

'Good.' He scraped some more loose soil. 'I could do with one if you can manage to bring me one out.'

She sighed. Nothing was going to lure him out of that hole. 'All right. By the way, Doctor Horne says Barry will have to stay in Shelderton a week or two.'

'He's mad.'

'No he isn't, just a breakdown, loads of people have them these days. I thought you said you believed that story about . . . about Rita, anyway.'

'I don't mean Barry — Doctor Horne. There's nothing wrong with Barry apart from grief. He saw Rita all right.'

'I'll bring you a cup of tea.' She turned away, didn't want to go into all that again. She might, with an effort, humour George over his shelter but certainly she wasn't going to kid him that she was idiotic enough to believe all that tripe. Once you were dead, you were dead and. . . .

She paused, didn't know why. A kind of awe like when you tip-toed into a cathedral and everybody spoke in hushed voices as though God Himself was there and they feared they might disturb Him. An uneasiness had her looking around her, a feeling that she wasn't alone. The silence, that was it. No, not *quite* silence, rather an absence of artificial noises that gave the impression of being very close to Nature, an environment that might have existed a million years ago when River View was heathland or forest and the occupants lived in caves.

Grasshoppers. A medley that grated on her nerves like an orchestra of miniature violin players who were getting tired and slowing down, an old record losing its momentum on the wind-up gramophone because the spring was getting weak. Eerie. She found herself stepping back a pace, searching the scorched lawn in front of her in case she trod on one of the tiny insects and squashed it. Remembering that dead locust in the jar. Now that was downright cruel of George leaving it to suffocate like that, the sort of thing the RSPCA took people to court for . . . and the sort of act that might make hordes of insects come looking for revenge! She gave a little laugh at her own stupidity and in that same instant the entire lawn seemed to heave up.

She stared. It must be the heat playing tricks on her. No, there it went again, a steady swell, the grating insect chorus rising and falling with it. Brown stalks that weren't dried and burned grass but thousands of tiny bodies that were almost identical replicas of that locust. And with that realisation Emily Brownlow screamed.

George scrambled up the ladder, pulled himself over the brink of the dug-out. 'What the hell's up?'

'*Look!*' She turned and he saw her anguish, an expression which he was becoming used to these days. 'The whole lawn is alive with . . . with grasshoppers!'

He scrambled across to her, saw that she spoke the truth. There were grasshoppers everywhere, hordes of them that squatted and sawed away to produce that melancholy music, every one of them seeming to watch the two humans, and if you looked long and hard you thought you recognised minute expressions of malevolence.

'Ugh!' Emily Brownlow reached for her husband's arm. 'They've cut us off from the house, George!'

'No,' he tried to sound flippant. 'They're harmless. You must've walked through them on your way out, not noticed them.'

Her stomach churned. She wanted to examine the soles of her shoes, see if any squashed dead insect bodies adhered to them. But she didn't because she didn't dare to look. The very thought was revolting. Frightening.

'I . . . I can't go back through them. You'll have to carry me, George.'

He stared at her dumbfounded. He hadn't picked Emily up since their wedding day when just to pander to the family's conventional sense of humour he had carried her over the threshold of their two-up two-down. Somehow it went against the grain. Just suppose somebody *saw* them. He'd be the laughing stock of River View. '*Hey, guess what I saw today, old Brownlow carrying his missus into the house like they'd just got married.*'

'There's no need for that, Emily. Just follow me, I'll see you safely back into the house.'

'George, I *demand* to be carried. I can't stand creepy-crawlies and you know it. I might have a fit or something.'

Angry, but he tried not to show it. He didn't want her to start screaming or else the neighbours might come round, a God-sent excuse to come and poke their noses into his shelter. 'It's all very nice, Mr Brownlow, but you're wasting your time because nobody'll ever *dare* to start a nuclear war. Ha-ha.'

He stooped down, swung Emily's weight clear of the ground, staggered a couple of paces to get his balance. Something crunched under his sandals like tiny twigs cracking and he had a vision of locust-like bodies being crushed out of all recognition. An urge to vomit. In a way it was worse than slimy frogs or wriggling snakes because the hordes just sat there waiting to die. Like lemmings. Try not to think about it, take your time and don't look down. The plague of pestilences is here and there's nothing you can do about it!

Emily stared up at the sky, screwing her eyes up because of the sun's brightness. This was not natural. There had to be cloud and rain before long to bring things back to normal. But there wasn't so much as a single fluffy white cloud in sight.

They were within a yard of the patio steps when George felt his right foot start to skid, a dry slipperiness that had him lurching. Even so he might have regained his balance had not his burden suddenly shifted, grasped at him in panic and despair, yelled '*George, look out!*'

Falling, hitting the ground with stunning force, Emily clawing at him, gouging his skin. A kaleidoscope of colours, breathless as she landed on top of him. Instinctively he tore himself free from her, pushed her away.

She screamed as she landed face downwards on the dry grass, a sensation of hundreds of insect bodies crushing beneath her, the survivors panicking and jumping for safety — *landing on her, crawling all over her!*

Frantically she beat at her body, tried to sweep the revolting little things from her but they dug in with their legs, resisted her. Lying there wide-eyed, watching them — not just grasshoppers, other insects as well; ants that stung with sheer hate, harmless ladybirds now awful in their bright red polka-dot shells. tiny greenflies that seemed bemused by it all, different species of insect life suddenly finding a human being at their *mercy*! Some stung, others just crawled to satisfy their curiosity.

George slapped at his bare legs, squashed a greenfly and a ladybird. Something flew at him, a dive-bombing commando-type raid, zoomed off again. A bumblebee. sometimes they attacked humans like that, for no apparent reason, almost as if their radar had gone beserk.

Emily had somehow got back on to her feet. She was flaying her arms wildly, trying to get something out of her eye.

George grinned in spite of his own predicament. Serve her right, she'd been asking for this for a long time. Leave her to her fate! A flitting temptation but now she had seen him, was staggering towards him with outstretched arms. He grabbed her, pulled her up on to the patio.

'Oh my God, George!' Emily Brownlow wiped at her eye again, smeared a black streak down her cheek. 'Let's get indoors quick!'

Inside the kitchen, slamming the door. A loud buzzing greeted them; black houseflies and a bluebottle swarming on the window pane as though madly trying to get out.

'We'll have to leave this place,' she began to sob. 'Move somewhere else.'

'No. It wouldn't serve any purpose. *There is no escape from the plague of pestilence. The whole of Britain will be crawling with almost every species of insect life before the week is out. Just as Egypt once did!*'

'Oh, for God's sake, shut up about Egypt!'

'I will not, for their ancient curse is now ours. Dalūkah and Āba-aner will be reborn and will die again because they were removed from their native land — and *almost* escaped from Set. Yet none can escape him in the end. Both you and I, Sheila and Barry, we are his chosen ones. We have a duty to perform during the last few weeks before civilisation is destroyed. Do not forget that. *We shall be saved when millions are dead and dying if we remain loyal to the serpent god and do his bidding!*'

Emily Brownlow forgot all about the insects, stared at her husband and was suddenly very frightened. There was a strength of purpose about him that transcended fanaticism, an obsession that would not be swayed. His eyes . . . she felt them boring into her . . . confusing her.

'Whatever do you mean, George? What's all this about Set? What's *he* got to do with it?'

'Don't speak of him flippantly, Emily, lest we feel the power of his wrath. They who were entombed by his priests to everlasting damnation were freed and brought to this country, to this very place. *Even then they might have escaped him but Set had foreseen such a happening and had put his own watchdog to mount guard over their wretched bodies . . . his amulet, charged with his own power, so that whoever stole the mummies stole it also*, that damnation would follow Dalūkah and Āba-aner whose child had been shut in the tomb with them while it died from a plague. Now we are faced with events beyond our control. The fools burned Rita's body and she is now one of his priestesses, her restless *khaibit* already having been seen by Barry. Should any of *us* die during the coming holocaust we must not allow it to happen again. The ritual of embalmment must be carried out, something which I must learn before it is too late.'

She had moved back to the window, was staring out across the desecrated lawn as though she had not heard him. Even the buzzing flies were still now; the bluebottle lay on its back on the sill. Perhaps they had killed it.

'There doesn't seem to be that many grasshoppers on the lawn now.' She spoke expressionlessly as though her thoughts dwelled elsewhere. 'In fact, there doesn't seem to be much happening out there at all, George.'

He moved alongside her. She was right. Like the frogs, the insects had bunched and dispersed.

'It was probably a warning,' he spoke softly.

'Yes.' Her voice still held that vacant tone. 'It was a warning, George. There can be no doubt about that. What are we going to do?'

He tensed, wished she would turn around so that he could see her expression, but she didn't. He felt his pulses quickening, that dryness in his mouth again. She should be spitting her contempt, lashing him with her tongue; at the very least disagreeing with him.

'I'd better get back out there,' he scraped the chair as he stood up. 'I've wasted enough time as it is.'

'I was going to make some tea. D'you want it here or shall I bring you out a cup?'

'You'd better bring it out to me now that those insects have gone. I don't have much time. None of us has.'

He went outside, closing the door behind him. The atmosphere smelled heavy, almost thundery. But he knew it wouldn't rain. The drought would not break before the end came, and after that it wouldn't matter.

George Brownlow had found an old camping lamp in the shed and had managed to make it work. Now that the actual digging of the shelter was completed it would be invaluable in assisting him with night work and no longer would he be restricted to the hours of daylight.

The walls had to be braced with timber and some of those lengths of three by two which those wasteful builders had thrown aside had to be sawn to fit. Then the polythene membrane had to be put in place like a kind of damp-proof course. There was an awful lot still to do. The skilled worker was about to replace the labourer.

Slower work now, requiring a much greater degree of concentration. Time passed unnoticed, didn't matter anyway; tiredness blended into fatigue, passed its peak and freshness came again. A continual cycle through the nocturnal hours, a body that for a few short hours needed neither sleep nor food, generating its own power, controlled by unknown forces and subservient to them.

George Brownlow sensed that he wasn't alone, a feeling that had him glancing back beyond the lamp into the furthest recess, but he saw nothing. If the gods watched him then he must be seen to work. He positioned another upright, began to hammer in a four-inch nail, cursed because it slanted and he had to bend it back. Yet his concentration was broken, his thought-wavelength scrambled.

'We must soon be together again, George.' Words that came out of that patch of darkness, soft gentle tones marred by remorse and sadness. George Brownlow listened, sensed a slight drop in the temperature. A force, not necessarily evil, but projecting itself at *him*, a distress call loaded with futility. *Rita!*

'They have parted us, George, just as they parted Dalūkah and Āba-aner who were my parents in another life. Now, again, they seek to destroy us. Beware the serpent with two heads! For it will destroy my Barry as surely as it will destroy you all!'

'Do not speak against Set!' George whispered. 'The serpent has eyes and ears and is everywhere. You seek to betray him although you are his priestess?'

'I am his unwilling slave and I care not for myself, only for my beloved who is also your son. Spare him, I beg of you. Do what is right, George, for otherwise he will rejoin me in eternal purgatory and far sooner would I have us parted so that his soul can travel to Sekhet-Aaru. Perform the rites and protect him from Set. Promise me this, I beseech you, for soon he is to die!'

'I dare not. I am not ready yet!'

'You must! Do you not care for your own son?'

A wave of dizziness flooded over George Brownlow and he recognised it as a mixture of fear and fatigue. Words of betrayal from his own lips were demanded by Rita's *khaibit*. A trick by the double-headed serpent to test his loyalty? Searching the shadows but seeing nothing, only sensing her presence.

'Hurry, for I dare not linger. Promise me this one thing, for your own son's sake!'

'I . . . promise,' he breathed, clutching at the wooden framework for support. Oh God, what had he done?

No answer. He did not hear her go but he knew she was gone and that he had given his word.

He stood up, shaking, wondered if he had the strength left in his body to climb out of this pit and make his way back to the house. Frightened, not just because he had made a vow against his master but because he knew without any doubt that Barry was going to die!

Chapter Nine

The Outcast

DUSK WAS falling when Adrian Capper walked down the sloping road that led into River View, a furtiveness about his movements almost as though he feared recognition. His features were strained where a fortnight's anxiety had left its mark upon him. Desperation now, fear because he had to know the worst, whatever. He had to speak to Sheila.

He saw the house, and it hurt, twisting his stomach up in knots, brought on a feeling of nausea, nostalgia gone sour. Her mother was to blame for all this, had put pressure and more pressure on Sheila, worn her down in the end. *'You can't let the family down by marrying a boy off a council estate. What d'you think all the people on River View will say? And it's making your father ill, given him high blood-pressure and now it's preyed on his mind so much that he's been digging a nuclear shelter. It's all your fault, Sheila. If anything happens to him it'll be on your conscience for the rest of your life!'*

Anger now as Adrian pressed himself back into the shadow cast by a willow tree. Last week and the week before he had made several trips to the supermarket to try and speak with Sheila, but she hadn't been there. One of the assistants had told him that she was away ill but she didn't know any details. Rita's death was sure to have upset her, but not to that extent. Now, somehow, he was going to see her. He wasn't leaving River View until he had, and if the worst came to the worst, Emily Brownlow was going to have a piece of his mind. They were ruining his life as well.

112

He tried to formulate a plan of action. It wasn't easy. The obvious approach was to ring the front doorbell only there were no lights showing at the front of the house. And in all probability Mrs Brownlow herself would answer the ring, in which case he would be sent packing. So he had to think of something much more cunning. It was almost like breaking and entering.

He tried not to be angry with Sheila. She had promised to ring on that Thursday but she hadn't. He could not understand it because she had never let him down before. A call, however hurtful and abrupt — *'I don't want to see you anymore, Adrian. This is goodbye'* — would have been preferable to not knowing.

He walked forward, looked furtively about him. The side gate was unlatched, half-open. Perhaps if he went round the back, knocked on the rear door, a kind of psychological advantage. He would take *them* by surprise.

A sense of guilt. It was like committing a felony sneaking in like this. But he had to know, once and for all. If Sheila told him to clear off then at least he could retire to lick his wounds, let time be the healer.

There was a light on in the kitchen, the curtains partly drawn. He edged his way up to the patio, had to force himself to peer inside. The room was empty, the remains of a meal still on the table. Now that wasn't like Emily Brownlow — she insisted on every plate being washed and dried before you left the room. It was all very odd, so uncharacteristic. Eerie.

Adrian stood there undecided. Surely they hadn't all gone up to bed and left the lights on. A movement attracted his attention, had him glancing behind him; something jumped, squatted, jumped again, a tiny body glistening in the ray of light which shafted out through the window. A frog. There was another one on the edge of that patch of shadow. Both of them were watching him and he could almost feel the intensity of their hatred. The little bastards knew that he was frightened of them, maybe they were survivors from that amphibian invasion three weeks ago and they *remembered. You killed some of us and now we're going to kill you!*

113

His breath quickened and he looked away. Insects were pounding the lighted window pane venomously, a concerted attack as though they were determined to break the glass and force their way in. Hard-shelled flying beetles that might be capable of inflicting a nasty sting.

He swallowed, almost turned and ran. The atmosphere was so oppressive, a hint of thunder but the rain wouldn't come. It would never rain again, ever. Nature was rebelling, strange forces plotting to overthrow civilisation, destroy an artificial way of life. Man had brought about his own undoing, gone too far, challenged forces beyond his control.

A sound, the sort of noise Adrian might have made himself, the scuffing of a plimsoll on hard ground or clothing brushing against some obstacle. He stared into the darkness, could just make out a shape on the lawn, a whiteness that moved and was still again. Watching him!

His skin prickled and he stepped back, trod on something that burst into a slimy morass. A flying beetle whipped against his cheek, zoomed on its way like a harrier jet in search of another target. Moths and midges vying for any area of exposed flesh. He ignored them, found himself walking towards that figure on the lawn as though obeying some irresistible force, a mute Pied Piper calling him.

A silhouette standing by that huge mound of rubble, a shapely female form, ghostly in appearance because it wore some kind of semi-transparent garment as though a mist was rising in an attempt to shield its nakedness, becoming familiar with each step he took until finally he recognised the other — *Sheila Brownlow*.

'Sheila!' Words that trembled, were an apology for trespassing in these grounds. The confrontation for which he had longed these past weeks he suddenly found frightening.

'Adrian, you shouldn't be here. What have you come for?' The same soft tones yet they lacked the kindness which he had come to know, her eyes searching him out. She clasped her flimsy nightdress to her in a gesture of embarrassment.

'You . . . never phoned me.' His voice was husky, loaded with tension. He didn't want it to sound like a reprimand.

114

'No, I didn't. I didn't think it really mattered.'

'I've been to the supermarket to try and see you but all they'd say was that you were ill. The last time I saw you was at the funeral.'

'We are wasting our time.' A half-sob which she tried to hide. 'You know nothing will ever come of our relationship, Adrian. It was doomed from the beginning.'

'But of course it will. I'll do anything for you.'

'Please, don't! It's better if we end it right now. I thought we had already done so but apparently I was wrong.'

'But why, Sheila? For God's sake tell me *why*!'

'I've already told you, we're wasting each other's time.'

'Your mother's behind this. She's finally got you where she's been trying to get you ever since we first dated!' Adrian could not keep the contempt out of his tone, his lower lip curling into a sneer.

'It's nothing at all to do with Mother. God's truth, it isn't!'

He stared at her in hurt amazement, knew that she spoke the truth. And in the faint light from the kitchen window he saw the way her eyes were misted up, how pale and distraught she looked as she wrung her hands together in obvious anguish.

'. . . Nothing at all . . . to do with . . . your mother . . .' Echoing her tones of sadness and finality, a wave of nausea sweeping over him. 'Then why? *Why?*'

'Because it's best that way. For your sake as much as mine. Things have changed here, Adrian.'

'Because of Rita's death?'

'No-oo-o.' She glanced away, back towards that digging almost as if she expected to see somebody there in the shadows eavesdropping on them, an expression of *fear*! 'It's just that . . . that things are going to be . . . *different* from now on.'

'You've got somebody else?' Voicing his worst fear that some boy off River View, more eligible than himself, had stepped into the breach. The Brownlows would really like that.

'No. There's nobody else, I promise.'

115

'Then what you told me wasn't true. You don't love me.'

Silence. Her gaze dropped for the first time, stared down at the parched grass, didn't even appear to notice a frog which had moved in close to her feet. Suddenly the night air was filled with their croaking as though they had come up out of the river and waited for this very moment. Those same two humans who had escaped before were here again. Sheila was trying to hold back her sobs. 'Can't we just leave it at that, Adrian?'

'No, because I think you're covering something up. If you don't want me anymore that's fair enough, but at the very least I think I'm entitled to an explanation. I'm beginning to think you're ill and that's what's worrying me.'

'I've been sick a lot lately. Mostly in the mornings.'

He tensed, stared in disbelief and said weakly, shakily: 'It's probably the heat . . . and all the upset over . . .'

'No, it's not. *I'm pregnant, Adrian!*'

Adrian Capper swayed on his feet, barely noticed another flying beetle ping against his cheek. A mixture of shock and euphoria. What Sheila said was virtually impossible, they'd been so careful, but if she was pregnant then she couldn't just throw him out like that. He'd have to face the Brownlows but he'd survive. In a way it couldn't have happened at a better time. All the same she had to be making a mistake. Maybe she was distraught, seeking refuge in fantasy.

'You're not *sure* though?'

'I haven't had it officially confirmed if that's what you mean but take it from me, I *know*. It's all a question of knowing what to do about it.'

'You know I'll marry you.'

She shook her head again, smiled wanly, and his hopes faded cruelly again. 'No, I meant what I said. Don't make my life anymore complicated, Adrian, *please*. Just leave me alone. It's also a big worry about Barry.'

'Why?'

'He's in a mental hospital. Mother's doing her best to keep it all hush-hush but it'll get out eventually. The irony of it all is there's nothing the matter with him. He saw and spoke to Rita, or rather her *khaibit*. Dad knows more about that than any of us because this last fortnight he's been studying Egyptology as though he's going to take a degree in it. But already he's learned such a lot about it and he's teaching Mother and I.'

Adrian's first inclination was to laugh. Instead a tiny shiver ran up his spine and spread out on to his scalp. George Brownlow wasn't the type to do things just for the hell of it, he always had a reason for everything he did. But this time his reasoning was illogical. Barry in a mental hospital, George soon to follow. And it was quite clear that there was something terribly wrong with Sheila. She needed help but in order to do that he would have to humour her.

'Have *you* seen Rita, Sheila?' he asked.

'No, but I'm hoping I will soon because we got on so well together and I miss her terribly.' Tears began to trickle down her cheeks. 'I've got to help Dad finish the shelter because there isn't much time left. If only Barry was here to give him a hand it would probably have been finished by now. There's not a lot left to do, though.'

'Maybe I could help.' Adrian was watching carefully for a reaction, his hopes plummeting when she shook her head slowly.

'No. Dad wouldn't like that because he says this shelter's a kind of *personal* thing and he doesn't want anybody except a Brownlow touching it.'

'I'd like to see it. Just a quick look. *Please*, Sheila.'

'All right,' she smiled faintly, peered past him towards the house, 'but only a quick one, mind. Dad would go beserk if he knew I'd let anybody see it. He's gone up for a bath but he'll be back shortly to give it a quick inspection before he goes to bed.'

An obsession that had got out of all proportion, Adrian decided. However, he was curious to see how George Brownlow's idea had worked out. Just a bloody big hole in the ground lined with a polythene membrane and sand-bagged, no doubt. If Emily was in on it she would have a carpet on the floor, a mirror and a doormat so that visitors didn't carry mud down there on their shoes.

'That's it. Now don't be long, Adrian, please.'

Adrian Capper stared at the dark mound of soil and rubble. No longer was it just an untidy heap, it had been levelled, shaped . . . *the top a kind of miniature pyramid!*

'Whatever's your dad shaped it like that for?' His mouth was dry, his voice a whisper.

'He refers to it as the pyramid of Dalūkah and Āba-aner.' If only she had laughed, made a joke of it, his spine wouldn't have tingled like it did. 'Like I said, everything in this household has to have an Egyptian flavour these days. I think it's rather a sweet idea, don't you? The ancient Egyptians were such a cultured race.'

The atmosphere didn't feel balmy any longer. Adrian sensed that same tension, an electrification, only it was too cold for thunder, a sort of icy heaviness and when the faint breeze rustled across the garden it was like dead fingers touching you. He didn't want to see what lay beyond that old door fitted into the mound. Maybe Sheila was right and he should just walk away and forget everything . . . while he still could!

'Hurry up, Adrian. Dad might come back any minute.' She *wanted* him to go in there now, moved behind him as though deliberately barring his escape route. 'Go on, what are you waiting for?'

His fingers stretched out, clicked the latch; the metal was icy cold. The door swung open as though wafted by some breeze from down below, but that was impossible. He stared into the interior, could just discern a flight of steps going down, a wooden rail to hold on to. It wasn't totally dark, a kind of gloom like a vestige of dusk before it blended into full darkness. Perhaps the reflection of polythene-lined walls was causing that.

'There's a light-switch just by your hand.' Sheila touched him, a gesture that was almost a shove, had him instinctively clutching at the rail. *Oh God, I don't want to go down there!* But he knew he would.

Instant artificial light came up the steps to greet him, a low-watt coloured bulb of some kind. Why the hell didn't George Brownlow fit a decent light? This was merely an extension of the previous gloom. And the smell, damp musty earth that cloyed nostrils and lungs like foul catarrh. He heaved, thought for a moment that he was going to throw up. *I don't bloody well want to go down there!*

But he did, staccato movements, ducking his head to avoid catching it on the roof, Sheila holding on to his arm and whispering: 'It's nice, isn't it?'

Airless like an exhumed grave, trying not to draw breath but being forced to, tasting that odour. He reached the bottom of the steps and stared in amazement. Oh God, all this was sheer madness, the product of a crazed mind!

The shelter was roughly the size of the living-room in the Cappers' council house except that the roof was lower, a stout timber framework supporting the earth walls and the weight of the soil above. A polythene lining, thick but transparent, probably 1000-gauge thickness, lighted by a single orange bulb, unfurnished except for. . . .

'What's *that*?' Adrian's whisper echoed as though a thousand invisible demons had taken it up, mocking him. *'What's* that . . . *that* . . . *that* . . . *tha* . . . *t?'*

A kind of box structure stood against the far wall, draped with some kind of frayed material that might once have been a tablecloth. It reminded Adrian of the plain altar in the Methodist church where his mother used to take him each week to Sunday School when he was a boy. Frightening in its simplicity because you knew it was something to do with God but you didn't understand and you were afraid to ask.

Something was propped up on this structure, a kind of polished metal disc that shone and glinted in the dim light, an emblem which incorporated a pair of snakes . . . no it was one, but it had two heads, both with shining red eyes that glittered and gave you the impression that they were capable of seeing . . . and were actually *watching* you!

'It's an amulet.' Sheila's voice sounded dreamy, far away. 'Something that Dad found when he was digging this place out. He says it has to be kept down here because of Dalūkah and Āba-aner.' She paused, he heard her intake of breath. 'I like it. Funny how these trinkets can get so that you can't stop looking at them. I could stay down here all day and just gaze at it . . . it gives you a sort of . . . warm feeling inside.'

Adrian shivered. The amulet was having exactly the opposite effect on himself. Those orbs were burning with a fire of sheer hatred, boring into him. *You have no right in here, boy. Be gone!*

'It's . . . *Set*, isn't it?' The words just seemed to flow from his mouth, another echoing whisper, hissing all around him. '*Set . . . Set . . . Set . . . Se . . . t . . .*'

'However did you know that?' Surprise and admiration in Sheila's voice, then her eyes narrowed suspiciously.

'I . . . don't know. I just know it is.' He spoke expressionlessly, couldn't take his eyes off those malignant serpent faces. The fangs appeared to move, it was becoming angry. 'I'd better be going.'

'Yes. Dad will be back soon. He hasn't finished in here, of course. He says he still has quite a lot of work to do, putting the finishing touches to it.'

Adrian found himself backing away, caught his foot against the bottom step and almost fell. Turning, he scrambled up the rough-hewn steps in a desperate flight, an awful fear that the door might have swung shut and imprisoned them both in that dreadful place. But it hadn't. He pushed his way out, gulped the night air down into his lungs. It had turned much warmer again. A temptation to spit, to try and get that taste out of his mouth.

'Are you all right?' Sheila was watching him anxiously.

'I'm OK.' He was sweating profusely. 'I guess I just found it a bit claustrophobic down there.'

'I got that way the first time I went down. But you get used to it, get to like it, in fact. It's cosy, you can think of it as a snug little house which protects you from the rest of the world.'

He grimaced. There was definitely something wrong with Sheila. The Brownlows' indoctrination had got through to her at last. He couldn't just walk out on her like that.

'Look,' he spread his hands in dismay, 'if I've got you pregnant then I'm determined to do something about it. Go and see the doctor, make sure, and if your test is positive then we'll talk again.'

120

'You just forget about it.' She was aloof again, folding her arms as though she feared lest he might be afforded a view of her breasts through her thin garment. 'Now go, because if Dad finds you here we'll both be in trouble.'

An awful moment of heartbreak and indecision for Adrian Capper, a nightly farewell that was suddenly final, devastating in its weirdness, an instinctive leaning towards her in search of a kiss that would burn as coldly as the eyes of Set in that underground chamber, only to be repelled by an upraised hand. Rebuffed, mutely pleading.

'Go quickly!' she snapped, and dodging his grasping arms she ran for the patio.

He stood there watching her, saw the frogs crowding on the lawn. Sheila did not appear to notice them. Twice she trod on an unfortunate animal with her bare feet but her pace did not slacken. Then she was gone, in through the door, slamming it shut behind her.

Adrian Capper slunk off into the darkness, a bowed figure that found its way back out into the lighted cul-de-sac of River View and sought refuge for the second time that night in the shadow cast by the huge willow tree. He was badly shaken, could easily have been sick, a feeling of acute despair. Jesus Christ, the horror of that shelter and the vile amulet it housed would remain with him forever. He'd never get the stench out of his lungs, the taste off his palate.

With an effort he pulled himself together, began the long walk back home. The Brownlows' had become a house of madness and he feared for Sheila's safety. She had told him to go at a time when she needed him most. Possibly he was the only person in the whole world who could help her, and now he was an outcast from River View.

By the time he reached the ring road he was crying unashamedly. And he was also very frightened.

Sheila Brownlow hadn't expected to find her parents sitting in the kitchen when she came in from the garden. The sight of them jolted her nerves, had her blushing with a flood of guilt. This was how it used to be at the old house when she was fourteen. A date with a boy and when she got back they were waiting for her, a thorough interrogation that overlooked no detail. We sat on a bench and *talked*, nothing else (I promise). You didn't *hold hands*, did you? You're sure you're telling the truth because if you aren't somebody will surely have seen you and we'll find out.

Now some strange time-machine was trying to rob her of her womanhood, a force that wilted her determination, was making her subservient to her parents again. And she couldn't do a thing about it.

'What were you doing out there, Sheila?' George Brownlow's eyebrows knitted, reminded her of some kind of hooded bird of prey.

'I . . . have been to the pyramid of Dalūkah and Āba-aner. I just wanted to look at it again.'

'I see.' George appeared to accept her explanation. 'But you weren't alone. We heard voices, you were talking to somebody.'

'Yes.' It was pointless trying to lie. And anyway, she hadn't invited Adrian here. Furthermore she had sent him away. 'It was Adrian. I told him to leave and never to come here again.'

Silence. Sheila felt herself cringing, wanting to pour out promises, pleas, total subservience. And deep down somewhere she despised herself for it. Her mother's features were tired and strained, looking to her husband as though she constantly needed his approval for her own presence in the kitchen. Sheila swallowed, tasted something rancid.

'We've heard you being sick in the mornings.' George Brownlow's eyes reminded her of those on the amulet in the shelter. You read the question before he asked it but you would not lie to him. 'Are you pregnant?'

Sheer psychological terror. A blurring of her vision, a wave of blackness spotted with red that had her holding on to a chair, then sinking down on to it because otherwise she would have fainted. Nodding, crying.

'By that boy?' A sudden lessening of his severity, more anxiety than anger, even gloating curiosity.

'I . . . I don't know.'

What d'you mean, you don't know? Have you gone with him?'

Nodding again like a string puppet whose ventriloquist master had suddenly been struck dumb.

'Then it must be. Unless you've been with anybody else.'

'No.' Almost a shout. 'I haven't. But I don't know for sure if I'm pregnant or not.'

George Brownlow's eyes seemed to glaze over as though cataracts had suddenly formed, his tone a recitation of words learned but the expression omitted. 'You are pregnant, my child. *For what is written cannot be changed. Dalūkah, of royal blood, gave birth to a bastard child by a commoner named Āba-aner. They were punished, yet temporarily escaped the curse of Set when their bodies were taken from their tomb to another land. But Set is all-powerful and it is decreed that Dalūkah and Āba-aner must live again so that they shall not escape their punishment. Another life, another death, even though the whole world is in its final hour!*'

Words that were suddenly no longer meaningless to Sheila Brownlow. The blackness came back at her with the hissing and roaring of a desert sandstorm, whipping her into unconsciousness. She slumped forward, fell from the chair.

Chapter Ten

The Tomb

SHEILA AND Emily Brownlow had remained in the kitchen for most of the afternoon. Just waiting. They had not spoken since George had gone outside, no sound except the steady hollow ticking of the clock on the mantelpiece. It was as though they were prisoners until his return.

Once the telephone in the hall rang, but neither of them made a move to answer it and eventually it stopped. They did not glance at each other, their thoughts elsewhere. Indeed they might have been oblivious of each other's presence. That call could have been from the hospital about Barry. *Your son is very much better, Mrs Brownlow; we think a spell at home would be good for him. I'm afraid we have some bad news for you, Mrs Brownlow. Your son threw a fit in the night, suffered a major stroke as a result. He's in a coma, could you come as quickly as you can please?*

Mutual concern but they would not answer the phone if it rang again. A sort of telepathy that saved them the trouble of conversation. Rita. Barry had seen her, all right. They did not doubt his word. Perhaps very soon they would see her too. At least they hoped so.

It was funny how things had changed, brought about a close-knit relationship in a family which hitherto had gone their separate ways. Emily was glad to relinquish her position as head of the family, she hadn't wanted it in the first place only George had needed somebody to motivate him, drive him. It had worked and now he was at the helm, making all the decisions. They would not question him. Furthermore, they would obey him. Sheila could not get Adrian out of her mind, sadness and guilt gnawing at her like the beginning of some cancerous growth. He was so kind and thoughtful but he really did not fit into the scene now. He always queried everything, had to have facts to substantiate facts. No way would he accept things as they were. *'Everybody's gone mad, She, and I want to get you away from them. A bedsit will be fine until I can get a job and afford a decent place for us.'*

Oh, the fool, albeit a lovely fool. He didn't understand and he never would so the only solution was to get rid of him. He'd find somebody else. As Mother would say, *'one of his own kind.'*

Emily permitted herself a faint almost unnoticeable smile. Sheila had seen sense at last. Thank God she hadn't done anything stupid like running off with that boy. Her features hardened, paled. But there was no getting away from the fact that her daughter was pregnant even if it had not been officially confirmed yet. George was quite apathetic about it, though, almost as if it was bound to happen, that he *wanted* it to, had *willed* it! Destiny, he called it. *One cannot control one's fate.* That was all very well, but who was going to look after the baby when it was born?

Emily Brownlow winced at the thought. She couldn't go through all that again — a continually crying infant, nappies hung on the clothes-horse in the kitchen because it was too wet to put them out on the whirligig (it was sure to rain again one of these days). And, most important, the shame of it all. There were lots of things you could cover up in life but there was no hiding an illegitimate child. A bastard! She squirmed, turned sideways to look at Sheila who was staring vacantly at those flies buzzing on the window. *In spite of all my warnings you made yourself cheap after all!*

Blushing with embarrassment because there was only one way a girl got herself with child. Disgusting, so primitive. Mating like a wild animal. She'd never have thought a daughter of hers would ever do anything like that. *Your*

*father and I never did anything before we were married. I
certainly wouldn't have let him even if he wanted to but he
had more respect for me than to try anything.* A sudden
fleeting memory of something that had *almost* happened
that Sunday afternoon when they had gone for a stroll
down the fields. A moment of impetuous passion on
George's part. Nothing *serious* by today's so-called
enlightened standards. They had been sitting on a grassy
bank outside a small fir wood, so peaceful, so remote. So
romantic! Just the place for a kiss and a cuddle. And then
George had spoiled it all by attempting to slide his hand up
her dress. Even thinking about it now had her going cold
and rigid. She'd frozen with shock and he had almost got his
fingers on their intended goal before she had slapped him,
dragged herself away from him. That had nearly been the
end of their engagement and at first she had refused to
accept his profuse apologies. Eventually she had relented
and it had all been smoothed over. But not forgotten, it
never would be.

Even on their wedding night Emily had demanded
respect. Of course she expected George to want to do *that*
the moment they put the bedroom light out but she was not
standing for a lot of playing about. It wasn't decent!

She had hoped she had brought her children up like
that, but evidently she had failed somewhere along the line
with Sheila. Where Emily had said '*no*' to George, Sheila
had quite obviously said '*yes*' to that council estate boy. It
was heartbreaking but when she had spoken to her husband
about it he had acted very strangely and replied in a flat,
expressionless voice '*One cannot alter destiny. What
Dalūkah did once she is bound to do again.*'

It couldn't have happened that first night the frogs
came up out of the river in their thousands, or if it had then
Sheila had already conceived. Emily was trying to work out
dates in her confused mind. It was all too complicated for
her and in the end she gave up. She hoped that Sheila's
pregnancy was just the result of one moment of madness,
that she and that boy hadn't done it before or since.
Anybody could make *one* mistake. And now the girl must

pay for her folly. The Brownlows wouldn't involve Adrian because that was inviting a scandal.

Her thoughts switched to Rita, brought a burning moistness to her eyes. Now Rita wouldn't have let Barry do anything like that. She would act exactly as Emily had acted that Sunday long ago if Barry succumbed to temptation. A girl to be proud of and yet she had to be snatched away from them all in the midst of life. It wasn't fair. There were dozens of hussies plying their trade unashamedly in town most nights so why couldn't the Lord have taken one of them? She shuddered as she recalled George Brownlow's answer to that question. *'It wasn't the Lord who took her, Emily.'* His eyes resembled those on that snake-thing in the shelter. *'It was Set! Because he had need of her, in the same way that he has need of all of us!'*

Set! She closed her eyes, saw four burning pinpoints of fire in the darkness, heard the hissing of that wriggling repulsive two-headed snake. Somehow that amulet had been the beginning of George's dominance over the family, had given him some kind of power. She felt it, so did Sheila. Maybe it was responsible for what had happened to Barry.

She began to panic in her own mind. Surely the thing was easy enough to get rid of. She could sneak down to the shelter when George wasn't around, take it and throw it into the river at the bottom of the garden. Nobody would ever find it then. It would remain in the mud and sewage forever.

A hissing. Unaccountable noises in her head which had her clutching her hands to her ears, writhing in her chair. *Oh God, she wouldn't do that because she dared not touch it! Had not that same snake bitten her husband?*

Sweating, she smelled that awful musty underground stench again, changing to her own body odour as she opened her eyes, staring fearfully around the room. Sheila was still engrossed with those flies on the window pane. Maybe if the window was open they would all fly away. Or else more would come inside to join them. But neither herself nor Sheila was going to get up and open the window.

Still waiting. Waiting for George Brownlow because he held the key to everything. He was the Master! Today his work would be completed, the final touches put to the shelter. Then they would be shown it.

The clock on the mantelpiece showed five minutes to five. The temperature seemed to have risen considerably and the chest freezer was labouring to keep pace with it, the floor vibrating as the motors changed up a gear. The flies were noisier, a lot more seemed to have joined them and Emily found herself wondering how they had got in because all the doors and windows were shut. Lately they had to be kept like that, night and day. A few nights ago the interior walls had been crawling with all kinds of repulsive nocturnal insects. The worst had been those hard-shelled flying black beetles which seemed to be imbued with a desire to attack anybody or anything that moved, homing in like miniature spitfires. Emily cringed, closed her eyes just thinking about them, anticipating a stinging facial impact, bracing herself for the sudden sharp pain.

Footsteps. The kitchen door opened and closed. Sheila started, half-screamed as she was jerked out of her reverie. George Brownlow stood there dressed in a soiled singlet and shorts, his features sweat-grimed, a film of dust covering his glasses and giving the impression that the sockets were black and empty. He smiled, a hideous stretching of dry lips. 'It is ready.'

Words that carried the impact of a physical blow, seemed to throw the two women back in their chairs. Emily didn't want to go down there into that awful claustrophobic shelter of George's where a double-headed serpent writhed in the dim light and watched their every move with a malevolent stare. Where it was deathly cold on the hottest day and the stench of sheer *evil* almost suffocated you. A week ago it had been a bare underground room; since then George had done *something* to it and she was afraid to go and look.

'No.' A weak protest, Emily's lower lip trembling.

'You must! You *shall*!' George's head was thrust forward, the veins on his neck standing out. 'It is for all of us.'

Emily rose shakily to her feet, saw that Sheila had also stood up, was hanging back.

'Come on.' He was impatient now, eager. 'This is a great day in our lives, particularly in mine. You said, everybody said, that George Brownlow was not capable of constructing this shelter. But I have proved you all wrong. Come now, and see for yourselves!'

They followed him outside, the concrete unpleasantly hot beneath their feet, even the lushest and most resilient foliage in the adjacent shrubberies was beginning to wilt. A solitary blackbird regarded them from a branch, chirped at them because the bird-bath was dry and the bird-table was bare. It had been accustomed over the past months to being provided for but suddenly it seemed that the humans didn't care anymore. In its own way it feared starvation.

That mound of earth and rubble had certainly been tidied up, Emily reflected. Levelled so that it resembled a . . . a huge *grave*! No, it was her morbid imagination playing tricks. More like a bunker on a golf course. An ordinary everyday heap of soil.

A barren parched landscape all around them. Surely the lawn would never recover, the shrubs would wither and die. Only yesterday the public had been urged to do everything possible to conserve water. Reservoirs were dangerously low, rivers were well below their normal level. The country could just run dry if it went on like this.

George reached the door, pulled it wide. The other two wrinkled their noses, anticipating that awful smell rising to greet them. He ducked his head, began to descend the steps, knowing that they would follow. Emily first, because it was her duty as a wife to accompany her husband, then Sheila because some compelling force other than curiosity was luring her down below.

That same dim light only this time it showed up every detail, possibly because now there were details to discern whereas before, apart from the amulet on the altar, the place had been bare. Cries of amazement came from the two women, gasps of terror because the stark reality of George Brownlow's project was now presented in its entirety.

Dexion shelving covered both long walls. Fixtures from the garage which unknown to the others George had dismantled and re-erected down here. Packed shelves, tinned and dried foodstuffs on one side, personal possessions on the other, resembling a small overstocked supermarket.

'That's . . . that's my jewellery box!' Emily pointed to a square black object opposite. 'I . . . it should be in the bedroom.'

'No.' George's tone was firm, his hand restraining her from reaching out for it. 'Its rightful place is here. Like everything else — books, clothing, food to sustain us on our long journey.'

'*Journey*?' Sheila stared aghast. 'But Dad, we're only twenty yards from the house. Even if the worst comes to the worst we don't have to stay down here for more than a fortnight!'

'That is where you are mistaken, my child.' He stood facing them at the far end of this strange room, one hand caressing the amulet, those eyes appearing to glow with pleasure in the manner of a contented feline beast. It was a trick of the light which had the serpent seeming to move. 'For this place, the result of weeks of toil, is the focal point of our destiny. When the end comes the Brownlows must all be together.'

'But isn't the idea of building a shelter to survive a holocaust?' Emily asked.

'To survive the follies of Man,' he laughed, a frightening sound that echoed, had the others stepping back in alarm, 'is one of the aims. But life is so temporary, at least in the form we know it. Whether we survive or not is a matter for conjecture, but even if we do, the world as we know it now will be gone forever. What is there to remain here for except to rule supreme over burned-up continents, smouldering wastelands? No, there are far better places awaiting us. Look upon this humble edifice as a ship that will convey us across the waters to a land where *Ra* will smile gently and kindly upon us, a place that is called *Sekhet-Aaru . . . the Land of the Dead!*'

Sheila clutched at her mother, fought back her scream, wanted to yell '*We're not going to die.*' George Brownlow smiled, a facial movement intended to convey an expression that was half-apologetic, half-reassuring.

'Please don't be frightened.' Softer tones now, almost a whisper. 'What is death but an extension of life, the chance to live again? Perhaps we shall survive, perhaps the Great Powers will back down before the ultimate confrontation. Only the great Set knows that and he will not impart such knowledge to his humble servants. We shall only know when the time arrives.'

He stepped forward, an orator aware that the climax to his speech was near, drawing himself up to his full height. 'If perchance we are fated to perish then we must be certain that we go to *Sekhet-Aaru* and that our *khaibits* do not wander in eternal darkness such as happened to poor Rita. Maybe we can even save her. We are in the hands of the great god Set!'

'We're going to die then,' Emily breathed. 'But you forget one thing, George, as a family we are not united for Barry has been taken from our midst.'

'He will be returned to us,' Brownlow smiled. 'Set promised me that in a vision last night and I know that our son will come back to us. *But in the meantime we must make our preparations, for the journey, if we are called upon to make it, will be a long one and we must carry food to sustain us, and our most treasured possessions to grace our new home when we arrive!*'

Sheila experienced a feeling of faintness, the underground room darkening, tinged with red reflected from those glowing orbs. The stench was overpowering, the atmosphere thick with the smell of ancient decay; dust that had her coughing.

And in those last few seconds of consciousness came the terrible realisation. George Brownlow had not worked for weeks in the unrelenting heat simply to construct a shelter to protect them in the event of a nuclear war. *He had built a tomb in which to incarcerate them, a prison that was also his own temple to the serpent of evil!*

BOOK TWO

THE DEAD

Chapter Eleven

Scorpions!

AUBREY HOUGHTON had worked at the council offices ever since he had left school twenty years ago. For him success was a challenge, the smallest promotion a cause for euphoria. A slow process, hiding his frustrations, yet they had left their mark upon him. Thinning hair, narrow features that were pallid from an indoor occupation and lines that had been etched by his hopes and disappointments. Nervous to the point of being neurotic, disliked by his colleagues and superiors alike, he had finally progressed to the planning office at everybody else's expense.

He implied to his associates outside his place of appointment that he was *Assistant* Planning Officer. Not wholly a lie, because certainly he assisted Mr Millichip, took the brunt of the chief's roastings, found himself landed with innumerable menial chores in addition to his routine paperwork. And if the boss didn't have faith in him he wouldn't have been continually lumbering him with these irksome tasks, Aubrey decided smugly. Staff came and went, were promoted to other councils elsewhere so his own best policy was to sit tight, become the planning officer's devoted and trustworthy henchman and in time the job *could* just be his.

Houghton stroked his dark moustache with obvious satisfaction and determined to pursue this route to promotion. Examinations were not his strongest point, never had been, but so long as he showed willing by attending evening classes, and reminded Mr Millichip frequently that he was doing just that, perseverance and hard work would do the rest. It was easier for a bachelor because he didn't have the ties and distractions of family life. Aubrey Houghton was toying with the idea of taking up golf, wondered if he could afford it. Often business success was achieved on the course and Mr Millichip took every Wednesday afternoon off for that purpose, in spite of what some of the others in the planning office hinted at. Now if somehow Aubrey could worm his way into that same club. . . .

'I've got a job here for you, Aubrey.' The bulky shape of the Planning Officer loomed over Aubrey's desk, had him tensing, swallowing instinctively. The use of his first name by the boss was usually an ominous sign.

'Oh yes, sir?' A sickly smile as he looked up into those craggy features, pale blue eyes that made you glance away anywhere so long as you didn't have to meet them. Overweight, but it suited the boss, gave him a sort of strong-man image like some tough New York cop who was capable of pulling out the punches when it mattered most. Nobody argued with 'Chip' — a living legend in his own area.

'There's some bloody nonsense going on up at River View and we'd better look into it.' The Planning Officer waved two pages of handwritten paper, but obviously had no intention of passing them over to his clerk for perusal. 'A complaint from one of the residents. The Brownlows at number twelve are sneakily building something in their rear garden. What the hell it is I've no idea but we'd better find out. According to this anonymous complaint they've been digging out some kind of footing for weeks. You'd better get up there and take a look. Don't stand for any nonsense and if you're refused admittance we'll get a warrant. They're funny people by all accounts.'

'Leave it to me, sir.' Aubrey stood up, buttoned his jacket. 'I'll soon sort it out.'

'You'd better. Go up and see what's going on and let me have a detailed report in the morning.'

Aubrey Houghton experienced a desire to run from the room, a schoolboy with an unprecedented opportunity to appease his headmaster. *'Fetch me some tobacco from the corner shop, boy, and don't be long about it. And I won't cane you for your next minor misdemeanour.'*

'I won't be in this afternoon.' Wednesday, of course. 'So leave your findings on my desk and I'll deal with it first thing in the morning.'

Bureaucracy was a fillip to Houghton, a delegation of authority which he would use to its fullest capacity, something which they did not teach you in the classroom at night school. The public were mindless morons and they had to be reminded of The System from time to time. Somebody stepped out of line so you made an example of them. Today Aubrey Houghton *was* the Planning Officer, deputised to investigate the Brownlows and he would make an impression on River View. They would remember him for a long time to come. Yes, sir, he would let them know that he was around.

He made a deliberate effort to check his excitement as he crossed the expanse of tarmac which served as a car park behind the towering block of antiquated council offices. He saw himself as tall and rugged, a figure that instilled instant unease into any who saw him coming. Millichip's Mercedes shimmered in the fierce sunlight, a symbol of prestige and success. Aubrey allowed himself a brief fantasy, a direct course towards it before changing direction and heading for the battered Mini which was parked twenty yards beyond it. That was the moment you came down to earth, remembered your own lowly role, a small cog in the mighty council wheel. That was the difference, a Mercedes or a Mini, the gulf that stretched between Houghton and his boss.

The interior of the Mini was stifling, the seat burned his body and he was compelled to wind both windows down. The starter motor whined, fired, and rattled the bodywork. A puff of black exhaust fumes, a grating of gears, and Aubrey Houghton was easing his way out of the car park and into the flow of traffic.

He did not drive right down into River View. When he had progressed to a Mercedes he would make regular calls in that exclusive part of town but in the meantime he would leave some conjecture concerning his mode of transport.

Council officials sometimes travelled by public transport for a variety of reasons; there were moves afoot to pedestrianise the town centre and an example had to be set by somebody — *'leave your car at home and travel by bus.'* A deliberate destruction of status.

Aubrey parked in a side road adjoining River View, hurriedly locked his car and tried to disassociate himself from it, a self-inflicted personality change in which there was no place for a Mini. An expression and posture of officialdom, head high, looking neither to the right nor the left, an umbrella because you were undressed without one even in an unprecedented heatwave. An air of contempt that increased as he turned down into River View, an inborn hatred for capitalists. But their day would come just as the Brownlows' already had.

He slowed his pace, studied River View carefully. Number twelve wasn't any different from the others except that it occupied an end position and its garden ran down to the river. At least, he thought it did. He would soon find out.

A few moments of final preparation. Straightening his tie which was nearly strangling him in the heat, sweat pouring down his face, eyes smarting. Blurred vision as though he was dizzy. He swallowed, mopped at his features with a handkerchief. Damn this heat, it didn't inspire confidence.

A determined mental effort and he was the Planning Officer again, the chief, not his assistant. Arrogance replacing that momentary indecisiveness, stepping forward on a direct course for number twelve.

The place looked deserted. Now that would be a real letdown. *'I'm sorry, Mr Millichip, sir, but there was nobody at home.'* *'Oh all right, Houghton, I'll pop up there myself this afternoon. Maybe it's best that I go in person, anyway.'* No bloody fear!

An impressive-looking oak-panelled front-door (probably made in Taiwan), with a polished brass knob and letterbox. Aubrey searched for the bell, finally found it set in the brick surrounds. It felt spongy as though the pull wasn't attached to anything. Probably the wire had snapped. Listening. Silence. Except for the buzzing of insects.

Flies, swarms of them appearing suddenly as though they had been forewarned of his coming and had lain in ambush in the bushes. He swatted at them but it had no effect. So undignified standing there in the middle of a cloud of flies as though something about him was attracting them. Christ Almighty, where was everybody? If that blasted bell wasn't working then they wouldn't know he was here. A sudden spasm of anger had him bunching his fist, thumping on the door. It was solid, just made a dull sort of noise that wasn't likely to attract anybody's attention.

He stepped back a few paces, took a good long look at the house. Again he experienced that envy of capitalism. This place was sure to be worth seventy grand. All the curtains were drawn. That could have been because of the heat or it might be because they had something to hide.

He took a deep breath, swatted at the flies again. He couldn't just stand here all afternoon, it was too bloody hot anyway. Maybe he should go back to the office and try again this evening. *'I didn't hang about, Mr Millichip, because there's always work piling up in the office, so I went back after tea. No, I don't want to book overtime or mileage, it's all part of the job, isn't it? Money doesn't enter into it.'*

Aubrey Houghton was on the point of turning away and retracing his steps when another thought struck him. The Brownlows could just be in the rear garden, snoozing the afternoon away in the shade of the willows down by the river. It was the sort of thing fat idle capitalists were likely to indulge in on hot summer afternoons. A quick glance down the side showed him a high wicker gate between the garage and the house. It was worth taking a quick look.

Trepidation now. He had no right to do this, he was trespassing. On the other hand, he was the Planning Officer and if the Brownlows were up to something then there was only one way he was going to find out. It would certainly be a feather in his cap if he uncovered something.

He eased the gate open, a steady creaking. If they were in the garden then they would surely hear him. Excuses, apologies started to cram his mind but he pushed them away. It was the Brownlows who would need to fabricate.

Aubrey wiped his eyes again, clawed at the flies which had followed him. The rear garden stretched away before him, a large gently sloping lawn that resembled an area of compressed straw. Then his eyes alighted on that mound of soil, sent a shudder through him in spite of the temperature. This was what the neighbours had been complaining about and no wonder . . . it looked like the Brownlows had buried somebody in a huge grave!

He approached it, looking all around him. There was nobody in sight so perhaps they really were away for the day. In which case he had all the time he needed to investigate. Flies crawled all over him unheeded as a host of possibilities presented themselves to him. Just suppose that thing really *was* a grave; that meant that somebody was buried in it. It was big, big enough for a dozen bodies. Oh God! His legs had gone weak and there was a tight ball in his stomach gripping him and threatening to make him vomit. '*It was like a grave, Mr Millichip.' 'Well, was it or wasn't it? Didn't you take a close look?' 'No . . . I didn't.' 'Why not?' 'Because I was shit-scared, sir, and I messed my pants, spewed all down my shirt as I ran. Vomited my promotion all over the lawn.*'

He pulled himself together. It couldn't be a grave otherwise it would have been hidden away somewhere. Therefore it was something else. And you'll only discover what by going and taking a closer look.

He spat some flies off his lips, thrust at them with his rolled umbrella, realisation that he had a weapon in his hand. It gave him the confidence he needed to creep closer, primed to run if he discovered some nameless horror, if his legs were strong enough.

A door! He stared at it in disbelief, felt a sudden surge of relief. Graves didn't have doors. Looking back towards the house again. A curtain at one of the upstairs windows appeared to waft slightly; it must be his imagination. To hell with the Brownlows if they were skulking indoors watching him.

The door swung open at his touch, delicately hung on well-oiled hinges. A rush of stale air that even had the flies scattering. Christ, it didn't smell very healthy down there.

Maybe the Brownlows had constructed some kind of septic tank. They had to be bloody crazy when they had mains sewage.

He propped the door open with a large stone, checked that it couldn't swing shut and imprison him in *there*. He stooped, moved to the top of the steps, tried to peer down into the darkness. Whatever was down there? *'I didn't actually go down, Mr Millichip, sir.'* 'You didn't *go down and look?'*

His hand brushed against something, flicked the switch even as he recognised what it was, and pale yellow light flooded up the steps to greet him. He stared down, puffed his cheeks out at that awful smell. Well, there was no going back now. A quick look, enough to enable him to file a report of some kind. From here it looked like some sort of workshop. Brownlow was running some kind of business on the side, avoiding rates, dodging taxes. That was what it was. He'd have to make sure though.

Aubrey Houghton reached the bottom of the steps, turned to his left and grunted his amazement aloud. Some kind of foodstore. More than that, like a well-stocked corner shop that was short of floor space. What the hell *was* going on?

Something attracted his attention, seemed to draw his gaze away from the loaded shelves, a compelling frightening force that created within him a sensation of helplessness. He could not hold back a little cry of fear, recoiled as he saw the writhing snake, its two heads bobbing from side to side like tulips caught in a gale. Blood-red eyes that saw him, glittered ruby hatred, fixed him with their stare. A pendulum that you found yourself watching until eventually you couldn't drag your gaze away. You felt the full force of its power!

Houghton stood there transfixed, aware that this underground room was growing darker as though the single bulb worked off a dimmer switch. He couldn't make out the shelving any longer, details slipping from him until finally the only thing he could see was that awful monstrosity bathed in the glow from its own eyes.

Timeless terror. How long he had been here he had no idea. Cold, so that the sweat chilled on his body, had him shivering like he used to do as a boy when the swimming instructor was being bloody-minded and kept them all standing about on the edge of the baths. A vibrating noise that jarred his brain, began to hurt. After a time he realised that it was the chattering of his own teeth. He had dropped his umbrella, he would never find it again. *'It's some kind of snake with two heads which the Brownlows keep down there, Mr Millichip.' 'You're mad, Houghton, stark raving mad!' 'Yes sir, I'm mad and I wish I was dead.'* Maybe I shall be soon.

Movements. He wanted to turn his head and look behind him but even if he had been able to do so then he wouldn't have been able to see anything in the darkness. A rustling sound, too heavy for flies. Mice? Rats? Aubrey Houghton wanted to scream, tried to, but no sound came from his lips.

Then something brushed against his foot, began crawling over it, making his flesh crawl with it. *Oh God Almighty, what the hell was it?*

The reptilian features were suffused with the glow from those burning orbs, fangs flicking from side to side in escalating fury, mouthing a hiss that fused like cold water being poured on to hot embers, infiltrating Houghton's brain and becoming words.

'Trespasser in the Temple of Set! Death should be your reward but it would be too easy. Behold, all about you is another plague come to scourge a dying land. The Plague of Scorpions is upon you and your kind!'

And in that instant Aubrey Houghton knew what it was that crawled about his feet and over them; *giant poisonous spiders — scorpions!* He was rigid with terror, wanting to scream, wanting to die. His crazed brain conjured up vague pictures of scorpions as he remembered them from hazy television programmes. One sting was fatal, an agonising death, a screaming fit that would last until the end came.

He could hear them, dozens of them circling him, closing in. *Oh Jesus, something was crawling up his leg*

141

inside his trousers, sharp feet that gouged holds like a rock-climber hacking his path with a pick! Up and up, sensations that shrunk his testicles into a compressed ball. Around his thighs, creating shivers up his spine and following them on up. And all the time he was forced to stare into those hateful lusting red eyes which mocked him, anticipating the fateful sting. If only he could faint, bring it all to an end. But unconsciousness was cruelly denied him.

That hissing voice, it reminded him of Millichip's sarcastic gloating. *'Have you discovered what the Brownlows are up to, Houghton?' 'Yes, sir, they're breeding scorpions in a dug-out.' 'Then let me have a full report.' 'I CAN'T, SIR, I'M GOING TO DIE!'*

But Aubrey Houghton didn't die. The unseen spiders crawled and scratched his flesh but did not administer the sting of death. He was slowly going mad. He could feel their sharp claws digging into him, anticipated the fatal sting which never came.

And suddenly he found that he could move again! A frightening anti-climax. The four red eyes had died down to a dull glow almost as though that repulsive reptile slept. This time he managed a scream, a hoarse sound that echoed back at him, lingered in the confined space as though it could not find a way out. *Flee, run while you still can!*

He turned, banged into a section of shelving and almost fell. Something hard crunched beneath his feet and he almost vomited. He had trodden on one of the scorpions, crushed it. The others would surely kill him now!

Then came the terrifying realisation that he had lost all sense of direction, was totally disorientated in this Stygian blackness. Feeling his way along the walls, afraid of what his fingers might touch. Canned foodstuffs avalanched, rolled. He trod on something else which split and crushed but he couldn't be sure what it was. Something still crawled on his back inside his shirt but he dared not try to dislodge it.

Those eyes were no longer glowing; indeed, he thought that reptilian monstrosity had gone, having squirmed its way into some hiding place and left him to his fate. Movements all around him in the darkness as though the giant spiders could see, were watching him, torturing him with some obscene game in which the loser's prize was death. Stumbling one way, then another. God, he must find the exit soon, surely!

Something caught against his shin with jarring impact, threw him forward, and even as he fell he knew that he had found those steps and sobbed his relief aloud. He clawed at them, tasted blood in his mouth as he pulled himself up. His hand brushed against something that moved and he snatched it away.

Scrambling on all fours, crying with fear and pain. His shin might be broken but he didn't care as long as he made it up there and out into the daylight unscathed.

Daylight! A tantalising oblong that might have been a mirage because it took him so long to reach it, fearful that at any second it might be blotted out by that terrible blackness again. *'You've gone the wrong way, Aubrey. Go back and try again!'*

But it was real. Blazing sunlight on parched grass, an emaciated blackbird squawking in alarm and taking off at his appearance, leaving behind the remnants of a huge grasshopper on which it had been feeding. Aubrey dragged himself clear of the opening, lay there with his eyes closed, didn't dare glance behind him.

His head throbbed and his crazed mind could not yet come to terms with the outside world. A noise that increased steadily in magnitude, a tuneless orchestra of minute violins tuning up for some awful symphony of death. He lay there wondering if that scorpion still crawled inside his shirt and if it did how he was going to remove it. But he couldn't feel it any longer and in the end he concluded that his terrible host had left him.

He sat up, began unfastening his shirt. It clung wetly to his body and when he tugged at it the material tore. Frantically he pulled, shredded it, anything to get it away from his body. A sigh of sheer relief escaped his lips as he discovered that the scorpion wasn't there anymore. Perhaps it had all been in his imagination — no, he could still hear them down there, scurrying about. He should have slammed the door behind him but he wasn't going near it again.

Blood! It trickled sluggishly from his nostrils in thick twin rivulets that congealed in the heat before they reached his lips. He rolled up his trouser leg, saw a bloody gash where he had banged his shin on the steps. His umbrella was somewhere down there but he wasn't going back for it.

He wiped his smarting eyes, stared across towards the house. There was no sign of movement, the curtains were still drawn. The Brownlows were definitely out and that was someing to be grateful for because he had no wish to meet them.

He rose shakily to his feet, swayed as a wave of dizziness hit him. What the hell was that noise? It seemed to be coming from all around him, a discord that filled the air so that there was no way you could shut it out. And even as he stood there the burned lawn seemed to move. A crazy shifting that might have been his own giddiness.

Grasshoppers! They were everywhere, millions of them, miniature violinists who sawed their bows and stared malevolently up at him with minute pinpoint eyes which were reflected in the glare of the sunlight.

Aubrey Houghton gave a strangled cry, backed away, felt dozens of tiny bodies crunching under the soles of his polished office shoes. And this time he vomited, bent double. His vision cleared, seemed to be drawn back to that open doorway beyond which those steps led down to hell itself. *He screamed, a weak noise that was lost in the cacophony of insect music, for coming out of that entrance were huge spiders, a dozen or more that moved jerkily, then stopped as though the intense heat had suddenly sapped their strength!*

But they weren't scorpions! Aubrey didn't know much about spiders but he knew these creatures were huge. Dark brown multi-legged varieties similar to those which wove their silky webs in the dark corners of most households, only very much bigger. Loathsome bloated bodies, overfed but still hungry. Hunting for food. . . .

The music changed instantly, a million fearful insect screeches mingled into one, waves of grasshopper bodies suddenly thrown into a turbulent wave of retreat, scattering in all directions. Aubrey felt their movements over his feet, a rush of tiny bodies, crushed them by the thousand as he broke into flight.

The patio, raised ground that offered a sanctuary from this lawn of seething revulsion. He grazed his shin again on the steps but barely noticed the pain. A door. Oh God, he knew it would be locked because the Brownlows were out. Banging his fists on the woodwork until his strength ran out, yelling for somebody to open up and let him in.

But nobody answered his call and when eventually he looked back towards that lawn it was still and silent. No grasshoppers, no spiders. Just a square of parched land that might have been an area of desert wasteland anywhere in the world except on River View.

Finally he moved away, a hunched trembling figure in a sweat-grimed vest and town trousers, face smeared with dried blood, glancing fearfully behind him until he was clear of Number Twelve. Then he broke into a run.

'And how did you get on up at River View, Houghton?' *'Oh, it was all a load of nonsense, Mr Millichip, sir. Blown up out of all proportion by the neighbours. The Brownlows have dug themselves a nuclear shelter, nothing to do with us or anybody else. A bit unsightly but once it's grassed over you won't know it's there. But we can't interfere with it. The leaflet that was sent round a couple of weeks ago, the one about not interfering with any nuclear shelter digging by members of the public, sir. Well, with this Libya business scaring half the population there's going to be an awful lot more of this sort of thing happening and you can't really blame folks, only nosey neighbours who report them. Somebody's wasted council time, but not to worry, sir, because I was intending to work over for a couple of hours tonight, anyway. No, I shan't be booking overtime.*

Aubrey Houghton did not even notice the stifling heat as he climbed into the Mini. Certainly he wouldn't wind the windows down until he was well clear of River View.

The Brownlows were mad but that was OK by him. Because he wasn't going back there again for anybody, not even Mr Millichip. And he would ensure that a return visit wasn't requested.

Chapter Twelve

Madness!

BARRY BROWNLOW was not sure how long he had been at Shelderton. Life had embarked upon a new course of apathy for him, an almost lazy existence like cattle on undulating meadowland, drifting aimlessly to and fro. He could not even remember much about Rita. She was gone and that was all there was to it. He did not need her. Maybe he hadn't needed her in the first place. Like a dream that faded with waking and eventually you forgot all about it. You just waited for the next dream and hoped that everything would be all right.

Those early days here had been unpleasant, but he was learning to forget them as the tall man in the white coat had promised him he would. Vague recollections of a bare room with white walls, and each time his visitors came in they hurt him a lot. In the early stages he had struggled but there had been too many of them, strapping him down and attaching some kind of strange machine with innumerable wires to his body. Sheer agony that left him weak and trembling but strangely contented. But now they did not do that to him anymore. They said there was no need and that he was getting better. One of these days, they assured him, he would be allowed to go home.

Barry wasn't sure that he wanted to go home. It was nice here, they fed you, they gave you a comfortable bed and they weren't everlastingly pestering you about the need to study for examinations. Shelderton was the sort of

146

place you could happily spend the rest of your life in. He wondered why Mother hadn't been to see him, but if she came she would only nag the whole time she was here so it was better if she didn't visit him. Just take each day as it comes, let everybody else do the worrying.

He concluded he was getting better because now they were quite happy for him to wander about the grounds, spacious gardens that became a wilderness of neglect away from the main buildings, the part where visitors never went. Four bells a day: breakfast, lunch, supper and bed, a matronly-like figure conducting her own roll-call in the dining-hall and checking your room last thing to make sure you were in. Apart from that you were free to mooch anywhere within those two acres bordered by a high pleached hedge. Almost like an open prison where nobody wanted to escape.

One day was much the same as another and Barry had mentioned to the doctor that life was becoming a bit boring. The grey-haired man had frowned, scribbled something on a slip of paper and that night his tablets were changed. Only a slight difference, red ones instead of green ones, but the next day wasn't monotonous at all. So much to see. Grasshoppers that plaintively bemoaned the scorched grass, especially a giant-sized one that regarded Barry steadily from the bough of a wilting rhododendron bush. The insect reminded him of the one Dad had caught that time. The cruel bugger had kept it in a jar with the lid screwed down tight and in due course the poor thing had suffocated and died. He ought to have been reported to the RSPCA for all the good that would have done.

Barry studied the one perched on the branch for some time, and it seemed to return his stare, masticating the whole time with a kind of brittle crunching sound. Eventually it appeared to become bored with his company and flew off.

There was an abundance of all kinds of insects. The tangled rosebeds were thick with greenfly which in their turn were being devoured by an increasing army of ladybirds. Nature was cruel, he decided, and moved on down to the pond at the furthermost corner of the grounds. More cruel than Dad, in fact.

So peaceful here, the croak of frogs from the thick rushes reminded him of the river at the bottom of their garden. Frogs were perfectly harmless. Sheila and Adrian had panicked that night. He grinned at the memory of their naked homecoming and in due course his thoughts returned to Rita. *Oh God, why did she have to die like that?*

Morose now, staring at the black muddy water between the rushes, remembering how it had been that night. Rita's flushed features, the dry soreness of her throat and how he'd felt the hotness of her breath when he'd kissed her that last time. He felt it again now, a burning in his own mouth, a dryness that demanded moisture and brought with it a sense of unreality as though he was merely a spectator to his own actions.

Water! Suddenly it was an obsession, his over-heated body screaming out for it. He would never make it back to the hospital, like a desert wanderer who had pursued a mirage relentlessly throughout the heat of the day and was now suddenly unable to go any further. Desperation took control. Water was within yards of him, cool natural water that flowed from an unseen spring.

A headlong rush took him to the edge of the pool, his feet squelching in the soft ground, stirring up mud and putting a fleet of water boatmen to flight. He flung himself headlong, his dry tongue starting to lap. Tepid water that tasted cool and sweet, no longer dark and brackish. Heedless of particles of dirt and algae that made him cough, he drank thirstily, oblivious to everything about him. The frog chorus changed note, the shrill triumph of the hunter who has lured his prey to the water-hole. Gloating.

Barely time to raise his head and draw breath, drinking again greedily, his thirst unassuaged. Clouds of insects homed in on him, midges that settled on every area of exposed flesh and bit deeply in their eagerness for the taste of human blood. A mutual seeking of satisfaction, Man and insect, but neither fulfilled their desire.

Barry Brownlow felt the water coming back up from his stomach in a rush, raised his head and vomited violently, drank again. A process of liquid regurgitation. And

148

somewhere a bell was tolling, a distant clanging but he ignored it. He could not leave the water, he could not live away from it.

Sometime later his body seemed to cool with the coming of evening, shadows lengthening across the reedy surface of the pool and turning the water to an inky blackness. He raised himself up, coughing and spitting out algae and drowned flies. So weak, he wondered if he would be able to make it back to the hospital. He set off, using the overhanging branches of trees and bushes for leverage and support, tottering across the burned lawn, the crazy-paving of the big mossy terrace hot to the soles of his flip-flops.

'So there you are!' There was relief and remonstration on Mrs Howe's lined face as Barry walked into the hall, grey eyes that scrutinised him closely, noting a flush that was more than just the continual heatwave. 'You didn't come in for lunch, and supper's almost finished now. I was on my way up to ask Mr Bale to go and search for you.'

'I wasn't hungry. I've been resting down by the pool.' Barry thought his voice sounded a long way away and his vision swam so that momentarily Mrs Howe had two heads like that snake amulet of his father's.

'You don't look well.'

'I'm fine, honest I am. I reckon the heat is getting me like it's getting everybody else.'

'Well there's still some supper left in the dining-room. You'd better go in and get some.' She watched him closely.

He almost snapped '*I'm not hungry*' but that would mean telling her how he felt and that could have unpleasant repercussions. Like having nasty painful things done to you and being kept in his room for days on end.

'OK,' he smiled. 'I feel fine now so I'll go in and get something to eat. I'm starving.' *And I'm also dying of thirst!*

She watched him cross the hall and enter the dining-room. It *could* just be the heat but she'd keep a careful eye on him, check how he looked first thing in the morning.

Barry Brownlow closed the door behind him, leaned up against it. The room spun, swam in a sea of kaleidoscopic lights, and when it steadied he saw that it was empty. Just a

149

trestle-table at the far end that served as an evening supper bar. A pile of dirty plates and cups, some sandwiches and a battered tea urn.

In that instant the thirst hit him again, had him staggering across the room. The milk jug first, it had maybe a couple of pints left in it. He lifted it to his mouth, began to gulp the white fluid down his throat, slopping it as he did so. Then he was sucking on an empty jug, biting the rim in his frustration.

If anything his thirst was worse now and he moved across to the big urn, thrust the empty milk jug beneath the tap.

He could not wait for it to fill, swallowing the thick brown lukewarm liquid while the untended tap still flowed, tea splashing and running on the quarry tiles. The urn was almost empty, it spluttered, was reduced to a steady drip.

Barry Brownlow grunted, rattled the jug back on the table. There was nothing to stay here for. The weakness hit him again and he had to cling on to the door as he eased it open and peered out into the deserted hallway. Thank God Mrs Howe was gone, she was always tittle-tattling to the doctors. A good night's sleep, that was all he needed. In the morning he would be fine. Maybe he would be better off at home. Surely they had to release him soon. Only for Christ's sake don't go and be ill and prolong the stay in here.

He thought at first that he wasn't going to be able to make it upstairs. It was as though his limbs had suddenly become jellified, his legs threatening to throw him to the floor. A concerted effort, spurred on by the thought of being confined to that small bare room again and another session of electric shock treatment, had him pulling himself up by the stair-rail, one step at a time. Sweat poured from him, had his eyes smarting so that his vision was blurred. Or he could have been dizzy. Or both.

Confused now so that when finally he reached the landing he had to work out which was his room, walking on the balls of his feet in case he disturbed somebody and they went and fetched Mrs Howe. He made it, slumped down to the floor, knew he had to rest before he tried to crawl across to the bed. His throat felt as though it was loaded with red-hot embers that needed to be quenched instantly but he could not do that because there was no tap in his room. The nearest was in the bathroom at the end of the landing and he would never make it that far.

He lay there on the floor in the darkened room for some time before he attempted to reach the bed. It was a slow process, but eventually he managed to pull himself up on the iron bedstead and roll himself on to the coverlet. That would do, it was too hot to cover his body anyway, and he didn't have the strength to get undressed. If only he had a drink, liquid of any kind would suffice. But he didn't and there was no way he was going to get one.

Logic interspersed with feverish thoughts in the manner of a child's waking nightmare. They'd said in the beginning that he was mad and they'd been right. A nervous breakdown was just another way of saying you'd gone out of your mind. This was all part of their plan to keep him here forever. Give you a little bit of freedom, kid you that you were on the mend and any day you might be going home. They plugged it so that in the end you liked it here and didn't want to leave, but when you finally decided you did, you couldn't. Crazy, Barry Brownlow didn't really understand it himself but, there again, he wasn't supposed to. He was a victim of The System. But he was going to fight every inch of the way.

One touch of home down by that pool. Oh Jesus, they'd set it all up so cleverly, gone into every tiny detail: the grasshoppers, the frogs, had even found a locust from somewhere. You loved it so much that in the end you had to drink that water, foul stagnant water covered with algae. Gallons of it so that it made you ill, so ill that you wouldn't be going anywhere. Mrs Howe knew as soon as she saw him, was already gloatingly informing the others. *'Brownlow will be staying because he can't leave. Like we planned.'*

Helpless rage that had him crying, real wet tears that he caught on his fingers and sucked, salty so that it made his thirst even worse. *They* knew so he might as well call them, at least they'd give him water. Or would they?

His anger subsided, to be replaced by fear. Just what the hell were they going to do to him? It was a frightening thought. Like Dad was doing to the family . . . he hadn't built that shelter just to protect them from a nuclear war. Oh no, there was something much more to it than that. That snake amulet was the key to it all. And no matter what they tried to say Rita had died because of it. A sequence of events that might have led to her picking up some hideous germ in the laboratory at work but it was all part of a plan. Dad's or. . . .

His thoughts were jumping now like those grasshoppers on the lawn at home and in the grounds here. He'd been sent to this place to keep him out of the way. Dad didn't want him around because it interfered with his plans, whatever they were. For the same reason that he didn't want Adrian around.

He tried to sit up, fell back. God, it would be easy enough to escape from here, you just walked out through the front gates, *if* you had the strength, and they made bloody sure that you hadn't!

Weeping his frustration, licking at his tears again. Then lying spent, just staring up into the blackness. Maybe he slept, he didn't know. It was difficult to differentiate between waking and sleeping.

But Rita wasn't really dead. She couldn't be because she had come to him in his room that night after the funeral. She had been different, though, so aloof. She refused to let him touch her, had evaded his intended embrace. They had talked for a long time. Mum and Dad had heard them, banged on the door but they couldn't get in because it had been locked.

He was worrying now, desperately trying to recall that conversation. It had been important, Rita had impressed that upon him. A warning of some kind, something he had to do to prevent something else happening. But they had ensured that he didn't remember by giving him that hellish shock treatment, a kind of hysterectomy of the mind that removed almost everything, but left you with the basic original thinking functions. Like starting all over again. Whatever Rita had said to him they had made damned certain he wouldn't remember. Already it might be too late.

He shivered. It had gone suddenly cold and the lather of sweat had chilled on his body. He was awake all right now and the thirst wasn't so bad. Perhaps he could make it as far as the bathroom and. . . .

There was somebody in the room! He had not heard the door open and close. Now he could see a silhouette between the end of the bed and the small barred window. He thought at first it must be Mrs Howe but it wasn't bulky enough. Slim, somebody young, definitely female because he could make out the delicate curve of her breasts as she stood sideways.

'Barry.' Soft husky tones that he would recognise anywhere.

'Rita!' Surprise and hope, fear of the disappointment brought by yet another will-o'-the-wisp dream, followed by a shiver that was not wholly due to the sudden cooling of the sweat on his body. 'My darling . . . is it *really* . . . you?'

'It is me,' she laughed, a little sadly. 'I had difficulty finding you. Indeed I have been searching since that night when we last spoke. But you are ill!'

'It's nothing.' He stared hard, tried to discern her features but her whole body was bathed in shadow. 'I have been ill, so they tell me. They gave me shock treatment to make me forget everything you said to me.'

'Set works in many mysterious ways,' she whispered, 'and even the well-meaning people at a hospital such as this may find themselves his pawns. But it is necessary for you to return home. Your father's plans are almost complete and it is imperative that we rejoin your family.'

'What has he done? What is that underground place for?'

'It is a tomb, such as the one in which I was incarcerated when I was Dalūkah, child of Dalūkah!'

'Oh my God, then we must stop him before it is too late!'

'No, for it is not necessarily an evil place, or it need not be, depending upon the forces which control it. *It is up to you and I to ensure that it is not evil.* Also, it is the only place in which we can be rejoined as we were in life.'

'I'm . . . I'm going to die . . . aren't I?' He spoke softly, a whisper that was both a realisation and a resignation to his

153

fate, a fear of death that came and then evaporated almost instantly.

'Yes,' she said. 'I am afraid you are going to die, Barry. In the same way that I died, the victim of a deadly plague that was rife in Egypt at the time of Dalūkah and Āba-aner. It is Fate, and we cannot alter it!'

He lay there in silence, numbed by her words, knowing that she spoke the truth. This, then, was really the end for both of them.

'You must return home,' she said. 'Tonight!'

'I . . . I don't have the strength. I can't even manage it across to the bathroom.'

'*You can!*' There was a determination, an insistence in her voice now. 'You will have the strength to return to River View. Go now, under the cover of darkness. Go back home, go to your bedroom and remain there. Make them take you down into the tomb and eventually I will join you.'

'My mother will ring the hospital and I'll be brought straight back here.'

'I don't think so.' She was facing him now and he could make out her features, pale and beautiful in the starlight which shafted in through the window. 'Fate cannot be changed, even your parents cannot alter it. It is decreed that we shall be together for eternity. My peace can only be assured if you join me. Only then will I be able to cross over to *Sekhet-Aaru.*'

He did not doubt her words and when he looked again and saw that she was not there he did not show surprise. She had said they would be together and that was how it would be. Rita had gone on ahead and he must follow.

He swung his feet to the floor, waited for the dizziness to pass. Physically he felt stronger now and the thirst had left him. He stood up, swayed slightly, began to walk across the room.

A low-watt bulb was always kept burning on the landing. Barry Brownlow paused outside the door of his room, listening. Just the sound of rhythmic breathing from the other rooms. His heartbeat speeded up and his pulses raced as he began the descent of the stairs. One or two boards creaked alarmingly, but nobody stirred and his confidence soared.

He clicked back the Yale lock on the front door, closed it softly behind him, and experienced a rush of euphoria — freedom! They would not catch him now, and even if he died it would have been worth it just to walk unhindered on this warm night. The stars showed him all he needed to see, a dark avenue of tall trees that led down to the entrance gates and out on to the road. From there it would be a matter of a couple of hours' walk back to River View. He felt slightly heady and his throat was sore but he knew he would make it now.

Only once during that long walk did he have to step back into the bushes to avoid being spotted by the twin headlight beams of an approaching vehicle. So serene, a land that was Nature's domain for a few hours while Man slept and was absent from it.

So humid though, an atmosphere that was *alive*. It touched you, stroked you so that your skin prickled and you kept glancing behind you. You *knew* you were being watched, a self-consciousness that bordered on fear, had you wanting to run, to lock yourself indoors until daylight. That primitive fear of the dark and *much* more. He began to walk faster.

Barry was soon out of breath, had to rest awhile to recharge his strength, but all the time he was getting weaker and that burning sensation was back in his throat and lungs. He was wheezing, fighting for breath.

Relief surged through him as he saw River View below him, a silent cluster of houses. As he approached his ears picked up that sinister orchestration, frogs vibrating the still night air with their ceaseless rasping croaks against a background of insect noises. Clouds of moths fluttered against a glass porch where a hall light had been left on, kamikaze divebombing against the glass, hard-shelled flying insects pinging against it like missiles from catapults.

He stumbled, almost fell as something struck the back of his neck and viciously buzzed off into the night. So weak now that he feared he might collapse within yards of his

155

own home. He fumbled in his pocket and found his key, the one item they had not taken from him at Shelderton.

The hall was stifling, suffocating, as though Emily Brownlow still had the central heating running. He gasped for breath and the burning and thirst returned instantly. He had been given just enough strength to return home. Now he was ill again, and he was going to die!

Leaning back against the door, instinctively trying to shut *them* out. But it was futile because *they* were already in here, unknown mysterious forces which fingered his sweating body in the darkness, whispered their evil in his ear so that the sound vibrated on his brain, had him wanting to flee. Only there was nowhere to go, no escape. He was at their mercy!

Somehow he managed to crawl up the stairs and into his room, dragged himself up on to the bed, his dry burning eyes searching the darkness, looking for Rita. But she was not here. Yet he was not alone for he sensed *their* presence.

And now he waited for death as that agonising inner fire began to burn and consume his body.

Chapter Thirteen

Homecoming

EMILY HAD gone down into the shelter shortly after breakfast, a kind of calling that preyed on her obsessions, a fear that she fought to overcome because of her duty. The place had to be cleaned, made habitable. George would ignore such details. It was up to her.

That awful smell made her feel sick at first, but somehow you became accustomed to it after a time and didn't notice it. And that double-headed snake watched your every move although it wasn't malevolent like it had been at first. Powerful, certainly, but once you gave subservience it would not hurt you. All it demanded was total obedience.

She went down the steps slowly, negotiating a mop and bucket with some difficulty. George hadn't considered when he built this place that it might need cleaning. She reached the bottom, stared in disbelief at the untidyness. Canned foodstuffs and packets littered the floor and somebody had trodden soil all over the place! Anger, directed at George because only he had been down here in the last twenty-four hours. An uneasiness that had her peering into the corners. Suppose it wasn't George who had done all this. . . .

Inevitably she found her gaze drawn towards the amulet. Those four eyes flickered into life as though they had been closed in sleep and she had disturbed them, a film that cleared, flickered. Saw.

Emily Brownlow experienced a sensation of instinctive embarrassment, did a half-curtsey, almost crossed herself in the manner in which she had been indoctrinated as a child whenever she came into contact with an altar. Her mouth went dry and she licked her lips nervously, found herself mentally apologising for this intrusion.

'Your son has been returned to you.' Those awful mouths moved, something which she had always attributed to a trick of the light, like the eyes. But she no longer sought logical explanations.

No, that isn't right. He's in Shelderton. He might be coming home in a week or two, though.

'He is home. He is ill, beyond help, and he will die of a plague that was old when Egypt was young. Do not send for help. You must hide him. And wait!'

She felt her breathing quicken. Barry was going to die. There had to be some mistake. Perhaps she ought to go and check. Ask George. She had never been in the habit of asking George for anything in the past but now her life revolved around him, a kind of symbolic worship . . . like Set!

'Cleanse this place for there has been an intruder. But he has gone and will not return.'

She began to brush the floor. A jar of coffee had shattered and she swept the broken glass into a small heap. Next time she came down here she must remember to bring a dustpan.

Those eyes had dulled, closed. She must not interrupt again. Moving silently as she went about her work, muttering apologetically when she dislodged a tin of beans and it crashed to the floor, glancing half fearfully at the thing that was Set, but the amulet did not stir.

A movement behind her that she sensed rather than saw, half-turned and almost screamed when she caught sight of the spider. A huge bloated thing, its body the size of a five-pence piece, legs thick and strong like bent pipe-cleaners. Watching her!

She straightened up, backed away. She had had a fear of spiders ever since childhood. A good housewife had no place for them in her home, she had once told a friend.

Some argued that spiders caught flies. Well, there were plenty of fly-killers on the market nowadays so that was no excuse. Spiders should be exterminated until they became an extinct species.

Her grip tightened on the broom. One swift blow and she could crush it, sweep its squashed corpse into the dustpan along with that glass. Slowly, carefully, she began to lift the brush, just enough to give her the necessary impetus to. . . .

'Stop! Do not kill it, for scorpions are sacred to the Temple of Set!'

Words that hit her with the force of a physical blow, had her dropping the broom so that it clattered on the floor. And with surprising agility the spider reversed, disappeared beneath a section of Dexion shelving so that it might never have existed except as a figment of her own imagination.

Emily Brownlow was sweating and trembling, very much afraid as she turned back towards the amulet just in time to see a fading dull glow like embers that had finally burned themselves out. Set slept, yet he was ever watchful.

She began to sweep the rest of the floor, her heart pounding and her flesh goosepimpling, keeping well clear of shadowy corners, relying on the length of the brush to drag the dirt back towards her. *Scorpions!* It had looked like an oversize spider to her, not like those scorpions she had seen on the wildlife programme on TV. Nevertheless it was a repulsive looking thing and needed to be kept at broom's length. In fact, Emily did not like coming down here on her own. But Set would protect her; suddenly she had unquestionable faith in that double-headed serpent, like she had once had in God!

It was twenty minutes to one by her watch when she finished. Sheila would have prepared the lunch by now. Salad. The whole nation was living on salad, but if the rain didn't come soon there wouldn't be any available even if you could afford to buy it. There would be food shortages. *Famine!*

At the bottom of the steps she turned back, almost bowed. Set was watching her all right even if his four orbs were dull lifeless metal. A quick glance around but there was no sign of that spider. She shuddered and almost ran up into the blazing heat of the day.

She paused on the patio and turned back to survey the garden. That part of the shelter which was above ground looked quite neat; you would hardly notice it once it had grassed over. That stupid blackbird was still trying to unearth a worm in the baked soil. It didn't seem interested in the hordes of grasshoppers anymore. Too much of a good thing, Emily decided. Just like the ladybirds didn't seem to be bothering with the masses of greenfly on the rosebushes, or the blackfly which were resolutely demolishing the remnants of that row of broad beans. Nature's last line of defence had been breached. Only rain, and a return to normal, would save civilisation now.

George would be in the lounge tuning in to the one o'clock news. Three plates and some cutlery adorned the scrubbed pine table in the kitchen. A bowl of wilted salad was the focal point, lettuce leaves that had browned around the edges.

She swilled her hands in the sink, thought she heard Sheila's voice upstairs. In that case George was up there, too. She ought to speak to him about that spider, not that there was anything they could do about it if Set had declared it sacred. All the same, it was unnerving.

Sheila came in, seated herself at the table, began to load lettuce and cucumber on to her plate, a habit learned in the Brownlow household, that unless you engrossed yourself in something you were inviting an interrogation.

'Where's your dad, Sheila? I thought I heard him upstairs.'

'No, he's in the lounge watching the news. Things aren't looking good. Dad says it's Cuba all over again only this time the Russians won't back down.'

'I heard you talking to him upstairs.'

'No . . . that was . . . *Barry*.'

'Barry!'

Suddenly for Emily Brownlow the whole room was spinning, Sheila upside down and still spooning salad out of the bowl, the crockery threatening to avalanche on to the floor and smash like that jar of coffee down in the shelter. And then a huge spider would creep out from under the sink unit. . . . The room came to rest again. Sheila was hunting for a quarter of tomato with the wooden servers. It slipped away from her and hid beneath a lettuce leaf, but she caught it at the second attempt.

'Did you say *Barry*, Sheila?'

'Yes, he's up in his room but he's very ill.'

Cold fingers like those down in the shelter clutched at Emily's heart and she fought for breath as though she suffered an attack of asthma. Movement wasn't easy, her limbs seemed to be weighted, her thinking muzzy. *Your son has been returned to you. Do not send for help. You must hide him!*

Sheila seemed apprehensive, glancing at her mother as though she feared she might make a dash for the telephone, moved her leg as though she would trip her up if she did so.

'I'd better go upstairs and see him.' Emily moved slowly, pale and trembling, knocked the table and rattled the salad bowl as she pushed past.

A glance through the half-open lounge door as she passed through the hall. George was hunched in the armchair, the television screen flickering away in front of him. He might have been asleep but she wasn't going to bother checking. She paused at the foot of the stairs, almost afraid to go up. She'd heard how Rita had looked when they took her to hospital. Oh God!

A stair at a time, having to pull herself up forcibly on the rail. That night came back to her in detail, the expression on Barry's face, she would never forget it. That was why she hadn't been to Shelderton to visit him. She didn't want to see him now because it wouldn't have changed. But she had to, it was another of her duties.

She stood in the doorway, clutching at the lintel until her fingernails began flaking some of the paint off, not sure that it was *her* son, trying to tell herself that those emaciated flushed features lying back against the pillow belonged to somebody else. And that smell . . . it made her want to vomit.

She recognised it, the same odour that lingered in that . . . that *tomb!* Not just the stench of dry dusty staleness but a smell that was nauseating. Like rotting meat . . . flesh that was decomposing while it still lived — *gangrene!*

'Mum!' A whispered croak from the bed, an arm that began to move but couldn't make it and flopped back on to the coverlet.

'You're ill, Barry.' He knew and she knew, so there was no point in trying to hide the obvious.

'Yes.' An attempted smile that made a hideous mask of those features. 'I'm ill and I'm going to die. But you've got to hide me and you mustn't send for help. Promise?'

'I promise.' Her skin crawled as she remembered Set's words. He had spoken the truth, then he had to be right about that spider being a scorpion. She shuddered. 'We'll look after you.'

'I can't stay here in this room.' Cracked tones, his lips blistered and oozing blood and a trickle of yellow mucus. 'They will have missed me by now. This is the first place they'll look.'

'I'll speak to your father about. . . .'

The shrill ringing of the telephone interrupted her, a brain-jarring sound that made you want to scream. Ringing. And still ringing. Christ, there were two of them downstairs and they were both too bloody idle to answer it! No, that wasn't quite right, they were *frightened* to answer it.

The angry ringing suddenly petered out but you still heard it as though its echoes could not escape from the house.

'That will be the hospital, checking.' Barry gave a laugh, coughed up some pink phlegm which trickled slowly down his chin. 'They'll be sending somebody round any time now.'

'We won't let them take you away again.' Emily Brownlow experienced a rush of maternal instinct which she thought had died out years ago. She would protect her offspring at all cost, sacrifice her own life for him if necessary. Even if he was going to die and she did not doubt that for a second. 'Is there . . . anything we can get for you?'

'Just water,' he grabbed the plastic beaker off the bedside table, sucked noisily at imaginary dregs in the bottom. 'The thirst . . . it's not as bad as . . . as it was. That time at the pool . . . I thought I was going to drink it dry, would willingly have drowned in it.'

'You drank out of a *pool!*' Horror on Emily's features. 'Then . . . then you could have . . . *diphtheria!*' *A plague that was old when Egypt was young.*

'No . . . it's something else. But hurry, you'll have to hide me down in the . . . the shelter that Dad made. They won't think of looking for me down there. There isn't much time. They'll come soon.'

She turned away, tripped and almost fell on the stairs in her feverish haste. George was still hunched in that chair, facing away from her. There was a weather chart being shown on the television screen. *'Sunny and very warm — outlook similar.'* Why the bloody hell didn't they just admit that it was never going to rain again? Ever. She shook him roughly, hated him for those few seconds. His head came round, an expression that was blank, his eyes glazed, reminding her of the amulet's orbs when they weren't glowing redly but they still watched you.

'George . . . there isn't much time.'

'I know. A week at the most. This madman isn't bluffing, he means it. He *wants* to start a nuclear war, and not just to wipe Israel off the map. If he dies then he doesn't care because he will be destroying what God Almighty created, one human wiping out the lot at the press of a button. And that'll make him BIG. Those few hours of life he has left will have made it all worthwhile for him. And suddenly the whole world realises that it's more than just a possibility. That leaflet which was pushed through the letter-box this morning, the government one on what to do if there is a nuclear war, that's proof enough. They've been sitting back too long and saying it could never happen, that no nation would dare to start it, but now we have a maniac who wants to do just that. For a lot of people it will be too late but *we're* all right. Our shelter's virtually ready.'

'I don't mean that. I mean Barry. We've got to get him into the shelter before they come looking for him. If they find him here they'll take him back to Shelderton.'

He stood up, his eyes clearing and revealing a determined glint, defiant and obsessive. 'We'll do it now, this very minute. I'll need you and Sheila to help me and we'll have to trust to Set that none of these bloody neighbours see us. The Calthorpes were up at their bedroom window with binoculars most of last week. I'll bet they've been ringing the council, trying to put the shit down for us.'

'You know how ill he is, don't you, George? Like Rita was. He's going to die but the doctors can't save him. Nobody can. I want him to die in there . . . *with us!*'

His hand found hers, squeezed it gently, the first time he had shown her any affection for years, a kind of mutual sympathy now that the chips were down.

'Let's get moving.' George Brownlow's complexion was a dark flush; it might just have been the stifling heat. 'They won't take him back, I promise you that, Emily. Set will protect us all, have faith in him, for we are his chosen ones.'

Sheila came through into the hall, still chewing on some dry indigestible salad. None of them spoke; there was no need because they understood.

Chapter Fourteen

The Death-Watch

IT WAS mid-afternoon before the expected car drew up in front of Number Twelve, River View. Emily Brownlow, watching from behind the curtains, experienced an acute sense of relief. She had begun to believe that they would never come, that Barry hadn't escaped from Shelderton, that it wasn't her own son lying down there in that improvised curtained alcove in the shelter. That they had all made one big terrible mistake. But now the men from Shelderton were here.

She let them ring twice before she went to the door. Two men; one of them was Dr Horne, looking strangely nervous, meticulously cleaning his glasses. The other was short and stocky with eyes that reminded her of a fish's. Or a frog's.

'We . . . er . . . tried to ring you, Mrs Brownlow.' Horne put his spectacles back on, adjusted them. 'There was no reply.'

'We were . . .' she almost said '*in the garden*' but checked herself in time. The last place she wanted to admit to having been in was the garden. Instead she muttered, 'out doing some shopping.'

'I'm afraid . . .' the tall medical man began picking specks of imaginary fluff off his sleeve. 'I'm afraid that Barry has . . . left the hospital!'

'Left the hospital!' Acting now, hoping it looked authentic, holding on to the doorpost. 'Whatever do you mean, Doctor?'

'Just that.' Horne let out a deep breath, relief now that the hardest part was over. 'He just got up in the night and walked out. Just like that.'

'But . . . but don't you . . . haven't you *any* idea where he's gone?'

'I was hoping that perhaps you might be able to help us with that.' Horne stepped forward a pace. 'We thought perhaps he had come home. In his state of mind it was the logical place to run to, but apparently he hasn't. May we come inside?'

She stepped back, let them push past her, saw that George had emerged from the kitchen. There was no sign of Sheila, obviously she was still lying down in her room.

'Gone!' George Brownlow's flush gave the appearance of indignation. 'Don't they operate any security system at Shelderton, Doctor Horne?'

'Yes.' The doctor was uneasy once more. 'If a patient needs it we lock him in his room for the night. But Barry had progressed so well that we didn't think it was necessary. He's had the freedom of the grounds by day for the past week and if he was going to run away then logically he would have left then. We were hoping that you would have visited him before now. That *could* be the reason why he ran away, like an adolescent in his first term at boarding school who feels abandoned, *needs* his parents.'

George Brownlow was tight-lipped. They were trying to pass the buck now that they hadn't found Barry safely at home. 'But he doesn't really *need* to stay in Shelderton, does he, Doctor? You said yourself how much better he is. I mean, it isn't a *prison*, is it? We could have had him back home if we had insisted.'

'Yes and no.' Horne glanced at his silent companion as though seeking moral support. 'We would have done our best to persuade you not to take him away because he is receiving a course of treatment which isn't completed yet. As it stands, now we are obliged to inform the police and every effort will be made to . . .' — he just stopped himself from saying *'recapture him'* — '. . . find him.'

'And what *is* his mental state?' George craned his neck forward

166

'It's difficult to be precise. He has certainly responded to the treatment but he has become morose, reluctant to converse with the other patients. But . . . Mrs Howe, the senior matron, informed me this morning that when she saw him last night he looked flushed and far from well. That is one of the reasons why we want to recover him as quickly as possible.'

'What can we do to help?' George's expression was one of despair and anguish, almost over-acting it.

'There is every chance he will come back home. That is usually the first place which patients head for, so I think that the best thing you can do is stay here. If he turns up, give us a ring. In the meantime we'll notify the police.' Horne took his glasses off again, put them back on and turned back towards the door. 'I will be in touch with you again shortly, anyway.'

Emily closed the door after their visitors. She was sweating heavily and it had nothing to do with the heat. 'Well, that's got rid of them!'

'They'll be back.' Out of the corner of his eye George saw Sheila coming down the stairs. 'And we can expect a visit from the police soon, as well. From now we'll begin using the er . . . shelter as our home, but we'll have to take it in turns to remain in the house to take telephone calls and receive callers. It wouldn't do for the police to come looking for us in the garden, would it?'

Sheila Brownlow stood at the foot of the stairs. Her hair was awry, matted and unbrushed, her jeans and blouse crumpled where she had lain on her bed in them. Her features were deathly pale, a factor which brought fresh concern to Emily.

'Are you sure you're all right, Sheila?'

'I . . . I . . .' she was going to say '*I'm OK*' but a sudden feeling of faintness had her sinking down on the bottom step, holding her head. 'I haven't been very well. I guess it was the heat and . . . and struggling to get Barry down into the shelter.'

'It's because you're pregnant!' George Brownlow's voice was terse, chiding. 'The bastard child of a commoner is growing fast in your womb!'

'George!' Emily snapped. 'How could you. . . .'

'Be silent!' He turned on her and she saw his expression, felt her stomach tightening into a hard ball, experienced a fear of her husband which was almost as great as her terror of the amulet. *Indeed, for a brief second his eyes seemed to glow with that same unholy fire.* She tried to tell herself that it was a trick of the sunlight which slanted down into the hall from the small window on the first landing but she knew that she lied. *George Brownlow was surely a man possessed of Set!*

'I'm going to see Doctor Horne first thing in the morning.' Sheila was close to tears. 'I haven't had a test yet but. . . .'

'Maybe it's a phantom pregnancy.' Emily was still clinging to vain hopes. 'Lots of women have them.'

'Stupid woman!' George whirled on her and for a moment she thought he was going to strike her. 'The girl is with child because she has mated, been fertilised by the sperm of a commoner!'

'Dad!'

'Do you deny it? Are you going to lie to me, girl? Have you, or have you not, mated with that boy? *Come on, answer me, and do not let the ears of Set hear a lie!'*

'Yes!' A stifled sob, backing away up the stairs in an ungainly crab-like retreat, sheer terror on her face. 'I have mated with him, as you put it, three times. And now I'm going to have his baby. *Does that bloody well satisfy you or do I have to put it all down in writing?'*

'Your admission of guilt is sufficient.' His voice was low and menacing. 'Now go to your room and rest. And you will not visit Doctor Horne, for we cannot tolerate the interference of outsiders from now onwards. You must rest. *Now I shall go to the temple for the Death-Watch must commence. There is not much time left for any of us!'*

He turned, walked through the kitchen and out into the dazzling sunlight. A strange silence seemed to hang over the garden. Even the multitude of grasshoppers on the dead lawn was silent. *A heat haze shimmered, appeared to be concentrated over that oblong of excavated soil like some transparent entity hovering there. And for a few seconds George Brownlow experienced sheer terror, a numbing of his brain that almost had him fleeing back indoors and locking the door, cowering and babbling under the table.*

Then it was gone, and the harsh chorus started up again, a rasping that for once was sweet music to his ears.

He walked steadily across the lawn, cared not whether he trod and crushed the insects beneath his feet for they were expendable, a pestilence that would die eventually just as they all would. He opened the door, felt a rush of cold air greet him, then that awful putrefying smell. It was stronger, more pungent than ever, had him recoiling and gasping for breath. Set's own odour and something more — *the stench of a rotting living body!*

At first George Brownlow thought that Barry was asleep, a naked pallid motionless body whose chest barely rose and fell on the frail camp bed. Then an eye flickered open, two. Seeing but not recognising, staring vacantly.

George approached the bed timidly, almost vomited. Festered sores that wept their pus, a rash beginning to spread out from groin and armpits; you almost saw it move!

'Water!' Breath as foul as a stinking marshland mist, a dribble of thick phlegm that he tried to spit out.

George lifted a two-gallon plastic container from the floor, unscrewed the cap and slopped some of the water into a mug, held it close to Barry's lips. The youth sucked fiercely, spilled most of it. The moisture seemed to revive him, started a wheezing in his chest like an ancient motor that stuttered into life after years of neglect. He took some more water, coughed.

'Rita?' A whisper, vocal chords stretched to their limits. 'Is she . . . here?'

'She will come.' George stole a glance at the amulet as though seeking confirmation, but those four eyes were dull and lifeless.

'She promised.'

Silence. He moved across to a chair, seated himself

on it and crossed his legs. The Death-Watch had begun.

Night or day, it made no difference down in the underground
shelter. A single bulb that flickered every so often,
threatened to go out, dimmed, came back on again. Just as
Barry Brownlow's eyes opened and closed periodically.

'They should not have burned her, the fools.' George
spoke softly as though talking to himself, angry words that
were scarely audible. 'Now her *khaibit* cannot cross over to
Sekhet-Aaru. It is too late to save her but we must not make
the same mistake with you, my son. I have the knowledge
to carry out the rites.'

'*No!*' Sudden strength, enough to bring Barry up on to
an elbow, anguish on his wasted fevered features. 'Not
without Rita, please. She promised that I would join her in
death.'

'And you would willingly enter into purgatory, a lost
soul condemned to wander forever, chained to this earth
which will soon become a burning wasteland, a veritable
Hades?'

'Anything . . . to be with Rita.' Barry's eyes closed and
he sank bank on to his pillow.

'Fool! I will not allow you to do this. When the time
comes I shall embalm you myself, and your mother and
sister will become the Body-Watchers. They shall act as the
Kher-heb, the *Sem* priest, the *Sa-mer-ef*, the *Tcherau-ur*,
the *Tcherausheraut*, the *Menhu*, the *Am-asi* and the
Am-khent. *It shall be the burial of Osiris again, and there
will be no mistake this time. We shall need a living sacrifice
but of all the gods only Set will be addressed. You will be
committed to his care for the duration of your journey to the
Land of the Dead!*'

Barry was mouthing protests but the words would not
come, only bubbling mucus. Desperation as his strength
ebbed, a mental battle, projecting his waning willpower at
the man who was now the High Priest of Set. The one who
used to be his father.

170

George Brownlow closed his eyes. It had been a terrible strain, an actor who somehow had spoken his part in the very throes of stage fright, an inner force that had taken over his body and brain. He was a puppet, afraid of what he had to do, frightened because when the time came he might not be strong enough.

Now he sat in fearful darkness, his eyes closed, feeling Set's power all around him, that evil stench so strong and foul that he could scarcely draw breath.

He sensed a presence, was aware of its hostility towards him, an icy draught as it moved. Not Set, because the serpent god burned him with those fiery eyes and this was like a breath of arctic wind. Somebody or something had infiltrated this hallowed place, was strong enough to defy the power of Set; and did not fear him!

George Brownlow trembled, squinted through narrowed eyelids, terrified of what he might see. At first he saw nothing. The light had been reduced to barely a glow, the shadows moving in to obliterate details. Just outlines. A bed . . . he started. A figure was bent over it and at first he thought it was his dying son in the midst of a miraculous resurrection from near-death. But no, the figure was female, shapely . . . familiar but his bemused brain was incapable of recognising it instantly.

Again he turned to Set. A hiss, it might have been his imagination for those four orbs remained lifeless and he heard only that which he made himself hear. *Save me, Master, for there is evil in our midst.*

He recoiled as recognition came, once carefree features that no longer smiled, dark eyes that smouldered their hatred for him. *Rita!*

'So you would sacrifice your own son to everlasting purgatory, give him to the snake god so that you alone might rule in *Sekhet-Aaru* like a lap dog at Set's feet.' Her face was pallid, corpse flesh which had not yet begun to decompose. The living dead!

Again George Brownlow looked to the altar but it was dark and lifeless, no fiery pinpoints glowing their anger at this sacrilege. Set had sentenced the child Dalūkah to everlasting hell on earth thousands of years ago and now he had no control over her beyond that original curse.

'You will not save your son, George Brownlow, but merely make him a slave of Set, as I once was. I have merely exchanged one hell for another. Ensure his safe passage to *Sekhet-Aaru* by all means, *but administer to him the rites of Horus!* Promise me this, I beg of you. For myself it is too late and I must suffer for eternity.'

George Brownlow reeled beneath her words. Light where before there had been darkness and evil, a glimmer of understanding. And his fear was all the more terrible for this knowledge because he had passed the point of no return.

His lips moved, his head went back to nod his agreement but in that awful moment he heard a hiss like a deflating tyre behind him, and froze. He felt the force of a terrible slumbering power aroused, its fury like the beginning of an electric storm, lightning capable of shrivelling one to a cinder, an unrecognisable nothingness.

'*Child, you defy me even as your mother, who was also named Dalūkah, did. You have dared to challenge the wrath of Set, dared to mention the name of his accursed brother in this temple!*'

'You cannot harm me, Set, for you have cursed me beyond your own power.' The girl drew herself up proudly, her slim body rippling sensuously beneath the transparent shroud which she wore. 'I have loved briefly in yet another life and now that is over, but you shall not have this boy for he is not of the line of Dalūkah and Āba-aner. He will die of the plague and his death will be yet another cancer on my conscience, but you shall not have his *ka*!'

'*Begone, child, return to the wandering dead!*' Four eyes blazed their hatred, two fangs spat their venom. '*In the Land of Osiris my power is challenged only by one, he whom you have already named, but I still rule the places of darkness. You are a child; in your last life you escaped me for a few years because of the protection of my brother but now that is no more. Here in the Temple of Set I can destroy you through this festering mortal who craves to be allowed into Sekhet-Aaru, the Kingdom of Osiris. Now his life is*

172

done and you are a child again, racked with the plague of your time. So be it!'

George Brownlow tried to scream but the shriek of terror came from the thing that purported to be Rita Hendon who was in turn Dalūkah, babe of the Nile. He saw her stiffen, her flesh suffused with a fiery radiance that shrivelled the frail garment on her body, her whiteness blackened as though she had been electrocuted by a high voltage current. Slumping to the floor, a crumpled hairless heap . . . *shrinking before his very eyes!*

Limbs so small and frail, gesticulating with pathetic futility, those screams turning to infant wails. The tender skin rippled, bubbled like molten lava, throwing up hideous boils that burst with stinking pus. The writhing babe stretched out its festering arms and for one awful moment George Brownlow almost went to it. Something held him back — the eyes of Set which were now focused upon himself. *'Fool, would you risk your own ka for one who has yet again betrayed me?'*

The child was growing weaker, its cries now barely audible whimpers of pain and terror, its body visibly decomposing even in life, emitting that same stench that had come from the dying youth on the bed — *gangrene, the living death!*

And suddenly she was no more, wasting away into the shadows until they, too, faded and made way for the artificial light from the gently swinging bulb. George Brownlow sat and stared, tried not to believe it but in the end knew that it had all taken place. And Set had retired to his somnolent posture, almost smug in his vengeance.

George moved, half afraid to approach that bed upon which his own son lay, but knew that he must. The head lolled to one side, those rivulets of foul mucus no longer trickling, beginning to encrust. Eyes wide and staring, static terror which had come with the plague and remained. *For Barry Brownlow was dead!*

George Brownlow sighed, a sound which incorporated remorse and relief because it was all over for his son's mortal body. Now the real nightmare was about to begin.

Set had demanded a *ka* and it must be given to him. Rita's futile attempt had failed because the child of Dalūkah, by Āba-aner, was fated to fester for eternity and the course of Fate could not be changed. And George Brownlow was a cog in that wheel. He had a part to play whether he liked it or not. He must obey the force which controlled him.

Wearily he mounted the steps, shielded his eyes from the dazzling sunlight. Outside nothing had changed except perhaps that the grasshoppers sawed with less resolution than before, their orchestration slow and mournful. Some of them looked much bigger than the others but it was difficult to be sure among the hordes. They just might have been locusts.

Emily was sitting in the kitchen when George entered. In all probability Sheila was still upstairs in her bedroom. He did not speak, went to the sink and swilled his hands under the tap as though he needed to wash some effluvium off them.

He turned back to the roller-towel on the door, met Emily's gaze. Her eyes were red-rimmed although if she had been crying she was finished now. Dry grief, the kind that hurt most and lasted longest.

'I *felt* him go.' Her voice was flat, just stating facts. 'A kind of burning that got so hot you couldn't stand any more. Then suddenly it cooled. But he's not at peace yet, I can tell. You've seen Rita, haven't you, George?'

'Yes,' he replied. 'I saw her but she's gone now and won't be coming back.'

'I see.' Maybe she did. 'What do we do now? They'll still be looking for Barry.'

'Who will?'

'The police.'

'Well, they won't find him and in the end they'll stop looking. Another listed missing person except that before many days are out the whole of civilisation will have gone missing. I pray that we'll make it to *Sekhet-Aaru* in time. The Death-Watch was shorter than even I believed it would be. Now we have a lot to do and I must not be disturbed. Sheila must remain in the house to deal with any

174

phone messages or callers. She can tell them quite truthfully that Mr and Mrs Brownlow have gone in search of their son.' He almost laughed at his own unfunny joke, but it would have been a sacrilege. 'I shall need your assistance, Emily, and what we have to do will not be pleasant, but it must be done.'

'What . . . what are we going to do?' Her voice was weak, almost inaudible, reminding him of the whimperings of the dying Dalūkah.

'The Death-Watchers have completed their task,' his words seemed to echo hollowly in the stifling atmosphere of the closed room, *'and now it is the turn of the Body-Watchers!'*

Chapter Fifteen

The Unborn

SHEILA'S RAGE had simmered as she lay on her bed. A build-up of frustration that was unable to come to a head and burst like a blind boil, agony that it was impossible to alleviate, a child in a tantrum determined to spite itself. Masochism, an inexplicable helplessness.

She wanted Adrian. She *needed* him here right now because he would not have pandered to Dad's obsessions. Or would he? It was impossible to tell. All her life she had rebelled but suddenly when it mattered most she was giving in, being swept along by a tide which she had suddenly given up fighting.

Run away! No, that was impossible, like she was physically chained here. Suddenly she was having to obey her father. She shuddered; his eyes, that was what it was. Similar to those of that amulet down in the dug-out. You didn't want to look into them but you had to and when you did you were glad as well as frightened. In some ways it was a sexual experience, like the first time she had let Adrian do anything to her. Resistance at first that grew weaker, reluctant enjoyment that escalated into sheer ecstasy and when you hit your climax you were a trembling slave to an overwhelming, burning passion. And you'd do it again. And again, even though you knew that you'd end up pregnant.

Dad, the amulet, did the same sort of thing to you. You were frightened but it was thrilling, little shivers running up and down your spine. Seeking excitement of some kind but you didn't know what. Curiosity. Hooked on some strange mind-blowing drug that sapped you mentally and physically, robbed you of everything except that unknown desire. If only Dad would agree to Adrian coming here to join them, to be with them at this triumphant yet terrifying time. A breathtaking thought that was interrupted by a sudden stabbing pain in her abdomen which had her clenching her fists, stiffening, almost screaming out aloud. Her unborn child!

Writhing in agony that was akin to orgasmic ecstasy, groaning as she remembered that night when Adrian had first taken her, feeble protests which echoed Emily Brownlow's warnings. *'Girls who do those sort of things find themselves with babies which they don't want.' 'I do want it!'* She clutched at her stomach, thought she felt a movement from within, tiny hands and feet trying to batter their way out, but that was impossible because it was too early. A sudden contraction as though she had gone into labour.

You must bear the child of a commoner because Fate has decreed it! You cannot alter destiny.

She stared apprehensively around the bedroom, thought for a moment that her father had sneaked in, had whispered his contempt, hissed it like she thought she had heard that repulsive two-headed snake hiss once. It was all in her imagination. Nevertheless, it was so *real*.

She lay there trembling, felt the pains dying away. Her eyes closed and she became drowsy, her thoughts flitting from one thing to another. Barry was going to die, they all knew that but somehow it wasn't so terrible as she had at first thought. It wouldn't be like Rita's funeral, the body sliding down that ramp to be burned, destroyed forever. They would keep Barry, he would always be with them. She didn't know how but he would, because nobody knew where he was. Dad had dug a special kind of family grave and when their time came they would all be together. If only Adrian could join them before the inevitable nuclear war broke out.

The room seemed very much darker. She struggled to open her eyes. The curtains had been drawn to try and keep out the heat but perhaps it had clouded over outside. Like Good Friday, now what made her think of that? She found herself looking at the alarm clock on the dresser but she was unable to discern the figures and the hands appeared to have lost their luminous glow. A feeling of depression, utter hopelessness.

Then for one fleeting instance she saw a face. It did not seem to have a body, appeared to float in the air up towards the ceiling, features which she recognised instantly. *Barry!*

Sheila sat up, made a despairing clutching movement towards him, mouthing soundless words. *Don't go, Barry, don't leave us!* No answering smile, his expression one of sheer terror as though he fought against some invisible force which was trying to pull him back. His lips moved but it was all a mime of some kind, a warning which he was trying to shout but his vocal chords were not functioning for some reason. A desperate struggle between brother and sister but there was some barrier between them which denied them contact, forbade them to speak to each other. Anguished eyes. Barry was becoming fainter, a slide show which has suddenly been destroyed by harsh lighting, a mirage fading as you approached it. Then it was gone!

She could move now, standing up on the bed, gróping the air but finding nothing. Sobbing, sinking back down on the cover.

She lay there for some time, numbed and frightened. It was as though . . . Barry had been on his way somewhere, a brief final farewell. And a warning that she did not understand. That was the most terrifying aspect of all. And she knew without any doubt that her brother had died.

After a time she got up, let herself out on to the landing. The house was hot and silent and she could hear flies buzzing crazily on the windows. Only the double glazing prevented her from hearing the grasshoppers outside. Revolting things, almost as bad as the frogs, their multitudes increasing daily.

Her mother was still in the kitchen.

'Where's Dad?' She knew but she had to say something.

'Out there. I don't know when he'll be coming back.'

'I'm going to talk to him.'

'Don't!' Emily Brownlow's features were even more pallid than usual. 'I don't think you should go down there.'

'Barry's dead.' An emotionless, matter-of-fact statement.

'How . . . how did you know that?' Emily half started up out of her chair but slumped back, a mixture of fatigue and despair.

'I just know, Mum. That's why I have to talk to Dad.'

'He won't like being disturbed. He's begun the Body-Watch.'

'I see.' She didn't really understand but her confused brain could not cope with explanations. 'I don't think he'll mind. Barry certainly won't. I won't be long, anyway.'

'Sheila,' she was almost at the door when Emily spoke again, 'can't you tell *me*? Nobody tells me anything.'

'It's about Adrian,' she dropped her gaze, felt suddenly guilty. 'I thought that . . . well, I'm having his baby and I think he ought to be here with us.'

'You'll have to ask your father.' Not angry, just non-committal. 'It all depends on him. Like everything else these days. We have to obey him now, you know. It's our only chance.'

Sheila went outside, closed the door behind her. It seemed hotter than ever. There weren't many insects on the lawn, they had probably withdrawn to the meagre shade offered by the shrubberies. The lawn was sharp to her bare feet but she ignored it and went straight across to the shelter.

She hesitated at the top of the steps, suddenly afraid to descend. The place had an atmosphere like a church prior to the start of a service. You were late and hoped that nobody noticed, creeping furtively inside, suddenly wanting to cough and fighting to control it. Guilty because God was in here, everybody praying with their eyes tightly shut in case they caught sight of Him. Civilisation was just a race of controlled puppets, everybody had to obey something or somebody.

'Who is it?' George Brownlow's voice, terse, greeted her from down below, a weird echo. 'What do you want?'

'It's me. Sheila.'

'What do you want?'

'I. . . . I wanted to talk to you, Dad.'

Silence as though he was thinking it over, taking his time reaching a difficult decision. Then, 'You'd better come on down.'

She descended nervously, wishing now that she had not come, seeing Barry's face again, trying to lip-read that stark vision, vainly attempting to interpret that warning. She reached the bottom, turned, and almost screamed.

At first she thought that it was not her father, instead some impostor who hadn't got the likeness quite right. The thick head of hair had completely disappeared, just a dark stubble on a shaven skull. Flushed cheeks that gave the impression of burning with some fever, dilated pupils that were not wholly caused by the thick lenses. Overall more imposing, more frightening. And when he spoke she knew that it was George Brownlow who stood before her. For some reason he had shaved his head.

'This is the place of the dead.' Tones that boomed. 'It is vital that this body is watched over. You, too, will have to take your turn, Sheila, for eventually I shall have to sleep. But not just yet. Now, what is it you want to speak to me about? Nothing frivolous at a time like this, I hope.'

She almost turned and ran. Possibly she would have fled had not her father's gaze held her, rendered her a prisoner down here by the sheer projection of his own willpower. 'I . . . I was wondering if . . . well, it would be nice if Adrian could join us, Dad. After all, I am carrying his baby.' She winced, expected an outburst, found her eyes drawn towards a still form on the camp-bed. *Barry's naked body, and stamped on his features was that same look of anguish which she had seen in her vision, that warning frozen on his dead lips.*

George Brownlow fell silent, pursed his lips. A few moments of deep concentration, his eyes never leaving her the whole time. 'Yes,' he smiled mirthlessly, 'in fact, I think we shall need him. Why had it not occurred to me before? Dalūkah and her child, albeit an unborn one, but we cannot appease Destiny without Āba-aner, can we?'

180

Amazement and suspicion registered on Sheila's face. Words of apparent madness yet they carried the message which she had not expected to hear in her wildest imagination. 'You may go and fetch him, Sheila.'

'I . . . I could telephone. . . .'

'*No!*' Brownlow's shaven head was thrust forward. 'That you must not do. Go and meet him secretly, and lead him here after darkness. Do you understand?'

She didn't but she nodded her head all the same. Such a concession by her parents was not to be spoiled by further argument over petty matters.

'Good. Go and get Adrian tonight. Now, leave me to my task.'

She turned away, gave one last glance back down into the interior as she reached the steps. Three expressions which seemed to be focused on her. The amulet, an inanimate thing which was fired by some kind of inner force, now had its four eyes glowing lustfully. Her father's had narrowed into a look of cunning.

And Barry Brownlow's. Staring eyes which still blazed their warning except that she could not interpret the message. Dead orbs screaming at her. When she reached the surface, she scrabbled in panic to open the door, broke into a run once she was outside.

But she knew she would go back down there soon and she would take Adrian with her. Together they would embark upon a Body-Watch!

Adrian's unease slowly infiltrated the euphoria of receiving a telephone call from Sheila. There was definitely something odd going on, he decided, as he made his way into the big recreation park. It was almost dusk, the atmosphere humid after what surely must have been the hottest day on record. And tomorrow would be even hotter.

An air of desertion, the playground empty, all the children having gone home to the discomfort of stifling bedrooms. A courting couple on one of the benches beneath the big chestnut trees, the girl swatting at relentless clouds of midges, the climax to their evening turning into an anti-climax.

Adrian paused, glanced about him. Nobody else in sight. He checked his watch, ten o'clock. He was a quarter of an hour early, fretting like he had on that first date with Sheila. Here. The same nervousness except that now anxiety had crept in.

So odd, that phone call that had hauled him from the very depths of his depression, he could recall almost every word of it. It had fetched him in from the garden where he had been lying in a small square of shade cast by a length of precarious council fencing. The bleeping of a call box, the person at the other end having to put a ten pence coin in again because it had passed right through without connecting the line. And in that split second before she spoke he'd known it was Sheila.

'Adrian?'

'Yes . . . I . . .'

'Now listen, and for the moment just answer "yes" or "no". Are your parents within earshot?'

'No. They're down at Uncle Fred's.'

'Good. That makes it very much easier. I want you to meet me this evening in the Park at ten-fifteen, down at the bottom end by the lake where we met the first time we went out together. You remember, don't you?'

'Yes. Of course I do.' Now this is bloody silly, as if I wouldn't remember. And, anyway, what's wrong with you coming here even if I can't come to your place because your mum thinks I'm common? 'I'll be there, She.'

'Hold on. Now I don't want you to tell a soul where you're going, d'you understand?'

'Sure. If you insist.'

'I do. Can you get out of the house before your mum and dad get back?'

'They won't be back till eleven. They're all going to the Farmhouse for a meal because it's Auntie Glad's birthday. And you and I could have gone as well.'

'Then that makes it even easier. Be there at ten-fifteen. It's very important.'

'Count on me, and. . . .'

The receiver was dropped back, leaving him with just the dialling tone, a sound like angry insects swarming that could turn into imaginary noises in the head if he didn't take a grip on himself. His first reaction was a sense of unparalleled ecstasy. He wanted to run back out into the garden, to yell out to the whole estate: *'She's phoned me, I'm meeting her tonight. Everything's going to be OK.'* But he didn't because everything wasn't OK.

He tried to work it all out logically. Sheila was pregnant so she needed him. Her folks wouldn't have him there so she had to meet him out somewhere. Adrian had not informed his own parents of Sheila's plight yet and maybe she didn't want him to, but it would all come out in the end anyway. And what the hell did it matter if they knew where he was going tonight? He shook his head in perplexity. Maybe she was panicking, wanted him to run away somewhere with him. Not that he was bothered about that, he'd go. He didn't have a job, no ties, and all he wanted in life was Sheila Brownlow.

It was getting dark. That courting couple had gone and he had the park to himself. Perhaps this was all some joke designed to pile on the heartbreak. Sheila hated him because he had taken her virginity, given her a child. She'd thrust the knife into his guts, now she was about to twist it, tug it about. *I love you — no, I don't. Yes, I do. No, I don't.*

'Adrian!'

He jumped, stared into the shadows cast by the huge chestnut trees. His heart missed a beat, his stomach churned, it was Sheila all right, her pale skin showing up in the gloom, dressed only in a bikini. Amazement, a faint sense of arousal over which he had no control, wanting to run to her, fling himself prostrate at her feet.

'I'm glad you came, Adrian.' She sank back on to the grassy bank, stretched herself out like she had that first time here when they had sat and talked, eagerly fantasising about a future which had all come to nothing. 'I was worried in case you didn't turn up.'

'You knew I would.' He lowered himself down beside her. 'God, I wouldn't have broken this date for anything.'

Subservient, humbling himself, putting himself at a disadvantage. 'But why . . . why *here*, and all this secrecy?'

She was staring at the saffron sky above, an expression on her face as though she had not heard him, was suddenly divorced from this place, lips moving, mouthing soundless words that he tried to catch by leaning over her, and failed.

'She, are you OK?'

She sighed loudly. 'I'm pregnant, nearer than even I dreamed. My time is approaching.'

'That's silly. You can't have missed more than one period. Your figure's still superb and . . .'

'Does it still excite you?' She turned her head, and her eyes seemed to narrow, boring into him, searching out his innermost thoughts, her whole bearing having matured decades since he had last seen her.

'Yes.' He gulped, could feel himself becoming aroused, made one half-hearted effort to check himself because there were more important issues at stake. Transfixed, momentary unease that turned into an overpowering urge. Her body, so sensuous — just the same as it had always been. And nobody but himself had ever lain on top of it, picked up its rhythm and shuddered with it to unbelievable peaks of sheer ecstasy.

Sheila Brownlow laughed, a staccato unfamiliar sound that sent a little shiver up his spine in spite of the heat, almost a snarl like a she-beast playacting some rigmarole in the mating season that was all part of Nature's unexplained courtships. Her hand came up, flipped behind her shoulder blades in a deft movement, an elasticated twang that had the bikini-straps slackening, the cups slipping from firm aroused nipples, flaunting them at him.

Again her movements were so perfectly co-ordinated, the downward sweep of both hands taking the brief lower garment with them, tossing it nonchalantly aside. Naked, so alluring, so *commanding*, eyes that had him wilting with a thousand inexplicable inhibitions that had not existed previously.

With trembling fingers and arms that had suddenly weakened he tugged at his damp T-shirt, somehow got it over his head, fumbled at the fastener on his frayed jeans, felt something tear and then it came free. Unable to remove his gaze from hers, almost overbalancing as he got free of the denims, stood there, a naked trembling servant in a state of full arousal.

She came to her feet in one lithe movement, stood there, arms akimbo, breasts swaying delightfully from side to side, so sensual and powerful. He found himself sinking back as though physically pushed down into the sharp dry grass, lying there on his back and watching her approach, a brief moment of terror stabbing into his heart for this beautiful seductress was far removed from the young supermarket girl he had seduced aeons ago.

She stood astride him, legs wide, forcing him to stare up into the blackness between, moist flesh that was bathed in shadow, a temptress sapping every last vestige of will-power that remained in him.

'I want you, Adrian,' she whispered, 'for you are my Āba-aner, my lover. We have been separated for so long and perhaps this is our last chance to be together for eternity.'

He nodded, swallowed, did not understand. Only that she would not leave him now because she needed him.

'You will come with me wherever I go.'

'Yes, I will. I promise.'

'Good.' Her body sank down so lightly, so weightlessly on top of him that he was not aware of physical contact until he felt her warm moistness swallowing him up. She leaned forward slightly, supported herself by gripping his shoulders, her lower half beginning to gyrate.

He closed his eyes but he could still see her, the purposeful movements, the rhythm which he strove to match. Two bodies in unison, hers a silent domination except for a slight quickening of her breathing, his own breath coming in gulps, his hands brushed aside when they instinctively groped for her as though her smooth milky flesh was sacred.

Guilt because he could not get their past matings out of his mind, the sordidness of love on the floor of a council house living-room, the lust of that night when the frogs of the river had come to lobby their own contempt. And now amends must be made, a new love had to be born in the same way that Sheila would give birth to a child amid the ancient pestilences which had returned to plague mankind.

Adrian's mind and body became engulfed in a storm of passion that destroyed all else: trivial thoughts and past fantasies were obliterated, his very soul seeming to be sucked from him in that final eruption, the mind-blowing ejaculation that had him flaying his limbs frantically and then reduced him to a trembling nothingness.

Sheila was moving about, retrieving her scattered two-piece and clipping the bra back into place with an expertise that had an air of finality, almost abruptness, about it.

He crawled, searched for his T-shirt and jeans, wondering if he had the strength to put them on. Humiliation, knowing that she watched his every movement, but enjoying it. *Oh, Dalūkah, I am your servant and your lover.* Now where the devil had he heard that name before?

'We'd better be going.' Her voice was soft, a whisper in the darkness.

'Where to?' His garments were damp with sweat and he half wondered if it would have been OK to leave them off in the dark. Clothing was yet another way of pandering to convention.

'Back to our place.' She took his hand, a firmness that would not be denied. An order which he must obey.

A courting couple going home now that their love-making was over, tired bodies that needed each other for support, the girl the stronger of the two. She dominated now just as she would in future years, a seductress who had had her way and would continue to do so.

'You're sure you didn't say anything to your folks about where you were going and who you were meeting?' There was an implication of reprimand in Sheila Brownlow's voice, a veiled accusation.

'How could I when they were already out when you phoned, and probably aren't even back yet?' he answered. 'Anyway, does it *really* matter if they know?'

'We cannot tolerate outside interference at this stage.' She spoke haughtily. 'You and I must share what lies ahead, a chance to repair a past failure. Perhaps before long you will understand, Adrian.'

His brain could not cope, he made no attempt to figure out the seemingly unending riddles in which she spoke. Suffice that they were together. Nothing else mattered; if she left him again he would kill himself for there would be nothing else to live for. Wherever she went, he would follow blindly, unquestioningly, right or wrong, in sanity or madness.

All the same he experienced a sense of foreboding when they came into sight of Number Twelve, River View. Some instinct deep inside him had his step faltering, almost drawing back but she tightened her grip and tugged him forward with her.

He made no further move to resist even when they walked down the drive of the Brownlow household, went through the side gate and entered a parched land that seemed to be cut off from the rest of the world, where the insects played an incessant mournful symphony of death.

A wilderness of no return.

Chapter Sixteen

Ancient Rites

ADRIAN FOLLOWED Sheila down the steps and into the dank bowels of the shelter, the mustiness which had greeted them at the top turning thick with a stench that had him fighting not to retch. Recoiling when he saw the body, the colour draining from his features, trying to turn his head away, but it was irresistibly drawn back to that still form on the camp-bed. Barry Brownlow's skin seemed to have darkened, almost a semi-tropical complexion but not quite, a kind of discoloration . . . *like meat that was starting to go bad!*

'How . . . how long has he been . . . *dead*?' Adrian Capper barely recognised his own voice, a hoarse whisper that echoed in the stillness of this chamber like the grating of insects somewhere behind the lines of shelving.

'Today,' she answered him emotionlessly. 'Sometime this afternoon. I don't know exactly.'

'But . . . but . . .' he began to stammer, a habit which he thought he had conquered in his early teens, 'you . . . you can't keep him *here*!'

'Why not?'

'Well . . . it's against the law.'

'*What* law?'

He swallowed hard, so confused now, frightened too.

'It is according to the law of the ancient ones.' Sheila's lips moved, uttered words beyond her own comprehension but she spoke them fluently. 'The Death-Watch has been

188

completed. Now we must mount the Body-Watch until it is time for the ancient rites. Father has taken his turn and now the Watch must be changed. I must go and rest. *You* must take the next Watch, Adrian!'

His senses reeled and he clutched at a section of Dexion for support, his whole body beginning to quiver with a mounting terror. *No*! He wasn't going to be left down here alone with . . . with *that*! This hell-hole had become a tomb.

'You must and you shall.' Her voice was low, menacing. 'I have brought you here so that you shall be with us all when the end comes. Now you are objecting to a small but vital duty, betraying us all in our hour of need.'

Again his resistance slipped away and he knew that he had no choice other than to obey. He nodded, tried to avert his gaze from her scathing stare but something else caught it, held it. A double-headed snake that flicked its fangs malevolently, sent his brain reeling again. *You will obey!*

She was gone. He hadn't heard her go but when he looked round there was no sign of her. *He was all alone!*

His fear was bordering on panic, the urge to flee but he knew he couldn't. He was a prisoner as surely as if he had been shackled and chained to the wall. Once more he glanced at that amulet but it was still, an inanimate object that neither moved nor glowed. He tried to tell himself that it had all been a trick of the light but he knew he lied.

Death! Something he had feared throughout his life partly because it had always been treated as taboo at home. You didn't talk about it; so-and-so had 'passed away' or 'gone'. Never died. Adrian felt sick. He had never seen a corpse before. Not quite: that time a few years ago when that accident had happened on the junction of the estate and the main road . . . he'd been first on the scene, had screamed at what he'd witnessed but nobody appeared to have heard him, at least nobody ever mentioned it. A motorcyclist travelling at speed had gone into a van that had pulled out without looking. The biker had been catapulted up into the air, almost vertically, had come down head first on the tarmac. Oh, Jesus Christ! The poor sod couldn't have been anything else but dead there and then although the newspaper report had said that the lad was found to be dead on arrival at hospital!

Adrian had hoped fervently that the guy had still been alive when they'd put him in the ambulance because that way he wouldn't have been looking at a corpse, a crumpled, blood-washed, virtually headless object which Adrian had tried to tell himself was mostly blankets that they had wrapped the victim in so that you couldn't really see what was what. Deep down, though, he *knew*, had woken up sweating several nights later after a dream in which he had seen a face spouting and coughing blood, trying to scream but the thick scarlet fluid had reduced those horrific yells to choking gurgles.

But this was far worse — death a stark, silent, motionless reality. The same Barry that he had helped tinker with motorbikes, those good-natured smiling features reduced to . . . to something else! Adrian wanted to look away but he couldn't. Dead orbs *watched* him! That was impossible. Any second now those lips would move, say something. The youth clapped his hands to his ears because he didn't want to hear. *For God's sake, shut up! You're supposed to be . . . dead!*

'*Your duty here is that of a Body-Watcher!*'

He whirled round but there was nobody there. Just the amulet, a polished metal lifeless thing. Turning back to the corpse, seeing that expression again, lips frozen into words that had never been uttered, eyes that mirrored a terror which even death could not destroy, a mute warning. *Flee before it is too late! I can't, I'm a prisoner here just like you, but you're the lucky one because whatever they do to you it won't hurt.* Those eyes seemed to bulge as though they were filling up with some invisible fluid, bubbles that would surely burst before long.

Body-Watching. You sat there with the dead for company, guarding a corpse to make sure it didn't . . . what?

A movement had Adrian flinching, cringing as something flicked against his ear and this time he managed a terrified gasp which turned to a grunt of temporary relief. Just a fly, a huge bloated bluebottle which must have got in from up above, possibly seeking refuge from the heat. So precise, landing on Barry Brownlow's upturned face, squatting there, seeing Adrian and almost taking off again. So alert, so wary. So revolting.

Adrian Capper felt anger towards it, hated it for its contempt of the dead. An idea crossed his mind to swat at it but he dismissed it almost immediately. Hit or miss, his hand would slap on dead human flesh, make a sound like a fillet of wet cod being dropped in an empty sink. The squashed fly, blood and excreta smeared across the dead face. He nearly threw up, just watched the insect, wondering what it was going to do, half-guessed.

It began to crawl, a purposeful reconnaissance, across an eye, down the bridge of the nose, watching him all the time. It paused by the nostrils, made a half-hearted attempt to squeeze itself inside but the cavity was too small and it withdrew. Hesitating, as though it was re-thinking its intended plan. Then it saw the half-open mouth and moved quickly, eagerly, across the upper lip, back along the lower one. Hesitated again, deliberately mocking its audience, tantalising the lone watcher.

Don't you bloody dare, don't you go. . . .

But the bluebottle was already inside the mouth, lost to Adrian's view. His stomach churned. Oh God, he could hear it buzzing away somewhere inside . . . feeding!

Time passed. Just an incessant drone which was playing on his nerves, his eyes riveted on Barry's face. The agony, the revulsion, there was no mistaking it, that mouth doing its utmost to move and spew the intruder out.

Another movement, much slower this time, a shape that shambled in an ungainly crab-like manner, coming out of the shadows on the floor, scaling a leg of the camp-bed with ease, hauling itself up on to the dead body via a stiff outstretched foot. A creature that dwarfed the bluebottle, a thousand times more repulsive as it became motionless, watching Adrian, almost challenging him. *A spider!*

Shudders convulsed his body. He had always had a fear of spiders, so much so that in early infancy his mother had had to stop reciting *Little Miss Muffet* to him because he had had gone into a screaming fit each time he heard it. Now he cringed, again would have fled if it had been physically possible.

The spider was a big one, bigger than any he had ever seen before. It had a face, too, and if you looked long and hard enough you thought you saw a similarity between insect and amulet. The eyes . . . it was mocking him, he sensed it, began to cringe, his mouth dry and his bottom lip trembling. For one awful second he thought it was going to come towards him.

Then, suddenly, the spider seemed to lose interest in him and moved on, an upward course that took it over the flaccid genitals as though its route was an intended insult to the dead. It did not look back, it knew that the sole spectator to its ramblings would not intervene because he was afraid of it.

The buzzing of the bluebottle was fainter as though it had gone deeper into the body and Adrian Capper tensed as he saw the spider pull itself up on to those lips, pause a moment as though trying to determine which inner route its intended prey had taken. Then it, too, was gone, scuttling across the half-protruding tongue until it was lost to sight.

Adrian sat there in that same chair which George Brownlow had occupied for the latter part of the day, hands clasped to his ears in a futile attempt to shut out that awful buzzing, trying to prevent his bemused brain from visualising the grim game of hide-and-seek which was going on deep inside Barry. He didn't want to hear, to see. Something hot and sharp burned the back of his throat and he hiccoughed bile. But no way could he shut out that revolting insect sound, louder, more persistent as though the bluebottle was screaming with terror.

Then, without warning, it stopped. The silence seemed to come at him in a wave of nausea, knowing full well what had happened inside there just as he had known that day what was the fate of that motorcyclist. Death in its most horrible form: strong spider jaws munching and squelching on a helpless body, dribbling bluebottle blood down Barry

Brownlow's lungs. The stench of putrefaction was much stronger again.

Adrian retched at the thought, would have vomited had he eaten that day, but lately food had become of minor importance to him. Just watching those dead lips, seeing them strain as though they, too, were going to throw up. And then the spider came back into view looking even more bloated than before.

This time it did not linger, a shambling multi-legged thing that took the quickest route to the floor and scuttled back beneath the Dexion.

'And the scorpions shall devour those who attempt to defile the bodies of Set's own!'

Adrian Capper hunched forward, resigned himself to an eternity in this chamber of death. For the vigil of a Body-Watcher was surely a long one and no harm must befall the corpse which belonged to Set for his vengeance was terrible to behold.

'I'm afraid there's no trace of your son to date, Mrs Brownlow.' Detective-Inspector Plant spoke to Emily Brownlow; you always addressed the mother in cases of missing sons, affected a sympathetic tone and didn't let on that thousands of people went missing every year and never turned up again. Mostly you found escapees from head-farms, though, because their movements were generally more predictable. Barry Brownlow was obviously an exception.

'Oh dear!' Emily closed her eyes, principally because she didn't want to give anything away, was afraid of making this policeman suspicious. She hadn't cried yet. Maybe that would come later but somehow it wasn't like *losing* a son. They still had him and wherever he was going they would soon be going there too. She had long resigned herself to that inevitable fact.

'I'm surprised he hasn't rung you or tried some form of contact.' Plant's gaze shifted to George Brownlow, thought Jesus Christ this bugger's queer too, shaving his head like a bloody Mohican! Or maybe he's got nits. The whole damned family's ninepence for a shilling if you ask me!

'Perhaps he will.' Emily had her head back and was intent on staring up at the ceiling, anything so she didn't have to look at that damned policeman. 'He was a loner as a child, never seemed to need our company.'

'You've got a girl, too, haven't you?'

'Yes,' George Brownlow cut in, half afraid what Emily might say. 'I'm afraid she's taken it rather badly since Barry was admitted to Shelderton. She's asleep upstairs in her room. It is rather late, you know.'

'Of course.' The inspector stood up and picked up his hat. 'It must be a trying time for all of you. Anyway, I'll be getting along now and as soon as we have any news I'll contact you.' In other words, don't ring us, we'll ring you. Maybe. It looks like the kid's scarpered and put as much distance between himself and Shelderton as possible. There's definitely something odd about the whole family.

'Well, with luck we shan't be hearing from *him* again,' George Brownlow muttered after the policeman had left. 'In fact, there's nobody likely to trouble us from now on. We shall be busy and we don't want to be disturbed.'

He went through into the kitchen and Emily followed him, wondering mildly to herself why her husband had torn most of her best linen into four-inch wide strips, had rolled them up like bandages; why he had sorted out a selection of carving knives and Tupperware bowls with snap-on airtight lids. And why he had meticulously shaved his head, even taken his eyebrows off so that he looked like some comic-book caricature. Except that there was nothing humorous about him.

There were an awful lot of things she pondered on these days, but she kept her thoughts to herself because it was not her place to speak out. She had been wrong to do so in the past but hopefully George had forgiven her. Even her thoughts might not be her own for George's eyes had become much more penetrating and powerful and that was not an illusion caused by the removal of his bushy brows. You could *feel* them boring into you, making you weak and wanting to please him, to obey him. Like that metal snake thing down in the Temple. Yes, it *was* a temple because you got a sort of "church-feeling" when you went down there, wanted to humble yourself, felt guilty about all sorts of things, the need to worship a deity. Set. And George was surely a disciple of Set.

'I need to rest.' George Brownlow paused at the foot of the stairs, bowed his head with weariness and sighed softly. 'Adrian will body-watch through the night hours.'

'Adrian?'

'Sheila fetched him tonight. Something that had completely escaped me until today for we shall need him.'

'Why? What for?'

He fixed her with a stare that had her backing away a pace, her hand going up to her mouth as though to stifle a scream of terror. 'Are you not aware, Emily, that we have a body on our hands and that there are ancient rites which must be carried out if our son's *khaibit* is to be able to cross over to *Sekhet-Aaru*? Set has commanded it, is waiting to receive him, and we dare not keep the Great One waiting. I shall need your help, Sheila's and Adrian's, too, *for they have an even greater part to play when that task is completed!*'

She watched him mount the stairs and only when she heard the bedroom door close behind him did she sink down on the bottom step and bury her face in her hands. Utter despair engulfed her, shook her with sobs of sheer hopelessness for she knew that whatever George ordered her to do she would carry it out, for she was his slave just as he was Set's.

Chapter Seventeen

The Ritual of Embalmment

IT WAS stiflingly hot down in the dug-out, Emily and Sheila huddling close together as though they sought refuge in each other's closeness. They stared at the naked corpse on its canvas bier, Adrian Capper sitting silently beyond it, a vague expression on his pallid features as though he did not understand what was happening. Black-ringed eyes were evidence of a sleepless night, his body bowed with weariness. His eyelids lowered, had to be forced open again, seeing but not fully understanding.

George Brownlow had constructed a trestle workbench adjacent to the camp-bed, piling it high with the impedimenta which had occupied the kitchen table on the previous evening; knives, strips of bedsheets and plastic bowls. He glanced at the amulet as though seeking a sign, but the four eyes remained dull and lifeless. The time was not right yet. They must wait. This was something which must not be rushed.

The stench of rotting flesh was overpowering. George was on one knee by the bed; he might have been praying to Set. His mind flipped to and fro, a series of unrelated events that moved on before he could grasp them properly. A news flash, it might have been earlier today. Or yesterday. Or the day before. A grim-faced newscaster who probably knew more than he had been instructed to say. *'Libya had issued its final warning to Israel. The mad Colonel would go ahead whatever.'*

Lies. All lies. George Brownlow's brain was numbed as though it had been injected with a mild local anaesthetic. So far he had been guided by Set, a vision that had been indelibly imprinted on his mind at the time but which was beginning to fade. Bandages, four containers of water to sprinkle around the corpse, bowls for the intestines. Their removal was not repulsive to him in any way, just a job which had to be done efficiently. He did not doubt his capabilities; as a boy he had gutted snared rabbits, prepared them for the oven. This would be the same but on a bigger scale. Nervousness because everything had to be done right and the sequence worried him. The Opening of the Mouth and Eyes. They were open now. Perhaps he should close them. He stretched out a hand, the fingers trembled, one second of revulsion but it passed. One lid, it moved easily like a minute shutter. He wondered if it would spring back up but it didn't. Then the other. Now the mouth. . . .

It was rigid, immovable jaws that refused to budge. A silly, rather frightening thought. Suppose they snapped closed suddenly, bit his fingers. No, Barry wouldn't do that. Using two hands now, trying to lever and push at the same time. Sweating, cursing beneath his breath, giving up. It wouldn't move. George sank back down to a kneeling position. It was his own fault, he should have closed the mouth immediately upon death. Now that part of the ceremony would have to be symbolic.

Emily watched expressionlessly, vaguely wondering what her husband was attempting to do. It was all beyond her. She regarded him steadily, saw how his hairless cranium shone with sweat in the light cast by that dusty bulb. Just a pair of khaki shorts, nothing else; he'd even removed his sandals. His body looked so much more lithe and muscular than she had ever known it. Perhaps all that digging had done him good after all; it had certainly removed that spare tyre which always bulged around his middle. He looked so much younger and even . . handsome! So capable that you no longer felt frightened down here because *he* was in command. Those snake eyes weren't glowing anymore; perhaps they would not come alive again because George had taken over, Set had delegated to his new high priest.

Sheila felt slightly sick and faint. It was due to the heat and her condition. She felt guilty, *real* guilt for the first time. A moment of weakness and temptation and she was pregnant — out of wedlock. Now she saw the whole thing in perspective. It *was* right what her mother had constantly drummed into her. She *had* let them down. The Brownlows had risen in the world, a stroke of sheer luck, a fortunate cross on a coupon had given them a new status, a magnificent home in an executive area and *she* had to go and grovel back in the council estates. Her eyes misted, burned with tears that wouldn't come. It was all Adrian's fault and she hated him for it, edged a few inches further away from him. *He* had persuaded her to have sex. She hadn't really wanted to, hadn't enjoyed it one little bit and now she was paying the price for her folly. Her place was here with her family, Adrian was an outsider, a *commoner*. He had no right to be in here with them. Yet suddenly Dad had wanted him here. They were all going to die, civilisation had but a few more days, perhaps hours, left. Her baby would never be born anyway. Oh God, she wanted to die *now* and wipe out her shame.

Adrian glanced sideways, wondered if Sheila was all right. Were *any* of them all right? Inner panic, trying to work out why he couldn't just walk out of here, take Sheila with him. It was as though some strange compulsion to stay gripped him, a sort of mental state like morbid curiosity, wondering what the hell old Brownlow was going to do. The bugger was breaking the law, could get put away for messing about with a corpse like this. And Jesus, how that body was stinking! It was going bad, decomposing by the hour like corpses did in tropical countries where they had to be interred within a few hours of death. There was something awful about Barry's death; it wasn't natural. Like Rita's. Something to do with that research laboratory, a bug which had escaped and the authorities were swearing that it wasn't contagious because they were covering up.

Some kind of plague that could spread, but they knew everybody was going to die within a few days so it didn't really matter.

He stretched out a hand to take Sheila's but she stiffened, shrugged him off. Christ, this didn't make sense. She had fetched him here, said she needed him and now he was being rejected. But he still couldn't leave. He. . . .

Something was happening! The light flickered, dimmed, so that those around him were merely silhouettes. They might have been statues. A kind of fiery glow was replacing the harsh artificial light . . . coming from those four serpent eyes. *Set had slumbered and now he was awake!*

Tiny jewelled pinpoints that scintillated, saw in all directions at once. Adrian felt their force, a kind of gamma-ray that burned into you, had you wanting to mumble your subservience to a living god, knew that there was nowhere you could hide.

George Brownlow was on his feet, leaning across the corpse, muttering incoherent incantations, doing something to the eyes . . . gently pushing the lids back so that Barry stared up at the ceiling once more. Pulling at the jaw, a click that made you wince. The mouth seemed wider than before and he was attempting to stuff that lolling tongue back inside but it flopped out again like a dead snake.

He had some kind of glass vessel in his hands, a sort of miniature decanter, was sprinkling liquid all around and over the naked body, still muttering. A smell, strong but pleasant, trying to overcome the stench of putrefaction. Adrian sniffed, recognised it. *Perfume!* Musk, Sheila used it when they went out together. It brought back memories, her beautiful naked body stretched out on the carpet of a council house living-room floor, trembling with nervousness. His own insistence, doing things to her which made her agree to go the whole way Selfishness that had got her a child, had ended in all *this*!

Guilt. Those tiny red eyes had singled him out, his thoughts were no longer his own. *I did it deliberately, I confess. I got her pregnant so that she would be mine, so that nobody could take her away from me!*

George and Emily Brownlow were staring at him now. Accusing. *You little bastard, you dared to do that to our daughter. She has conceived by a commoner's sperm! You'll pay the full penalty for this, along with her, for you are both guilty!*

His lips moved in a mute incomprehensible apology. Pleading for both of them but there was no mercy in those expressions.

George Brownlow was moving again, arms upraised, facing Set.

'The Temple has been made pure,' he muttered. 'We are ready now to help the dead one on his journey to *Sekhet-Aaru!*'

Adrian tensed, felt a rush of air like a dry desert wind whipping his face with particles of sand, threw up his hands to protect himself but no way could he shut out those penetrating eyes of fire. Then the gust was gone and it was calm again.

George Brownlow's features were tense, his glasses reflecting the fiery glow of the amulet, his expression fearsome. 'Are we all here?' A booming deafening voice. 'Speak to your *Kher-heb*, let him know that you are present. *Sem* priest do you hear me?'

Another rush of hot desert air that seemed to whisper 'I hear you, *Kher-heb*'.

'*Sem?*'

'Yes.' Adrian's lips moved, he heard his own voice somewhere far away, a frightening experience, a sensation as though his whole being had been taken over.

'*Sa-mer-ef, Tcherau-ur* and *Tcherausheraut?*'

'We hear you, *Kher-heb*.' A whispered chorus that came from everywhere yet nowhere in particular.

'*Menhu*, the slaughterer?'

A reply that came in George Brownlow's own tones yet his lips did not move.

'*Am-asi* and *Am-khent?*'

A distant rumble which might have been thunder

200

outside, slowly dying away, the metal shelving vibrating. The shelter darkened temporarily and then the dull red glow came back.

'We are all here.' George turned back towards the amulet, began sprinkling more strong-smelling perfume. 'The temple and the dead one are now purified and I am ready to begin!'

Adrian felt his bowels move, his stomach muscles tighten into a hard ball, tasted bile in his mouth. Oh Christ, he guessed what Brownlow was about to do, anticipated it even before the long knife-blade scintillated redly. He didn't want to look, didn't want to hear, but he had no choice.

Steel sank into that flat abdomen, squelched and grated on bone. You could almost see the vile vapours of rotting intestines rising up, their stench a physical body that spread out and came at you. A deep incision, the Kher-heb's *hands pulling at slippery offal, stringing it into one of the Tupperware bowls, clicking the airtight lid shut. More intestines, yards of them, another bowl filled. Adrian wasn't trying to hold his vomit back any longer, spewed bile down the front of his T-shirt, still compelled to watch as George Brownlow dug and hacked for the dead heart!*

Set's priest worked steadily and competently, as emotionlessly as a doctor carrying out a post-mortem examination, transferring the severed heart to a separate small container, then looking to the amulet to seek its approval. The light brightened, dimmed again almost immediately as though the watchers had been afforded a brief glimpse of the mutilations and now they must see no more.

Adrian managed a glance at the two women. They were watching emotionlessly, hypnotically, and there was no sign of the revulsion which he felt. He wanted to scream *'Don't you understand what he's doing to your brother, your son? You can't embalm him because he's decomposing already with some vile disease that we're all going to die of.'* But he didn't because that feeling of guilt came back again, as though it was all his own fault. I ought to be lying there being gutted because I deserve it.

Your time will come!

George Brownlow was struggling with the swathings, strips of linen becoming entangled and having to be unravelled, beginning with the feet; one leg then the other, up on to the torso. Something gurgled, followed by a long expellation of air as though the corpse still clung to a vestige of life. Now only the head remained, features still transfixed with that pre-death terror, still trying to shout that warning. It was too late now because bandages were being bound tightly over the mouth, pulled flat on to the contours of nose and forehead.

A mummy! George Brownlow stepped back to admire his handiwork, but was interrupted by Set, a shaft of ruby light arrowing on to him, a rebuke for his vanity.

'May the dead one cross over to *Sekhet-Aaru* and may we soon follow our son to the Land of the Dead.' George dropped to his knees, uttered a sound which might just have been a sob. 'Let our son enter the Kingdom of Osiris.'

Silence. Two women fought to hold back their sorrow and one youth suffered the agonies of his own terror, a feeling of hopelessness because he had been a part of all this, struggling to retain what sanity remained to him.

'We commit our son, Barry, into the care of Set.' George Brownlow's priest-like mumble, 'that he may take him for his own in *Sekhet-Aaru* and . . .'

A scream cut through the semi-darkness and the suffocating stench left by the disembowelment, a shriek of unearthly fear that came from the depths of a tortured soul. And there, a yard or so above the crudely mummified thing the watchers saw the unmistakable head of Barry Brownlow hovering, those same white agonised features, only now the mouth moved, spat out those words which had hitherto been frozen in death.

'You fools!' Wide eyes blazed hatred and remonstration. 'Do you realise what you have done to me? You have transported my *khaibit* into the land of darkness, beyond

202

the void in which my beloved wanders, and now I am an eternal slave of the double-headed serpent god who is known as Set. You have condemned us all to this *because in your folly you did not address Horus and Thoth!'*

An angry hiss, a flicking of venomous fangs, and Barry was fading, trying to scream but it was no more than a dying whisper. Darkness. Emily and Sheila were sobbing, holding on to each other, George Brownlow was slumped against a chair, silent with his own thoughts. Adrian just stared into the blackness. His mind having failed to cope had become a void; it needed to switch off and recharge.

The bulb came back to full power with stark reality, revealed the true horrors of what had happened. It was no nightmare. The bandaged body, a shape that only vaguely resembled human form, a monstrous anonymity that was lifeless and soulless, the stinking pots of offal beside it a gruesome token of ancient Egyptian emulation, the room reeking with the stench of a long-forgotten plague which terminated in gangrene. And death.

The amulet slept, metal-lidded eyes that needed to rest after their exertions, the snake mouths smug and gloating, a thing that had fed and was temporarily contented.

George Brownlow looked at each of them in turn with huge distorted eyes behind the thick lenses. His lips curled in contempt when his gaze finally rested on Adrian Capper. 'This is all your doing, boy. And *yours*!' He glanced at the cringing Sheila. 'Between you, you have brought plagues and death to this land. And it is not finished yet. *The suffering and strife has only just begun!'*

'Don't . . . don't you think we should . . . go back to the house, George? Emily spoke weakly.

'You and I, yes,' he laughed, a malicious sound that had Adrian cringing again. '*For we must wait again until the time is right, until Set is ready, and Menhu, the Slaughterer. For Dalūkah and the commoner, Āba-aner, must pay the penalty for their betrayal. The Wheel of Fate has turned another full circle!'*

Adrian watched them go, heard the outer door grating, being forced shut. He stared at Sheila, saw her glance away. There were a lot of things he wanted to say but this was neither the time nor the place, and he doubted his physical capability of being able to put them into words.

The two of them were trapped in here as surely as if George Brownlow had locked them in a dungeon. They had witnessed the fate of Barry, the living decomposition, the agony of after-death.

Now it was their turn and Set would keep them waiting until he was ready to call upon *Menhu*, the Slaughterer.

Chapter Eighteen

Dalūkah's Child

ALONE IN a tomb that reeked of gangrene and death, a plague that still lived and devoured the flesh of a mummified body, watched over by an amulet that slumbered but could come to life at any moment and if it did it was terrible to behold. Adrian forced his brain to work, a machine that grated and stuttered, threatened to cut out.

Facts first. A combination of coincidences. The drought had brought the frogs and the grasshoppers, an odd locust or two, nothing to get excited about. In due course the rains would come and everything would revert to normal — unless the Americans blasted that missile ship to Kingdom-come in the meantime. But in all these crises somebody backed down, started a long session of talks that eventually ended in some sort of compromise. But down here in the Temple there would be no compromises.

George had let his obsessions get the better of him. And that was where reality ended! All this was tied up with some powerful ancient curse that had come over from Egypt with those mummies which an old clergyman had buried right here, somewhere in the garden of Number Twelve River View. And Adrian had got caught up in it all, escalating madness that had led to a corpse being mutilated and subjected to mummification rites. There was no knowing what was going to happen to himself and Sheila if they didn't get out of here fast.

He looked at the amulet again. Just a bit of metal. It couldn't hurt you on its own. All this business was some kind of hypnotic influence engendered by George Brownlow and if you let it get to you it was like a psychic force controlling you. It was all in the mind, Adrian Capper decided.

Sheila was sitting on the floor, her back resting against some shelves loaded with canned foodstuffs, eyes closed. She might even be asleep, so exhausted by recent events that she would submit to anything her father came up with.

'She?'

At first he thought she hadn't heard him, then her eyes slowly opened, regarded him with a vague expression, looked as though they might close again. She didn't speak.

'She, we *have* to get away from here.'

'We can't.'

'Yes we can. We've been hypnotised but I think I've shaken the effects off now. Let me help you.' A mental struggle, fighting all the way, sheer exhaustion threatening to swamp him. 'Your dad's crazy, he'll kill us both, your mum as well.'

'No!' A hoarse cry, a flicker of terror in her eyes. 'We have betrayed them once. We dare not risk it.'

'You're coming with me!' Tight-lipped he took a step towards her, swayed slightly as a wave of dizziness hit him.

And in that instant she moved with incredible speed, a bound from her sitting position that took her across the room as far as the bed on which the mummy lay, grabbed something and brandished it above her head — *that long-bladed knife which George Brownlow had used to disembowel his own son, a string of entrails still adhering to it!*

'Don't be a fool!' Adrian checked his advance, backed off a couple of steps.

'I'll kill you if you come any closer!' A hiss that was reminiscent of that foul serpent. 'I swear it.'

He took a deep breath, knew that she meant it. 'All right, if you won't come, then you won't come and I can't do anything about it. But *I'm* leaving right now while I still can. I'm going to get help. I'm going to bring the police back here and I just pray that I'll be in time before that crazy father of yours does anything else!'

She lowered the knife, held it at hip level, poised and ready to strike but she made no move towards him. She didn't speak, didn't need to because the expression in her eyes said everything: her hatred for him because of what he had done and what he was about to do, a fanatical gleam in those pale blue orbs which might have belonged to George Brownlow himself.

Adrian Capper backed towards the steps, watching her the whole time, fearing a sudden rush forward and a frenzied attempt to stop him leaving. But she did not move.

He reached the steps, turned, moved quickly. Almost ran up them. The door, oh God he'd almost made it. Once he was outside they wouldn't be able to stop him. He'd run all the way to that telephone kiosk at the far end of River View, dial 999, tell the police what had happened to the missing Barry Brownlow. Then . . .

His fingers had closed over the latch, were in the act of lifting it when he heard Sheila's scream, a sound that seemed to come up from the very bowels of the earth, an embodiment of the ultimate in physical pain and mental stress, a cry that died away to a dull groan. Then a thud, the unmistakable noise of a falling body.

For a second or so Adrian's brain was fogged again, seemed to cut out and prevent him from thinking clearly, an inbuilt device by Nature which spared him blinding mental agony. Then he was turning back, holding on to the rail with trembling hands, descending those steps, knowing in his heart what he was going to find. *In her desperation Sheila Brownlow had taken her own life!*

His mind almost snapped at the scene which greeted him. She lay there, writhing, groaning, clutching at her stomach. The knife lay beside her, an instrument of death and mutilation which had claimed yet another victim in the name of Set.

Despair, panic. An instinctive desire to pick up the weapon, plunge it into his own heart. That way they would both die together, deprive *Menhu* the Slaughterer of his pleasure, and George Brownlow could do what the hell he liked with their dead bodies.

But Sheila Brownlow wasn't dead yet. Moaning softly, gripping her abdomen, rolling from side to side. He grasped her wrists, pulled them away, anticipated an ugly gash pumping her life's blood away. Instead there was nothing, no wound, no mark, no tear in her tight-fitting jeans. Shock turned to anger.

'You little bitch!' he breathed. 'It was a trick to stop me from . . .' Adrian's words died away. There was no doubting her expression, the pallor on the screwed-up features, the way she shuddered and whimpered, eyes closed as though she was on the brink of unconsciousness, desperately ill.

He knelt over her, shook her gently. 'She . . . Sheila, what is it?'

'Adrian,' the convulsions steadied, her clammy fingers clutched at him. 'Adrian. . . . I've . . . gone into labour . . . contractions . . . *I'm going to . . . to have the baby!*'

He stared in sheer amazement, relief surging over him, again suspicious that it might be a trick of some kind, instinctively checked that the knife was not within her reach. 'That's absolutely ridiculous!' A sudden desire to laugh his relief aloud. 'You're nowhere near. You can't possibly be having a baby yet!'

'I am,' she whispered. 'Oh God, I *am*! I know it, I can feel it coming.'

And at that very moment the bulb above them spluttered, plunged the whole shelter into pitch darkness. Adrian's first thought was that this was death, the black nothingness into which Barry and Rita had been condemned to wander for eternity. Then he heard Sheila moaning, clawing at him, calling for him.

'I'm here, my darling.' He experienced a moment of peace, a lull in the strife, until her fingernails gouged his arm and brought it all back again.

'Oh, help me, Adrian. It's starting to come fast!'

Helpless, unable to see, not knowing what to do even if he could do anything, he knelt and slipped an arm beneath her. He tensed, she felt somehow . . . different. Her clothing, instead of a blouse and jeans was soft and silky, voluminous so that it flopped and fell away from him. Beneath it he felt her nakedness, a belly that was suddenly rounded and moving, her body shuddering in the latter spasms of labour. That smell, it was no longer putrefying, more of a dusty dryness like somewhere that had been shut up for years. Strange surroundings but he could not see them, only sensed them.

She was crying softly, murmuring her love for him, gasping at the sharp pains. And even as he knelt there trying to comfort her he became aware of a difference about himself, his own clothing. Gone were the T-shirt and jeans, in their place a skin of some kind, a furry garment that enveloped his body down as far as his thighs, a tail flapping in his wake. This was all sheer madness!

The room was growing lighter, but not from the suspended electric light bulb above them; rather a faint red glow that was becoming brighter all the time, four tiny pinpoints of fire giving out an ethereal radiance like a rising sun showing itself gradually above an eastern horizon.

Adrian cried out aloud as he saw his surroundings for the first time in this strange illumination. The shelter, but all the shelves had gone, just four bare walls with strange pictures and designs painted on them. And in the centre of the floor stood a raised coffin, an identical smaller one beneath it. Frightened, he looked slowly around. In a recess, almost hidden by the shadows stood another coffin, much larger than the other two. Cold fear clutched at his heart but he still kept looking.

Of course the amulet would be here because it was impossible to escape from it. Four burning serpent eyes that lighted this chamber, the snake body seeming more polished, burnished and glistening. Beside it stood a carved head, a black shiny skull the size of a tennis ball. With a start he recognised it, remembered where he had seen it before. The Castle Museum! So strange that he should remember it, those obsidian features sinister in the half-light, forbidding, as though they resented his presence here, a kind of guardian of the amulet though surely Set needed no keeper.

Adrian saw but he did not understand. During those moments of blackness it was as if he had been transported to another place, another chamber where everything was so old. And Sheila. . . .

He stiffened, wondered for a moment if it was indeed her. Her hair was longer, several shades darker, her skin dry and cracking as though desert sand was ingrained in it. She wore a long flowing yellowish garment, her stomach ballooning up into it, quivering with the strain of an impending childbirth. But it was Sheila all right.

'Help me, Āba-aner,' she whispered, managed a faint smile. 'Any minute now . . .'

He nodded, glanced down at himself, rubbed at his bare arms and legs as though the duskier rougher texture of his skin might be removable, some kind of dried grease-paint but it was real enough, just as the worn and frayed leopardskin garment was, the tail swinging and brushing against his legs. He gave up trying to work it all out.

'Look, Āba-aner, *look*!' For a moment the girl seemed to forget her contractions, snatched her hand free from him and pointed behind him. 'See, it is a sign from *Khepera*!'

He turned, saw where she pointed, a small black beetle scurrying across the floor, checking, darting one way then another like it was lost, finally making it to the shadows where it was seen no more.

'Do you see it, Āba-aner?' There was exultation in her tone. 'Oh, surely you see it!'

'Just a beetle.'

'It was no ordinary beetle. That was a *scarab*. Did you not notice its rich metallic colours? It has been sent here by *Khepera*, the god of creation, a sign that a birth is nigh, a new creation is imminent.' She broke off, gave another gasp of pain. '*It is here!*'

His mind was spinning and there was no time to think logically. He must help her deliver the baby!

Adrian grasped her dress, tore it and tore it again, strips and squares of material that would be needed soon.

210

Water . . . there was none, he must manage without, relying on an age-old instinct when man and his mate delivered their offspring in a barren cave and the children survived amid the filth.

She was pushing hard now, straining and crying out, gripping him and cutting into his flesh with long fingernails. The baby, he could see it, hear it, but he was afraid to touch it in case he injured it. It seemed to be coming well. Its head was free but the tiny features were bathed in the shadow of those pushing thighs and he was unable to see them.

One final scream, a shriek of sheer maternal pain, and the infant was clear of the womb, a wriggling crying thing on a square of torn silk, still dark and featureless. Adrian bent to lift it clear, reaching for that knife to cut the cord. He found the knife, saw that it was different, an ivory-handled short-bladed dagger, but the edge was keen and that was all that mattered.

'Give it to me, Āba-aner. Is it a boy?' A mother's hope for a son and heir; she cradled her still wet baby to her bosom, felt at it in the darkness. 'Oh, Āba-aner, *it is a girl!*' Sheer despair, the sobs shaking her body. 'I prayed to *Khepera* when I saw the scarab that it would be a male child but even he, it seems, cannot alter the course of fate. Dalūkah has once again given birth to another Dalūkah and there is no hope for any of us!'

'Sheila, pull yourself together!'

'Sheila? And who is this Sheila you refer to, Āba-aner? You know I am called Dalūkah.'

He nodded. He did not know, but any name would suffice. 'I wish we had some water . . . Dalūkah.'

'It does not matter. I am drying her on my torn clothing. She will be all right. She is . . .' She stiffened, gave a sudden cry of anguish, almost dropped her baby. '*Look, Āba-aner, do you see its features, its skin. The babe is barely a few minutes old and yet it already has the accursed plague!*'

Adrian paled, recoiled. *And at that very moment the four eyes of Set glowed brightly, cast their red light upon the tiny creature which hitherto had been hidden by shadow. A face that might have been that of a monkey, rough and*

211

flat-featured, eyes that seemed to understand, glinted with a malevolence towards the mother who had given birth to it, mutely asking to be spared the misery of a misshapen existence, pleading for mercy. Euthanasia, it was the only answer but no parent would have the courage.

The skin was blistered, wet with pus from the festering sores, oozing yellow rivers dripping and forming their own sea on the floor. Flesh that burned and decomposed in its first few minutes of life, gave off that putrefying stench which had its mother holding it away from her, her screams drowning its own cries of pain. It vomited scalding bile, tried to fight its way back to those full breasts but the girl known as Dalūkah could not bear its closeness. If necessary it must starve. What did it matter when they were all going to die? Was not *Menhu* the Slaughterer due back at any moment?

Adrian covered his face with his hands, peeped through splayed fingers. For one brief moment he saw the baby girl's face, an instant of *recognition* that had to be a lie sent to torture him, a cruel trick by the amulet which gave light or darkness according to its mood. *It could not be, his imagination was adding to his own awful inexplicable terror. For in that split second he saw a tiny replica of Rita beneath the running plague mucus, the agony of one beyond mortal help who writhed in everlasting purgatory.* Then she was gone, and the wriggling shape held in Dalūkah's outstretched hands was once more a diseased child afforded an awful temporary life.

She set it down on the carpet of filthy cloth, grateful that the radiance was fading again and she would not be able to gaze upon it. It screams were louder and she found herself edging her weakened bleeding body away from it, groping the blackness for her lover, seeking the protection of his body in case her offspring came after her.

Adrian felt her go limp, lowered her gently to the floor. The light was gone now and the blackness had returned, the cries of the infant growing weaker as though already she was succumbing to the dreadful burning plague.

Then silence, except for faint scurrying sounds. The heavier ones might have been rats, the fainter ones beetles or spiders. His skin crawled as something brushed against his bare foot and moved on. In the distance he thought he could hear that awful familiar cacophony, an orchestra of grasshoppers and the deeper vocal chords of hordes of frogs preparing to leave the reed beds.

Dalūkah was unconscious. He stroked her fevered face gently, bent forward and kissed her lips. They were burning hot, her breath stale. But at least she still lived.

He fumbled around trying to find the knife again but it had gone, snatching his hand away as he touched something small and hard that darted away in fright. If he had found the weapon he would have used it, cheated the forces which mocked them in the blackness. But he did not and they still lived.

The living death, this was it, he was certain. He wondered if they would see Barry and Rita; perhaps it was better if they didn't after that one fleeting likeness which had materialised on the newborn's face.

The muffled noises from outside were louder now, the frogs had left their daytime refuge to conquer the land, the insects greeting them joyously, a multitude of pestilences joining forces against Man. There would be locusts out there too, like the one that George Brownlow had imprisoned in a jam-jar and left to die from suffocation. Just as Adrian and Sheila were dying now, if they were not already dead.

A vibration on the stone floor. Adrian's tortured senses picked it up, felt it gathering strength. Heavy footsteps, somebody was coming. *Menhu* the Slaughterer had arrived!

Chapter Nineteen

Dead Scarabs

EMILY BROWNLOW sat staring at the patterns on the kitchen wall, experienced a kind of after-funeral feeling — numbed shock that gradually turned to relief. Funerals were therapeutic, a climax to grief, and afterwards you felt better. That had been the case after both her parents had died, the same with Rita. Now she had to condition herself once again. The consolation this time was that everybody was going to die. Death was but a process of change, a transfer to another life. *Sekhet-Aaru.*

But she was changed already. Different. And it was all rather frightening, so much so that she deliberately tried to work out those patterns on the wallpaper over the unit, her confused brain fighting to adjust to something mundane. Squiggly lines that could have been anything and the more you studied them the more difficult it was to determine exactly what. Like those lines and symbols in the optician's that you squinted at trying to make up your mind which ones were level, and which were thicker, and eventually you finished up with eye strain anyway so they sold you a new pair of lenses.

They were like insects, that was it. Smug satisfaction now that she had come to a positive decision. Tiny dots that were flies on the wall, motionless because they were caught up in the criss-cross sections which couldn't be anything else except spiders' webs. And you wondered how on earth you had failed to spot the spiders themselves, big fat lecherous insects that squatted, waiting. They were in no hurry because their victims weren't going anywhere.

She started, her heart missed a beat, changed up a gear and accelerated. Like George. He was the spider, they were the flies: Sheila, Adrian . . . herself. Barry and Rita had already been devoured.

She sat up, gripped the arms of the chair, a sensation as though she had been manacled, shackled for a long time and suddenly for no reason at all her chains had loosened and fallen from her. A wave of sheer horror hit her, almost threw her back into a semi-comatose state and she had to clutch at logic. It almost eluded her but not quite, a will-o'-the-wisp but she caught it and dragged it back.

Shock again but not the same. She was not numbed any more like a mindless zombie, could actually *reason*. Oh God, it all had to be a dream, it couldn't have happened.

'Less than an hour to zero hour.' She hadn't heard her husband enter the room because he moved almost silently on bare feet. 'Libya isn't backing down. Israel will be blasted to hell and that'll be the signal for the Americans to trigger off their armoury. Maybe we won't even make it until tonight. The Prime Minister is addressing the nation at seven. A lot of good that'll do!'

She didn't reply, didn't want to look at him. George Brownlow was dead, months ago. This . . . *thing* was an impostor, not even much of a physical resemblance any longer. Something created by that devilish metal object in the shelter. Or was everything all in the mind? No, it was real enough, a nightmare that was reality.

George was standing staring out of the window as though transfixed. Out there, in River View, a quiet upper-class suburban backwater, people were starting to panic. One heavily laden car was already being backed out into the road, the luggage on the roofrack precariously tied with string. The vehicle seemed to groan under the weight. Next door a Transit van was in the process of being loaded up, loose items being flung in through the open rear doors, there was no time for suitcases. And so it would be at number sixteen . . . and number eighteen. Everybody was fleeing, but where to? George smiled smugly to himself. Running was no good, you had to go underground and sit it out. It gave him a sense of superiority.

'Did you hear what I said?' A touch of annoyance in his tone, an edginess that hadn't been there before, fanaticism bordering on panic.

'I heard. Does it really matter?'

'Maybe and maybe not but we need time. Not a lot, just enough so that *Menhu* can finish his work but Set isn't ready yet. If they bomb us first it could be too late and then we'd never make it to the Kingdom of Osiris. But Set will not be hurried.'

'What about Sheila and Adrian?' Staring again at the wall patterns, the flies not even struggling, the spiders not hurrying.

'They will wait just as we have to. They won't be going anywhere.'

She stiffened, hoped he didn't notice how her flesh crept and goosepimpled. He spoke the truth. Sheila and Adrian would stop in the shelter because they had been brain-blasted too, imbeciles who didn't even have the minds of children. She wished George would go away, go and lie down on the bed upstairs for a while. His presence was starting to fog her mind again, destroying that sudden flash of logic.

The door closed and she heard his bare feet on the hall blocks, a sort of slithering noise that sent a shudder up her spine. Just one creak on the stairs told her that he had gone upstairs. Maybe he *was* going to rest for a while. Her pulses were racing alarmingly and she wondered if she had high blood-pressure. It was quite likely.

Silence. *Proper* silence. It was unnerving, something which rarely ever happened if you stopped to think about it. There was always noise, the drone of cars in the distance, those damned grasshoppers never letting up, frogs croaking so that you couldn't shut them out because they got on your brain so much you heard them anyway. Flies buzzing on the windows.

216

Now silence. *Real* silence. Emily Brownlow swallowed, strained her ears in an attempt to hear something. But there was nothing. *Something was very wrong!*

The flies were all dead! She saw them lying on the windowsills, on the sink unit, all over the floor. Not one was buzzing, they were all dead, every one of them!

It was illogical, she tried to tell herself, the way her terror came back and once again she was engaged in conflict with her own brain. Run! No, I'm not scared. Yes, you are because everywhere you look there's death!

But they're only flies, a fly's life-span is only a day or so. Maybe, but Nature ensures that they breed rapidly so that there are always flies. But there aren't anymore. They're *all* dead!

Grasping at logic, a masterstroke by a frightened and confused brain. Somebody had sprayed the kitchen with fly-killer! That was why they were *all* dead. Emily expelled her breath in utter relief, tried to shut out that argumentative little voice inside her. Then why aren't hordes of them mobbing the windows on the outside trying to get in?

Maybe they were, she crossed to the sink unit. Oh God, there wasn't a fly to be seen, only thousands of dead ones littering the patio outside that would need to be swept up with a broom. A bucketful at least.

She trembled, held on to the sink, thought about Sheila and Adrian again, more positively this time, bringing in a new dimension. *Anger!*

She opened the door into the hallway, stood listening. That same awful silence but not quite. A distant faint kind of intermittent humming as though a generator somewhere was struggling in the heat, almost cut out but managing to hold on. Emily tried to dismiss it, crept towards the stairs, mounted them one at a time, stepping over the fifth step because that was the one that always creaked. Barry had said so once. Her eyes burned hot and dry at the memory.

She reached the landing, fought to overcome the urge to flee back downstairs, to fling herself into that kitchen chair and try and count the number of flies caught up in wallpaper webs. On tip-toe, easing open the bedroom door, a crack just large enough to see through.

217

Then she almost laughed her relief aloud. George Brownlow lay on the bed, stark naked, mouth wide, giving off a staccato snore which terminated in a grunt that almost woke him up before he began to snore again. A human generator struggling to cope with a heatwave.

Oh God, he looked pathetic without his shorts and glasses. It was a long time since she had seen him like that. Dirty, too, and with his head shaven he reminded her of a little old man nearing the end of his days. Nothing to be frightened of, just repulsive senility, the end product of an obsession that had burned him out.

A sense of shame, wondering how he could have dominated her like he had, not really knowing. Set's servant, a vessel that had been used for a purpose and now that it was empty had been cast to one side. Jesus, how she hated him! Her knuckles whitened, the remaining colour drained from her features. She thought about that knife down in the Temple . . . no, the *shelter*. There were others in the kitchen, not so big but they would do what she wanted.

Her rage boiled, came to a head. George still had a slight pot-belly, she'd slice through it, pull his guts out like tripe out of a butcher's bin, dig and hack for his heart. Then she'd. . . . With an effort she pulled herself together. Later, the children first. She had to get them out of that vile stinking grave, get them to safety before she took her own revenge.

She turned away, resisted an urge to dash downstairs, forgot about the fifth from bottom step. It groaned loudly, gave a slight crack. She stopped, listened. That generator was still working, picking up momentum. Thank God!

Back in the kitchen. That wallpaper didn't look like flies and spiders any longer, just meaningless criss-crossed patterns and dots. They had all died, becoming a nothingness on the wall like the real dead flies on the unit and floor. She felt them squashing beneath her feet, experienced a sense of satisfaction, deliberately crushed some more.

A reluctance to go outside, agoraphobia. She paused, had to make a mental effort, then struggled with the door. George had locked it and the key was stiff, had to be forced, using both hands so that it bent, almost snapped. The heat again. She edged the door open, peered fearfully through the open gap. So still and silent and . . . *the sun wasn't shining anymore!*

Black clouds, a bank of sheer depression, so menacing as though ordering her to go back inside. *Traitor, you are betraying the Master!*

She trembled, hesitated. Another idea. The phone was in the hall. Three digits: 999. The police would come. She left the door partly open, crept back the way she had come, squashing more flies on her way.

She almost dropped the receiver, had to dial a second time because her finger slipped out of the hole and the nine sprung back as though it was deliberately trying to thwart her. Nine . . . nine . . . nine. . . . Waiting, listening to her pulses roaring, half-thinking that she might be boiling up for a heart attack. Or a stroke, struck down by the awful Set who had brought darkness to daylight in his terrible wrath.

Still nothing. She didn't replace the receiver, just left it dangling on the end of its cord because like everything else around her it was dead. She knew she had to make herself go back out there, there was no other way.

Lowering skies, black shapes that became giant multi-headed serpents, massing as though to attack. She almost ran back indoors. No, she had to go through with it now that she had wrenched herself away. A noise had her starting, looking about her with frightened eyes. Thunder, a long low rumble that suddenly had every nerve in your body tensing. Man's oldest fear. Emily shielded her eyes, searched the skies but there was no sign of lightning. Yet. It would come, though.

She trod on something, felt it split like a dry hazel nut, her weight crushing it into a fine black powder. She looked down, grimaced. There were dead beetles everywhere, dozens of them, mostly lying on their backs on the patio, about the size of a thumbnail, black shelled but with a sort of metallic hue as though somebody had meticulously polished them. All dead, every one of them. There had been numerous beetles out here when she and George had returned from the ritual of embalmment.

'*Scarabs*,' he'd pointed at them, laughed softly. *Khepera has sent them as a symbol of creation. The birth of Dalūkah's child is imminent!*'

She hadn't been listening properly, her numbed brain recording his words but not interpreting them, throwing them back out now. *Scarabs!* No, they were just ordinary beetles, the kind that you found almost anywhere. At least, she thought so. Whatever species they were, they were horrible creepy crawlies like. . . .

The grasshoppers were all dead too! There was no doubt about that, the lawn resembled a parched area littered with piles of tiny dead twigs. Something larger from which feathers were strewn as though somebody had made an attempt to pluck it and had abandoned the idea. That blackbird, the one that lived in the shrubberies and had been feeding on the insects this last fortnight. Now it was dead, too. *Everything was dead!*

Not so much a movement as a presence had her glancing up, giving a cry of fear as she looked into two yellowish-green orbs. It was a bird, a big one, perched on an outstretched branch of next door's rowan tree, so still it might also have been dead except for the eyes, moving slightly as they fixed on her. Some kind of a hawk, she couldn't be more exact because she had never been interested in ornithology. At first she thought it might be a golden eagle but it wasn't big enough. Some kind of harrier maybe, cruel sharp yellow talons that would hook up an unsuspecting victim, rip it to shreds . . . glancing again at the dead blackbird, that area of exposed and torn flesh, the cluster of fluffy feathers. Emily threw up her hands instinctively to protect her face but the bird never moved, just continued to watch her.

She ran, heard the insect corpses cracking and crunching beneath her feet. Thunder like distant cannon-fire, the black sky tinged with streaks of yellow, any moment the heavens would be ripped asunder with jagged stabbing forked flame and the rains would deluge on to a parched landscape.

Emily Brownlow found herself at the door of the dug-out, a frayed and peeling piece of panelled wood which had lain behind the shed for years and was now of vital importance to her, a matter of life and death to her children.

She seized the latch, lifted it and pulled, felt an immobile strength resisting her frenzied efforts, had known all along that the door wouldn't open, that it would foil her just as that useless telephone had done. There was no lock so it had to be stuck. She tugged again but it didn't give. Panicking, kicking and banging on it, looking for a padlock or a bolt with which her husband might have secured it but there was neither. Just a door that refused to yield because its task was to imprison Adrian and Sheila.

'Sheila . . . Sheila, can you hear me? Adrian, open up. Open up, it's Mum!' I'm your mum now, Adrian, and I don't care if you only come from a council house home. I love you. I love you and the baby you've given my Sheila!

There was no answer, not even an echo. Nothing. *Oh Jesus, they're both dead, too. I know they are. Oh God, let me die!*

She fell to her knees, let her tears come with full force, another storm that had to burst sometime. A sudden fear that George might have heard her, come running from the house, *Menhu* the Slaughterer in full fury. She didn't care. All the same she glanced back.

That hawk bird, it was still there watching her, huge yellow eyes that belied the ferocity of those devilish talons if you took the trouble to look at them long enough. Pity, maybe it knew how to cry, too, had a lost mate to weep for.

Emily made a determined effort, forced herself back up on to her feet. They weren't necessarily dead in there, probably just in a bemused hypnotic state like she had been this past . . . oh God, she didn't know how long, time had lost all meaning to her. She just knew that she had to get help quickly.

Turning away, the sky beginning to spit its wrath at her, heavy spots of rain that felt icy cold. One last look back at that hawk bird perched on the branch. Its very presence seemed to give her comfort, then its eyes narrowed. A warning? *Run while there is still time!*

221

She was running blindly, raindrops splattering all around her like enemy bullets attempting to mow her down. Treading on dead things, a slug that squashed and left a black skidmark behind her, a frog that burst like a child blowing bubblegum. Sobbing for breath, struggling with the latch of a gate. Like everything else so far it wouldn't work, it would be rusted and . . . it clicked, the gate swung open and as it did so she gave a cry of despair. *In her panic she had fled in the wrong direction. This wasn't the side gate leading out into River View, it was the rear one at the bottom of the garden which opened out on to the river bank!*

Emily's scream was drowned by an overhead clap of thunder, followed immediately by a flash of lightning which shimmered across the sheeting rain. A deluge, bouncing on the hard-baked ground like invisible demons trying to bar her way, attempting to drive her back to the kingdom of George Brownlow, high priest of Set.

But she wasn't going back. She would sooner die out here in the open. There wasn't any need to die, though! There was a way back into River View, along the river bank for about three hundred yards and take a path leading off at right-angles. It was steep but it brought you out at the bottom of the cul-de-sac . . . by the telephone kiosk!

Muddy water splashed up her bare legs as puddles formed in seconds, indentations in the ground filling up with water, dead insects and frogs floating in them. *Dead things everywhere!*

She was forced to slow her pace, gasping for breath. The thunder was incessant now, so dark that it was impossible to see more than a few yards ahead except when the whole scene was eerily lit up by wicked prongs of earthbound fire. She thought she could smell burning somewhere but it would be impossible for anything to ignite in this.

She stopped again, looking desperately about her. An avenue of willow branches beaten down across the narrow path, soaking wet tentacles that tried to encircle her and pull her back. *You shall not escape the vengeance of Set!*

I shall! A sudden fear that she had missed the track, panicking in case she had to retrace her steps in this awful flood of death. Unrecognisable objects floated and lodged against her ankles, dead bodies that might have been grasshoppers or spiders . . . or *scarabs!*

Fighting those clinging branches, hurling them from her so that they sprang back and whipped her viciously across the face. She tasted blood, spat.

A deafening explosion that had her staggering back with hands clapped to her ears, staring skywards fearfully. It was night, surely such blackness could not happen at any other time. *The sky above her swirled, a maelstrom of angry clouds forming into a shape that was unmistakable — an elongated body that wriggled and writhed with seething fury, a point that grew from it and parted, became a double head with four flashing eyes, embers that were fanned into flames by the rising wind so that they glowed with evil. Twin fangs, jagged forked fire that swished from side to side, venomous thunderbolts of burning death that singled out their cowering victim on the flooded river bank, and struck with unerring accuracy and power!*

Emily Brownlow knew that she was going to die even before the double-headed serpent spat its crackling fiery venom, fell to her knees in one last gesture of humility, a plea on her lips that Sheila and Adrian might be spared, that her own sacrifice would be sufficient.

She felt the impact, slumped forward into a spreading pool of water, heard a hissing which might have been her own scorched body. Or it might have been the serpent mocking her.

Instant pain that faded so that her numbed body appeared to be floating in a black void. Faces all around her but they came and went before she could recognise any of them. Mutely screaming for Sheila and Adrian, Barry and Rita, but only a hissing answered her. And once she thought she heard George's voice, angry and shouting.

Then silence.

And some distance away a huge hawk-shaped bird flapped its wings, glided from the topmost branches of a

223

towering oak tree and fought its way back through the lashing storm towards River View. Even in the buffeting gale it was graceful and majestic, a purposefulness about its flight.

The snake shape in the sky spat fire again but the hawk was gone.

Chapter Twenty

Menhu the Slaughterer

THE ELECTRIC light was back on again in the shelter, so unexpected that it had Adrian shielding his eyes, blinded by its artificial glare. Those vibrations were deafening now, a pounding of fists on the door up above. For Christ's sake it isn't locked! What the hell was George Brownlow playing at?

Then, as suddenly as the noise had begun it died away. Silence. Adrian Capper squinted through half-open lids, waited while his eyesight adjusted to the brightness, closing them again because he was frightened to look, didn't want to see in case he saw that awful festering baby, dying from a plague before its life had begun, screaming in agony.

He couldn't hear it though. Perhaps it was already dead. He hoped so, it would be kindest that way, a merciful release. And Sheila, or Dalūkah as she had suddenly taken to calling herself, where was she?

He smoothed his hands down his thighs, an instinctive action to remove the wet sticky feel of afterbirth from them, was suddenly aware that something was wrong again. He looked down, let out a grunt of disbelief. No longer was he wearing a rough leopardskin garment with a hanging tail but he was clad once more in his old working jeans and grubby T-shirt, the way he should have been!

'Hey, She . . . Oh, Jesus!'

Sheila Brownlow was lying on the floor, half-propped up against the shelving, her jeans tugged down to her ankles, her bare thighs smeared with bloodstains. And on the floor beneath her was a small pool of scarlet blood.

225

'My baby,' she groaned, opening her eyes but they swiftly closed again. 'Where is my baby?'

Adrian glanced about him. There was no sign of that horrific newborn creature with its weeping sores although its shrill cries still rang in his ears. Gone was the bare chamber with its atmosphere of dry decay and its sinister coffins, replaced once more by the Brownlow dug-out and its crammed metal shelves, the mummified form of Barry with its putrefying stench. He didn't understand, made no attempt to.

'You haven't had a baby.' His voice was firm, insistent. *'You've had a miscarriage!'*

'No!' she screamed, opened her eyes and stared about her in panic. 'My baby is here somewhere and. . . .'

'Shut up!' He slapped her hard, the flat of his hand striking her cheek and throwing her head back so that it hit a steel upright with force. 'Pull yourself together. You've aborted at a very early stage and if you see a doctor quick there's probably no harm done. But we've got to get out of here before your father comes back. We've both been the victims of some strange hypnotic force and for the moment I've managed to throw it off. Now, if you can lean on me I can maybe support you. I don't want to risk leaving you here while I go for help.' He glanced at the motionless bandaged form on the camp-bed and grimaced. No way was he going to leave her; if necessary he would stay behind with her. His gaze moved on up to that amulet. The eyes were still closed and lifeless. Set slept, but for how much longer?

'We cannot go, we have to stay,' she whispered. 'It is written in the Book of Fate. Dalūkah and Āba-aner must die and their child with them, in this very tomb!'

'This is ridiculous.' Adrian Capper wondered if he had the strength to carry her up those steps and out into River View. 'We can escape if we go now.'

'We can't desert Barry and Rita.'

'They're dead, gone.' The words hurt but he knew he had to speak them.

'No, they have not gone.' Her fear-filled eyes became glazed as they looked into his. 'They are cursed to wander

forever in the darkness, *for my father is Set in human form!*
The ritual was Set's, not the revered *Rituel de
l'Embaumement* as written on the original papyrus. For
Barry was committed to Set's power and Horus was
ignored, not called upon.'

'Can you not call Horus?' Perhaps if he humoured her
she would accompany him willingly.

'I dare not. I do not have the power, for once I was a
high priestess of Set and I must pay the price for my folly,
accepting your love, Āba-aner, bearing your child. I am a
traitor, too, in the eyes of Horus. Mayhap the hawk-
headed god, elder brother of Set, would take vengeance on
us too. I dare not risk it.'

Adrian hesitated, glanced at the amulet again but
there was still no life in that repulsive serpent body, those
eyes were still dull. A rumbling vibration somewhere above
made the cans on the shelves vibrate, glass jars rattled.
'There's a storm brewing outside. Perhaps the drought is
over.'

'If it is, then it is the end for all of us for it is prophesied
that after drought, plagues and famine the world will end.'

'Let's go.' He bent to lift her, saw that she was still
bleeding, the sticky flow heavier now. She closed her eyes,
seemed to go limp, opened them again, narrowed orbs that
now reflected the cunning of a beast from the wild.

'All right,' she whispered, 'but you'll have to help me up.'

He nodded. Her hand went behind her as though to
seek the support of a shelving stanchion to heave herself up
on, but instead found a heavy can of tinned fruit, grasped it.
She paused, got her balance, then without warning her arm
shot forward.

Adrian's reflexes froze in that split second, a moment
when everything was reduced to slow motion but he was
powerless to take evasive action. A hurtling object, he even
saw the label, a cluster of yellow cling peaches. No way
could he dodge it, braced himself for the impact. Pain and
kaleidoscopic lights, a bizarre firework display that lit up
the darkness all around, then gradually petered out and the
blackness came in at him. He was unconscious even before
he hit the floor.

George Brownlow came out of his deep slumber with a start, hauled himself up to a sitting position. The room was dark and his first thought was that he had overslept, that night had come and Set was already angrily awaiting his arrival in the Temple. But no, it wasn't night because you could still see the tops of the withered trees down by the river. It was raining hard, a cloudburst, the sheeting raindrops spectacularly illuminated by a downward plunge of forked lightning. A rumble of thunder like an overhead bursting bomb had the walls vibrating.

A moment of fear. He covered his face with his hands, and then that flash of primitive terror was reduced to a feeling of unease. Foreboding. This was it, the prophesied hour was nigh. Civilisation was at an end and his presence was needed down in the Temple. Dalūkah and Āba-aner must pay for their treachery.

He pulled on his shorts, ran barefooted from the bedroom, down the stairs and into the lounge, a trembling finger pressing the control knob of the television. Something he had to know. . . .

The screen was distorted, shimmering lines across it so that you had to try and work out the picture behind it. A face, vaguely familiar like your own reflection in a fairground hall of mirrors. A newscaster, features grim, staccato vocal sounds that were almost drowning in the crackling and buzzing.

'. . . Report that the . . . missile carrier . . . been sunk by a missile fired from . . . submarine . . . hope to have further details very soon. We. . . .'

The explosion, a shattering blast of thunder that seemed to rock the set itself, a blinding flash that blacked out the picture, left a greyish-brown screen which still hissed its agony. Dead, like everything else would soon be.

He turned away, experienced that feeling of foreboding again, knew he would find the kitchen empty even before he opened the door. He looked around, saw the empty chair where Emily had been slumped in a daze. He stared at it, bewilderment and anger, trying to will her to appear but she didn't.

'Em . . . ily.' A croak, grasping the chair, rattling it,

228

shaking it, finally throwing it over on to the floor. 'You've gone, just when I needed you most.'

A hissing sound that might have been the television in the other room, a cry of electronic agony from a dying symbol of Man's ingenuity which was frail and useless when pitted against the forces of Nature. Or it might have been Set, the amulet demanding his presence at the final hour. A rumble of angry thunder, the kitchen lit up by a dazzling flash of lightning.

He crossed to the door, opened it, looked out on a flooded dancing patio, the steps down to the lawn a raging miniature waterfall that carried tiny dead bodies in its rushing current. Frogs . . . locusts . . . scarabs . . . the ultimate plague had arrived — DEATH!

He stood there, the torrent up to his ankles, water cascading off his shaven head, impervious to its coldness.

'*Emily . . . Emily, come back, I need you!*'

There was no answer. Even if there had been it was doubtful if he would have heard it. Indecision. Would Set grant him just a few more minutes to find Emily? Where had she gone? Oh God, he needed her now more than he had ever needed her before.

He set off on an aimless shambling course across the flooded lawn. Tiny bodies floated everywhere and he felt them being squashed beneath his bare feet. She wouldn't have gone back to the Temple on her own, she wouldn't dare. She had fled blindly, panicked when the storm had started. He should not have left her, he must find her.

George Brownlow could not see more than a few yards into the deluge and the gloom, shapes that taunted him, had him rushing towards them only to grasp the sodden boughs of bushes, cursing them for their trickery. A sudden movement above his head had him cringing. A bird of some kind, a big one with heavy wing-beats but it was gone before he could identify it.

He came to the lower garden gate, saw that it hung open and knew instantly that this was where his wife had gone. Oh, the fool, she did not realise!

'*Emily . . . Emily!*'

Noises that swamped him, sounds that came out of the

storm like the cries of the damned, the lightning now almost incessant. He stepped out on to the path, floundered in the thick mud, almost slipped and fell. The river would be rising, it would burst its banks before long, an unprecedented flood that would sweep the River View houses away with it, but that would not matter because there would be nobody left to live in them.

Which way had she gone, left or right? Panic, looking up into the storm as though seeking guidance but there was nothing but unending blackness and lashing rain.

'Help . . . me.' Words that he might not have uttered, might only have existed in his tortured mind — *but they were heard and answered!'*

The sky seemed to converge, the black clouds concentrating together, mushrooming upwards like a pall of smoke from burning rubber, merging into a giant shape that twisted and writhed as if in agony, a monstrous serpent that grew a double head, flicked its fangs angrily, spat jagged fire that was reflected in the malevolent eyes.

'Go back, Menhu, for death is your business!'

Brownlow tried to cover his eyes but he could not shut out the blinding light, heat that seared his brain, had him crying his terror aloud, vowing obedience. He turned, slipped and almost fell on a morass of unrecognisable dead things. Fighting his way back into the garden through a wind that was reaching almost hurricane force, the driving rain now hot and burning his flesh. Water everywhere, puddles spreading into larger pools, the dead lawn a black lake and still rising.

He wanted to run but it was impossible, glancing back fearfully at the sky behind him but the serpent had slipped back into obscurity. It was still there, though, he could *feel* it watching him, angry with him because of his human frailty, his concern for his mate.

He reached the shelter, groped his way along to the door. The water had risen above the broken slab he had used as a step and he could hear it cascading down the steps inside. There wasn't much time left for any of them.

Again something attracted his attention even as he

lifted the latch and he cringed. A shape in the dark sky, hurtling down at him. He screamed, instinctively threw up an arm to shield his face, felt the rush of huge wings and shrieked again as talons raked his bare forearm. The bird hit him and was veering off again, affording him just one glimpse in the darkness of a huge hawk that screeched its fury and disappeared into the darkness. A vivid flash of lightning illuminated the flooded landscape, vicious prongs of live fire that shrivelled the tall rowan tree, reduced it instantly to a blackened skeleton.

George Brownlow fell inside, slammed the door behind him, wondered if it was strong enough to keep that bird out. A faint ruby glow emanated from down below, a familiar radiance which would give him the light he needed to do what he had to do. *Set was here and ready!* George trembled, his mouth sour and dry.

The rainwater was flowing down the steps, forming a spreading pool at the bottom. Before long the whole shelter would be flooded. He laughed to himself. He had provided a damp-proof course against rising water but Nature had beaten him, found a way in from above.

He picked his way down carefully, holding on to the rail. He didn't want to go down there, was afraid of what he might see, suddenly aware of the task which must be carried out in the name of Set. A high-priestess called Dalūkah had betrayed her god thousands of years ago; she had been punished but an old clergyman had freed her and her lover, Āba-aner, from their eternal purgatory. But Set was omnipotent, had followed them into exile and now they must be punished again as they had been before. Only then would the cycle be complete.

Brownlow reached the bottom, stared in horror at the scene which greeted him. Adrian Capper lay unconscious on the rough floor, blood pouring from a jagged wound across his forehead, a bloodied Sheila cradling his head on her lap, weeping uncontrollably. She looked up, screamed as she saw her bedraggled father standing over her.

Menhu the Slaughterer had been summoned and now he had arrived!

231

Chapter Twenty-one

Horus!

SHEILA BACKED away, knew that it was now too late. Oh God, she should have fled with Adrian while there still had been time. She had wanted to go but some inexplicable force had dominated her, made her strike him down.

'Dad,' she shouted, tried to make herself heard over the noise of the raging storm and the pouring water. 'Dad . . . don't . . . *please* don't!' A feeble plea which she knew would be futile.

'Dalūkah, you must die.' His eyes were bloated behind the rain-splashed lenses, his mouth an awful black cavity where he had forgotten to replace his dentures. 'Your treachery is exposed. You must die, Āba-aner, too . . . and your bastard child!'

'My child is dead!' she screamed. 'I've had a miscarriage.'

But he didn't appear to hear her, moving slowly and deliberately across to the bed on which the stinking mummified corpse rotted, picking up the longest of the knives which lay beside it, holding it in the manner of a sword. He hesitated, turned back towards the amulet on the crude altar as though seeking guidance, bowed, straightened up again.

The two-headed serpent seemed to writhe as though at any second it might free itself from its casing, burning red eyes glowing, fangs flicking to and fro, hissing words that listening ears were compelled to interpret.

'*You are here at last, Menhu. I have been waiting, for*

232

there is not much time left. Where are the other priests and priestesses of Set?'

George Brownlow was mumbling his reply, trying to tell Set that Emily was lost, maybe dead in the raging storm, that there weren't any others.

'I summon the others. They dare not disobey!'

A sudden burst of thunder shook the underground room, toppled some cans from a shelf. A glass jar splintered into fragments across the floor. Set's glowing eyes flickered, threatened to extinguish like some damaged electrical appliance, spluttered as the shadows moved back in.

George Brownlow covered his eyes, had resigned himself to death or worse, was already anticipating the next burst of thunder. But it never came. And the ensuing silence was a thousand times worse.

That same illuminating glow lit up the interior and at first he thought it was some trick of the strange light. The shelving, the furniture, they were gone. He stood in an almost empty chamber, saw the amulet and a carved head of some kind which was vaguely familiar.

In the centre of the floor stood a small sarcophagus, another larger one over in the far corner almost hidden in the shadows. He experienced a sense of sadness that was stronger than his terror, heard the weeping, unrelenting sobs that grew in volume.

And then he saw the girl, his own daughter except that she looked somewhat different in those long flowing robes, both her skin and her hair several shades darker. She was kneeling beside a prone figure clad in some kind of tunic made from the skin of a wild animal.

George Brownlow licked his lips, tried to work out where everything had gone, why he could hear the storm no more, why this place was so dry and dusty and the rainwater was no longer pouring in.

There were others in here too, a multitude which kept to the shadows, were whispering to one another but he couldn't understand what it was they were saying. Waiting. For what?

233

'These two are traitors, Menhu. They have betrayed me. Put them to the sword for their treachery, then seal this tomb and begone and never dare speak the names of Dalūkah and Āba-aner again!'

Panic and terror knotted his stomach. He glanced down, saw the blade which he held in his hand. No longer was it a carving knife of forged steel but instead a sword which scintillated in the ruby radiance, its hilt jewelled and sparkling. He tried to hold back but his feet were already moving, slow purposeful strides towards the centre of the chamber, the sword raised, a human robot being sent on a mission of death!

Dalūkah screamed, tried to drag her unconscious lover away but he was too heavy for her. She sprang to her feet with a cry, her features a mask of defiance, her eyes flashing. 'You are too late, Menhu, for I have already borne the child of Āba-aner. Kill me if you will but I will not plead for mercy. I have no regrets!'

George Brownlow fought to overcome the power which controlled him. He tried to step back, instead his feet moved forward. He wanted to drop the sword, kick it away, but it came up, poised delicately, menacingly, in his hand.

I cannot murder my own daughter. 'Dalūkah, you must die!' Whispered applause for his words filled the chamber, echoes that were reluctant to die away.

'Kill her, Menhu. Āba-aner, too . . . Āba-aner . . . too . . . too . . .' They were all screaming at him now.

She faced him, her dress falling away to reveal smooth naked breasts that were perfect in every way. Her head was held high and the smile on her features was one of contempt. 'Kill me then, my father, and may it be on your conscience forever as my blood will be on your hands.'

'I am not your father. I am Menhu the Slaughterer and you are Dalūkah of whom I have heard but never seen before. Now *die!*'

He struck, tried to close his eyes but they refused to close. Everything before him was happening so slowly, the point of the sword taking its time, piercing the soft flesh

234

below her left breast, penetrating, going deeper and deeper until it grated on bone. She sagged, held upright like a skewered joint of beef from which the blood seeped, then spurted, that contemptuous smile still on her face, fighting to hide the pain. Slowly she fell to the floor, her weight dragging her free of the blade, rolling over on to her back, still looking at him with accusing sightless eyes. *'You have murdered me, father!'*

He wanted to scream, heard the shouts of the assembly in the shadows, *'Well done, Menhu. The traitoress is dead. Now kill Āba-aner and let us be gone from this place of death!'*

Adrian stirred, his confused brain trying to work out who was shouting and what they were shouting for. He opened his eyes, vaguely recognised this place of ancient death. Sheila was lying a few feet away from him; she'd hit him with something off one of the shelves . . . he rubbed his head, shook it. Oh, Jesus Christ Almight! The *blood!* There were pools of it everywhere, thick sticky crimson rivers that were slowing, would soon be congealing.

He stared aghast at Sheila's mutilated body. There was no doubt that she was dead, her capacious clothing ripped open showing a ghastly wound, a bloody incision that surely went right into her heart, her mouth still wide, her eyes still open, frozen in an expression of defiance.

There were other people in the chamber, clusters of them standing back in the shadows, watching, gloating. And . . . it *had* to be George Brownlow standing only a few feet away. At least, there was a resemblance. A wild-eyed human shape lathered in sweat, splashed with blood, wielding a dripping sword, muttering whispered incantations, still wearing those stupid heavy glasses with the lenses misted up so that they gave the appearance of huge sightless eyes.

'You, too, must die, Āba-aner!'

Everything seemed to stop like a still photograph taken from some awful movie, a moment of timelessness which bridged the abyss between life and death. Except that Adrian's brain was working, not understanding any

235

thing except that Sheila was dead and this madman intended to kill him next.

'You bastard!' he breathed. 'You filthy murderer!'

'Do not defile the sacred Temple of Set with your foul cursings.' George Brownlow advanced a pace, raised his sword. 'Set demands that you die, that you are sacrificed to him so that your soul may serve him for eternity. Even now Dalūkah has gone to him.'

The amulet, it no longer seemed to be an object of metal, a captivated serpent chained to its frame. It writhed, spat, flicked its wicked fangs, reared itself up on the shelf alongside that awful obsidian head. Adrian felt the power, the revulsion that motivated the creature that was Brownlow, had the hidden watchers murmuring their subservience to a mighty power. *'Kill Āba-aner, Menhu!'*

And in that instant Adrian saw Dalūkah, not the bloodied corpse lying on the floor but a shimmering translucent shape that hovered on the opposite side of the chamber close to the larger sarcophagus, her expression one of anguish, trying to attract his attention, struggling as though invisible hands were pulling at her, trying to drag her away before she could speak to him. Her lips formed one word, said it over and over again, until finally there was no mistaking her mute message. *'Horus . . . Horus . . . call Horus, Āba-aner, for now there is nothing more to be lost!'*

Suddenly she was gone, vanishing as though she had never been, had only existed in his own mind.

'Die, commoner!'

Adrian saw the sword go back, the point of the bloody blade aligned on a course for his own heart, heard the chorus from the dark shadows: *'Kill him, in the name of Set!'*

Somehow Adrian forced his stricken vocal chords to function, a whisper to begin with, growing in volume until the words were both a plea and a shout of defiance. *'Horus, Horus save me before it is too late!'*

George Brownlow checked as though he had met with an impassable physical barrier and even those glasses wet with condensation reflected his terror. His toothless mouth opened, a croak of fear, desperately looking about him.

The two-headed serpent was now a living thing, no longer part of the amulet, hissing its rage, slithering forward and dropping to the floor with a soft thud. Eyes of fire, anger and hatred, but if you looked closely you saw a tiny flicker of fear in them as it looked about.

Brownlow screamed and his sword clattered to the floor. He tottered back, fell, sprawled across the dead body of his daughter, clung to it as though begging forgiveness, sobs shaking him.

And in that instant the raging thunderstorm seemed to penetrate this underground chamber, a vivid flash of fire which blinded, a rumble that shook floor and walls. Adrian felt the ground heave up beneath him, stones splitting, a rush of hot wind tearing at him, threatening to pick him up and sweep him along like a dead autumn leaf.

He saw a vision that might have lasted a few seconds or several hours, it was impossible to tell, the scene stark and terrible, illuminated by crackling streaks of fire.

Set was reared upright like a snake-charmer's exhibit, his double fangs spitting fire and venom as he attempted to drive off the attacking bird which swooped and veered, raked with its talons, gouged with its wicked curved beak. Stabbing, slashing, a conflict in which there would be only one victor.

The serpent climbed for a better advantage, wriggled itself up on to the still, charred body that had once belonged to its servant, *Menhu* the Slaughterer. One head was damaged, a jagged wound that oozed a vile stinking dark fluid, the fangs hanging down limply. Even the larger of the combatants, the huge hawk, had not escaped unscathed, feathers billowing from its plumage and being whipped away in the wind.

Back and forth, a duel of fang and claw that was terrible to behold as serpent god and hawk-headed god battled out their fraternal hatred on each other. Adrian lay there half-blinded by the flashing forked fire, felt the rush of wings time and again.

Then darkness, a thousand times more terrible because the battle still raged but it was impossible to see how it fared. Adrian lay there, covered his head with his hands, listened to the fury of it all and knew that his own life, his very soul, depended upon the outcome.

Perhaps he slept, he did not know, only that some time later he awoke to a stark black silence. Utter darkness but he knew it was the Brownlow shelter because of that awful putrefying stench instead of the ancient dry smell. His outstretched hand touched something and he snatched it away, caught the sob in his throat because he knew without any doubt that it was the body of Sheila who had been slain for the sins of Dalūkah in distant times.

So hot and stifling, his entire skin seeming to smart as though it had been sprinkled with acid. He struggled to draw breath. Oh Jesus, if only he could die! But he had been granted life because he had beseeched Horus to let him live. He began to weep, screamed that he wanted to die but the huge bird did not return. It had answered his call and was gone forever. There was no sign of the serpent either. Perhaps it lay dead somewhere in the darkness. Adrian's flesh prickled with revulsion. All around him was death, a tomb in which only he lived, dying like Dalūkah's child thousands of years ago, its skin festering and weeping. Like Rita's and Barry's had done.

He found that he could move and sat up, was aware that where previously there had been shelved walls now there were just piles of rubble, dust that had him coughing and retching. And the atmosphere was so hot. . . .

His eyes hurt so much that he shut them in an attempt to alleviate the pain. It didn't help but he could not see anything in this pitch blackness anyway. Crawling, groping, snatching his hands away every time he touched something that was cold and soft.

Eventually he found the steps, at least he thought it was the exit, a slope of rubble that slid and avalanched with every movement so that he had to take his time, easing himself up on all-fours, grazing his legs and arms, bleeding. The door was smashed and he tried to see beyond the debris. Perhaps it was night because through the split woodwork he saw a dark dusty swirling fog. His whole body smarted as

238

though it was on fire and he barely had the strength to rip away the jagged panels.

Eventually he was forced to rest. He dozed with exhaustion, perhaps he slept. He didn't know, but when he looked again it was lighter outside, the fog having thinned considerably. He stared. *The house should have stood twenty yards or so immediately opposite but there was nothing, just rubble that smoked and gave off that burning fog. All around there was nothing but a smouldering landscape, the rancid stench of death!*

He began to claw his way out, gave up after a few minutes. What was the purpose in going out there? Everybody was dead, just himself left to suffer the agony of a smoking hell. He'd fought for life and in the end he was the loser.

Day blended into night once more and after an eternity morning came again. At least it might have been morning, it was difficult to tell, that grey smoke-haze creeping in, getting thicker and hotter.

And still he couldn't die. His chest hurt and he was spitting blood now, eyes swollen so that he could barely see out of them; crouched by that hole in the door. Waiting. Scanning the swirling grey fog in the hope that he might catch a glimpse of a huge fierce graceful bird with a ragged wingspan, but there was no sign of it.

He waited because there was nothing else to do, the eddying smoke creating strange shapes, raising his hopes, dashing them. Taunting him.

Horus wouldn't return because the curse of Set had been fulfilled. Dalūkah had died by the sword and only Āba-aner was left and soon he would be dead too.

The cycle was complete.

Bestselling SF/Horror

☐ The Labyrinth	Robert Faulcon	£2.50
☐ Night Train	Thomas F. Monteleone	£2.50
☐ Doomflight	Guy N. Smith	£2.50
☐ Malleus Maleficarum	Montague Summers	£4.95
☐ The Devil Rides Out	Dennis Wheatley	£2.95
☐ Cities in Flight	James Blish	£2.95
☐ Stand on Zanzibar	John Brunner	£2.95
☐ 2001 – A Space Odyssey	Arthur C. Clarke	£1.95
☐ Gene Wolfe's Book of Days	Gene Wolfe	£2.25
☐ The Shadow of the Torturer	Gene Wolfe	£2.50
☐ The Blackcollar	Timothy Zahn	£1.95
☐ Speaker for the Dead	Orson Scott Card	£2.95
☐ The War for Eternity	Christopher Rowley	£2.95
☐ Contact	Carl Sagan	£3.50

Prices and other details are liable to change

ARROW BOOKS, BOOKSERVICE BY POST, PO BOX 29, DOUGLAS, ISLE OF MAN, BRITISH ISLES

NAME . . . .

ADDRESS . . . .

. . . .

. . . .

Please enclose a cheque or postal order made out to Arrow Books Ltd. for the amount due and allow the following for postage and packing.

U.K. CUSTOMERS: Please allow 22p per book to a maximum of £3.00.

B.F.P.O. & EIRE: Please allow 22p per book to a maximum of £3.00.

OVERSEAS CUSTOMERS: Please allow 22p per book.

Whilst every effort is made to keep prices low it is sometimes necessary to increase cover prices at short notice. Arrow Books reserve the right to show new retail prices on covers which may differ from those previously advertised in the text or elsewhere.